Sorrow's Forest

Sorrow's Forest, Volume 1

Kaitlin Corvus

Published by Shadow Spark Publishing, 2022.

SORROW'S FOREST

First edition. July 16, 2022.

Written by Kaitlin Corvus.

To Shane, Blue's first fan. Thank you for all your friendship and sup-port

Chapter 1

Life is full of hard truths and soft lies.

The sky is blue, the sun is bright, and the stars are more than just pretty lights in a darkened sky. The forest that encompasses Lakeview Township is off-limits because it's teeming with vicious people-eating wolves. Shawn Macintyre, bike thief and bully, is mean because mean is in his blood. The river that snakes through the forest and widens in town never fully freezes in winter, and that's why so many people fall through the ice and never come back.

It's not always ignorance and lies, though. Lakeview *knows* the climate of the forest pressing against its borders. Mackie caught Father Callahan dousing his steps in blessed salt just this morning, muttering to himself about devils and a coming storm.

"Stay inside tonight, Mackenzie," he said when he caught Mackie staring. "Weather's changing."

Of course, Mackie ignored him and now stands, hands flexing apprehensively at his sides, before the aforenamed forest.

"What are you waiting for, King?" urges Shawn. He's practically salivating, looking for affirmation from their twelve other classmates, all standing in a semi-circle around the gigantic pile of blue Pixy-Stix they've built at the bottom of Mackie's backyard. "Thought you weren't a pussy?"

"I'm not." Mackie waits for this lie to curl in his belly the way lies usually do. He feels nothing other than a small twinge of nervousness. He loves the forest. Has always loved the forest, as he loves most things that scare him: horror movies, the park after dark, leaping from Muller's Bridge mid-summer, wondering if the water is just shallow enough to see the bottom but deep enough to catch him without breaking his back, or if he's going to hit rocks and hurt.

"I get all the Pixy-Stix, right?" Mackie confirms. Blue is the best flavour. He likes it when his tongue, teeth, and lips are stained with the colour, and his heart beats fast with the sugar rush. He feels like he can do anything.

"If you make it out alive." Shawn follows his ominous proclamation with a feral grin.

No one jeers because no one is pretending the forest is just a forest. Something *is* different tonight. The grade sixes sense it as well as Father Callahan did. Mackie's classmates shift from foot to foot and look nervously into the trees. The forest merely sighs quietly, waiting for them to offer it a meal.

"Good luck, Mackie," says Bree Lock, who is always looking at him from under her thick black lashes with her blue, blue eyes.

Mackie quarter smiles and faces the trees.

He's peered into the forest plenty of times after dark. He's sat at his bedroom window at the back of the house, watching the trees move like people, yanking their roots up and sliding across the grass. If he gets bored of that, he can spend his time picking out the bright eyes that study him from the shadows. There's no shortage. *Devils* he calls them, because what other word is there for the peculiar beasts that roam beneath the trees?

It looks stiller than usual tonight, however, and that stillness fills him with a sense of unease.

With a breath, he goes forward. Not one of his classmates tries to stop him.

Beneath the overhanging cage of branches, an icy chill overcomes Mackie, and he forgets it's a humid summer evening. It could be April, or early May, not late June. He checks over his shoulder. His classmates watch him from their half-moon circle a safe distance back. They're silent and sombre, except for Shawn, who sneers and covertly flips Mackie off by rubbing his middle finger against his nose, and Bree, who watches from beneath her lashes again; the expression she wears is much more complicated than a twelve-year-old can be expected to decipher.

Already, they seem too far away to return to. Like the lawn is a lake he's swimming across, and he's closer to the far shore than the one he began from. He must press on, so he doesn't drown.

Mackie squares his shoulders and goes deeper.

The forest eats things, though no one will dare say so in as many words. People and pets get lost, their bones turning up days later, picked clean and piled neatly for authorities to find. When the police step between the trunks, searching for lost children, they get turned around for hours, only to come out the other side in the town of Owensboro, confused and scared.

The ban restricting travel into the forest at any time has been in place for years, well before Mackie was ever born. *Wolves* are what people say instead of *monsters,* because wolves, though feral, are more easily understood than the horrors that call Sorrow's Forest their home.

Under the claw-like branches, Mackie is surrounded by something that feels very much like magic. It's in every breath he takes, filling up his lungs and clouding his thoughts. It guides him onward.

Vines crawl from one thick tree trunk to the next, and lilies with bone-white petals shoot up from the soft ground, flowering even in the darkness. He thinks it's his imagination when they turn their heads and follow his progress.

Looking back, Mackie can no longer see his classmates, only branches and ferns and stones.

Discarded tree limbs roll beneath his feet, but the ground and leaves are just the right amount of moist to mask his footsteps. He feels utterly alone. He may sneak up on something unsuspecting and scare it into a fight. Or something may sneak up on him. How will he fare against one of the forest's red-eyed beasts? He's tall and gangly without much muscle, though he can *run*.

Fireflies glow all around, bright, bright, bright, and tangle together into a long glowing rope, leading Mackie deeper into the trees, to an unknown prize.

Mackie follows.

Trees watch him with their knot eyes. And something in the dark holds its breath for his progress.

A little whip-poor-will cheers encouragement from on high as Mackie crouches beneath a soggy log and enters a grove so full of magic, that he must breathe shallowly in through his nose and out through his mouth. His fingertips tingle with it, and the skin on his face feels raw and sunburned.

The feeling that he's in a place he does not belong is overwhelming. He should turn back. He should never think about this place again.

But Mackie is pulled forward by an unseen force and continues.

The grass is knee-high and the pale silver-green of gemstones. Through trees as tall as skyscrapers, a brook meanders. Its water is glass-smooth and crystal-clear until a forked tail, sharp like a shark's, pokes up through the surface, scattering whirligig beetles. It disappears. The beetles still again. The water settles.

Movement draws Mackie's eyes to the left where a boy sits streamside with his hands in the water to his elbows. His hair is a blonde so pale, that it seems blue, like the blue star flowers in Mom's gardens.

His eyes flutter up to study Mackie, and Mackie can see they are black. No pupils. He has a birthmark that starts in the corner of his nose and moves up across his right eye like someone has taken soot from a fireplace and smeared it on him.

Mackie thinks they're near the same age.

The boy's limbs are long and thin, like the branches of a willow. When he stands, he'll be taller than Mackie by a few inches, at least.

Suddenly, he yanks his hands from the water, producing the biggest diving beetle Mackie has ever seen. In a flash, it's gnashed between his teeth. Every time the carapace crunches, Mackie cringes. The boy seems indifferent—just a boy alone in the forest, eating what the water gave him—no fear of the dark and no fear of the monsters watching from the trees.

Perhaps *he* is the monster.

"Who are you?" Mackie hears himself ask.

The boy swallows and pulls his arms from the water. He has another beetle pinched between his fingers. He holds it out to Mackie like a present.

Mackie curls his nose. "Gross."

Despite Mackie's denouncement, the boy waits for another moment, arm outstretched, water dripping from his elbow to the ground and the beetle worming in his grasp. When Mackie still doesn't take it, he shrugs and pushes it between his teeth. For a second, Mackie thinks they seem sharp. Too sharp. Then the boy runs his tongue over them, and Mackie sees they're the same as his, middle-class straight and white.

Mackie steps closer. "Why are you sitting out here alone?"

The boy still doesn't answer; it occurs to Mackie that he can't speak or doesn't know how.

"You know the forest is off-limits, right? I was just dared to come in here."

Nothing.

He doesn't look like the other people in Lakeview. He's too pale. Too thin. Too much *something* Mackie can't quite place.

Mackie asks, "Do you live here?"

Again, the boy blinks at him.

"Can you hear me?" There is a deaf boy in his school. He has to have special classes and can read lips if the person talks slowly enough. Mackie tries forming his words carefully with his hands and his mouth. "What. Are. You. Doing. Here?"

The forest breathes in, tree branches wriggling, and sighs out as if exasperated. A second of silence passes, and then the trees start quaking, though no wind rustles the trembling limbs. Acorns and loose leaves tumble down and thunder on the forest floor. Some hit Mackie in the head. The grass sways at his feet, and the water sloshes against the stream banks as the very earth rumbles.

The boy falls back on his rump and Mackie crashes to his knees; hands planted in the dirt. Through his fingertips, he can *feel* electrical currents moving through the ground, vibrating up his body.

An earthquake, he thinks. Though they don't live in an area prone to them, he's seen a lot of National Geographic.

All around, worms struggle out of the dirt, trying to get away from the shifting ground as the grass blades crawl with disapproving insects. The trees shiver, then start leaning forward, closing in on them like a tightening noose, and Mackie knows, suddenly, if he doesn't leave now, he never will. He will become part of the forest, leaving behind only his bones.

"Come on!" He gets his foot wet splashing across the river. When he grabs the boy by the wrist, the boy's skin is slippery and cold. Mackie holds on tight enough; he's sure he'll leave behind finger marks.

They run.

The fireflies are still out, flitting in front of them with a golden-green light that shows some sort of path across the carpet of grass. The forest tunnels around them, forming a chute. Brambles, thorns, thick branches, and wide tree trunks block them from both sides, making it impossible to deviate from the predetermined pathway.

Mackie can't help but think they're being *herded,* corralled forward. Through this next thicket is likely a witch's house or a devil's layer, the kind of place that can't exist without the oppressive weight of the forest hanging overhead.

I won't stay here, he thinks desperately at the trees. *You can't keep me.* It's not where he belongs.

In contradiction, branches stretch like hands and scrape at his chest and cheeks. Roots get beneath his feet and rise unpredictably. He falls once, barely hitting the ground before he's back up again and pulling the boy forward with renewed vigour.

A deep wail resounds through the trees and an unseen shockwave shudders from root to root, leaf to leaf. They curl, searching for each other to lock together and keep him there.

Paralyzed by fear, Mackie stalls. Sensing a moment of weakness, the forest surges forward to trap him in its shadow.

The boy crashes into Mackie's back and propels him forward. Together, they break through the branches and suddenly onto the mowed grass of the Kings' backyard.

It's like coming out of the water after too long in its depths. The air tastes different. Fresh and clean and boring without the distinct tang of forest magic.

Mackie spins to eye the forest, sure it's still hungry for him. Trees shudder one final time before straightening, then the fireflies disperse, and the forest seems normal once more if you don't look at the red burning eyes of the devils hiding as they peer out from the deepest shadows.

Mackie doesn't want to.

He examines his backyard. The circle of his peers is gone. They took the Pixy-Stix, too. *Assholes.* There is just his house sitting up on the hill. The only lights on are inside. Outside is dark, making the house seem more remote and shabbier than it really is.

Mackie still holds the boy's hand. Their fingers feel welded together. He is so thin, Mackie is afraid that if he lets go, the boy will slip back into the forest, into whatever magical cove he crawled out of.

Mackie's mother rushes to the door when they enter. Her hair, dark like Mackie's, is pulled up high on her head and her face is clear of makeup this late in the evening. A half-smoked cigarette smoulders between her long, nicotine-stained fingers.

"Where have you been?" she demands. "There was an earthquake. We were scared."

Before Mackie can answer, Mom's attention slides to the boy behind him. At first, she seems confused by the intrusion. Then, like magic, the lines on her face smooth out. "And Blue, you're covered in mud."

"Sorry, Missus King," says the boy. His voice is soft and light and reminds Mackie of wild things. Mackie scrutinizes him. Whatever prevented him from speaking in the forest, he sounds fine now.

Mom's face softens more. "That's okay. Get cleaned up and ready for bed, boys. I'll make the spare room."

Chapter 2

Mackie draws on his cigarette. It's a gross habit, he knows. His father smokes two packs a day when he remembers he enjoys smoking, and has a wet, wheezing cough that makes Mackie cringe to hear it when he goes home for holidays. But Mackie is what he likes to call a *social smoker*. Parties, family gatherings, and when he just needs something to do with his body while he gathers his thoughts. It's a reprieve he needs more and more nowadays as exams come to an end. He considers quitting altogether before a dependency builds.

"Your brother is really weird," says Carley Hunts in the indignant voice of someone scandalized. Sitting on the picnic table at Mackie's side, she glares across the courtyard to where Blue's animatedly telling a story.

Mackie forgoes telling her they're not really brothers. It's wasted breath. He follows her gaze and watches Blue tell a story beneath the awning of the pub, one heeled foot kicked back on the brick wall, the image of casualness. His pants are tight, purposefully drawing eyes down his lean frame. Similarly, his long-sleeved shirt clings to his long limbs and ropy muscles. Girls and boys look him over, and Blue does his best to flirt with them all, though boys are more his flavour. He has no qualms about making everyone fall in love with him. He's larger-than-life-pretty, the way boys aren't supposed to be, and he's so unapologetic about it, it's inspiring.

While Blue's crowd laughs at something witty he's said, Mackie studies his own hands. The thumbnail on his right is black and purple after being squished between his wrench and carburetor, and his knuckles are scarred. Bruised. Contrarily, Blue's are manicured and neat. Blue and Mackie, they contrast. They always have. Blue is clean-shaven, while Mackie sports three days of stubble. Blue is runway glam; Mackie wears a faded T-shirt he bought in his last days of high school three years ago, and jeans with a long, narrow tear at the knee.

It's a wonder they're friends at all.

More raucous laughter from across the courtyard. Blue has his own fan club, and he acts as though it's the most natural thing in the world. He *loves* the limelight. Thrives in it the way Mackie cannot. Yet for all the people who love him, there are plenty who tighten their eyes and mutter nasty things within earshot; like they're the first ones brave enough to accost him for the unconventional clothes he wears and the things he believes in, as though they're fighting some bloody battle for humanity's soul.

It's stupid. Mackie has always thought it was stupid and has never been afraid to say it.

"Did he buy those heels at a woman's store?" Carley continues. She's deaf to Mackie's mood. "I didn't think they made them in men's size."

"Special order," Mackie says with a smile he doesn't feel. He didn't think he'd love Carley when, at the beginning of the semester, she gave him her number and asked him to tutor her in their elective Aboriginal Anthropology class. He didn't think his resentment of her would grow so quickly, either.

She seemed nice at first. Then she learned that Mackie shared his residence with Blue, and he saw a crack in her façade. The day she learned it wasn't just the convenience of housing that brought them together, that Blue was the Kings' ward and Mackie's friend, she really started falling apart.

Now she comes in with little stinging shots here and there, doing anything she can to belittle Blue without directly saying his being offends her.

Mackie knows it's his fault—he didn't shut her down immediately—but she smiles to Blue's face, and Blue—who thinks everyone can change if they're just given the chance—tells him *she just needs to get to know me. Once she does, she'll realize bigotry sucks. Trust me, Mackie, she's not all bad. She likes you, remember?*

No one ever is *all bad*, though. It's just that Carley's kind of bad is toxic. He's slowly been distancing himself from her because he doesn't want to be one of those guys with a thing for toxic people.

Carley smacks her gum loudly. "Andy says he's in for the keg."

Mackie draws his eyes away from Blue. Carley is looking at her phone and scrolling through a text conversation. "What keg?"

"The one for your birthday." Carley rolls her eyes. "I *told* you that."

"My birthday was last week."

"Yeah, but you never told anyone. You didn't have a party."

"Me and Blue watched a movie and played video games."

She huffs exaggeratedly. "That is *not* a party."

Mackie takes another stinging draw on his cigarette and holds the smoke in his lungs, preventing him from snapping back with something mean. When he can do so civilly, he says, "That's alright."

Carley doesn't seem to hear him. She still scrolls through her phone, too fast to be focusing on anything. "We can have it at my residence."

Mackie's irritation spikes and he says with more force than he would normally, "I don't want a party."

Carley shoots him such a vexatious look he almost recoils. "That's too bad. I've already invited everyone."

Across the courtyard, a thin guy with red hair laughs hysterically at something Blue has said. Mackie tries to remember if he's seen him before. Blue has a lot of people that come in and out of their apartment; it's hard to keep track of who is who.

Blue smiles at him, casual, calm, in his element, and Mackie's hit with the sudden desire to be somewhere else. *Anywhere.*

The pub door bangs open, and a group of students pours out. They're boisterous after celebrating the end of exams with some beers, though one voice pierces above the rest, echoing off the brick building many times. Joe Redding is big in every way, loud, tall, and thick, with the knuckles of a scrapper.

It's subtle, but Mackie sees Blue tense. That's his only tell, though. He continues his story as though nothing major has changed. The people surrounding him are not as steadfast. They shift uncomfortably and shoot glances in the approaching crowd's direction.

Altercations between Blue and Joe have been going on since first year and have been getting progressively more aggressive. The last time they had an actual faceoff was just a little over a month ago, at a party on the first Friday of spring reading week. Blue narrowly escaped without a fight, succeeding only because a second-year girl stumbled into the room and was sick on the floor. He slinked out amidst the ensuing chaos.

There's nothing to offer distraction now.

Mackie grips his cigarette between his fingers and crushes the filter, prepared for it but still shocked when Joe whips his voice above the others and disperses the fleeting joy of Blue's group. "Holy shit. Are you still here, faggot?"

Blue diligently continues his story, only faltering for a heartbeat.

Joe won't be ignored. "Hellooooooo, hear me?"

In the place where Blue pauses for laughter, there is only silence and then Joe's mocking guffaw as he uses his elbows to get through the crowd. His friends are talking excitedly and following close behind.

"Oh my god," Carley leans into Mackie and gushes. Her party plans are forgotten. "Are you seeing this?"

Mackie can't look away.

"What the fuck are you still doing here?" Joe continues in his larger-than-life voice. He's not used to being ignored. He positions himself in front of Blue, forcing Blue to acknowledge him. Joe's cheeks are fever-red, and his eyes dance maliciously. His friends snort. Blue's fan club has backed off some, except for the thin redhead. He bravely tells Joe to fuck off and Joe pushes him hard into the wall as though he weighs no more than a bag of flour. Probably doesn't, to be honest.

"Don't touch him," Blue warns.

"Or what?" Joe makes a show of looking around the circle. His friends now outnumber Blue's, and they both know it.

Mackie sighs and mashes his cigarette out in the butt can beside the table. He stands. His legs are sore from yesterday's run.

"Don't get involved." Carley grabs Mackie's arm and looks up. Her expression is reminiscent of Joe's, hungry for something bloody.

"Fuck off, Carley." Mackie shakes her off. She has the gall to look wounded.

Mackie's taller than most, not heavily muscled like Joe but wiry and strong enough for his own purposes. He usually slouches to stay out of sight, though. He isn't like Blue. He doesn't adore the rabid attention. If he can pass beneath the radar, all the better.

That won't be an option today, he thinks as he draws himself up to his full height and crosses the courtyard with long steps that make his muscles scream with adrenaline.

Blue has valiantly answered Joe's *or what* by standing between them. Mackie wishes he wouldn't. He's taller than the redhead, but he's not much bigger by any means. His frame is slight. Almost delicate. It reminds Mackie of a bird. He wouldn't be surprised if, under all those sparkly clothes, Blue's bones are hollow.

As Mackie draws closer, he can hear Blue say, "Your fight's with me. Not him."

Stupid Blue. He thinks Joe's like the other homophobes back home, mean until they get to know him, and if that fails, because sometimes mean people are just *mean,* and there's no fixing it, he expects spitballs, jeering and the occasional fistfight.

Things are different with Joe. Last summer, Mackie heard he caught a raccoon in a live trap and burned it with his lighter until almost all its hair was gone, and its skin was a red rash. He probably would have killed it if his sister Trinity didn't take the raccoon and call the police on him. He got a fine, supposedly.

The world's an unjust place.

"Finally, the queer says something sensible." Joe's grin splits his face as he folds his hands into fists. Mackie's heart throbs four beats for every step he takes. He's still too far away.

"Are we already onto pet names?" Blue flutters his long lashes, seemingly unaware of the danger. Sunlight gets caught in the glitter he's powdered on his skin, and his red and black eyeliner looks darker. "If I'd known, I would have thought up something original, like you."

"Fuck you." Joe punctuates his verbal assault with a physical one. Mackie's mind is a racehorse and all he registers is Blue's head cracking back against the wall. Blood gushes out his nose and mingles with his blue lipstick. Mackie's stomach drops; cool madness befalls him. His head empties of all thought as he closes the last bit of distance. Mackie grabs Joe by the back of the shirt and reels him around.

Joe's eyes widen in surprise just as Mackie hits him as hard as he's ever hit anyone.

Joe folds to the ground almost comically. He's drunk enough that he doesn't feel the pain, doesn't scream, doesn't curse, though his face swells immediately.

Mackie drops down on top of him and pins him where he lays. He grabs Joe by the collar and shakes him until Joe's rolling eyes settle on his.

"Apologize."

Joe's face folds in with anger. His eyes slit, so everything about him seems venomous as he slurs, "Fuck you. I'm not apologizing to a queer."

Thoughtlessly, Mackie again punches him for the insult. Bloody spittle slips from Joe's mouth, and he writhes to get away.

"Apologize."

"Fuck you."

Their audience has grown to twice its original size, and as one, they chant *fight, fight!* like a mob of screaming grackles. Mackie doesn't care. He cares about bringing justice to the world. He cares about stains like Joe Redding going out into society with their Big Opinions and Big Mouths, using their little cocks to make little people with Big Opinions and Big Mouths.

Mackie's cheekbone stings and his eyes water. It takes a second to digest why. Joe's still prone on the ground and his arms are trapped beneath Mackie's knees.

His friends, though.

One of them grabs Mackie's shoulders and yanks him back while another winds up with a ham-sized fist and punches Mackie square in the mouth. His teeth bite into his cheek. He tastes the blood on his tongue, sweet and salty and thick. He spits it out and thrashes, trying to get free. It's no use, the guy behind him is holding him tight. The one in front hits him again. Stars dance before his eyes and his ears ring.

The voices in the crowd are all distant, except for Blue. Blue's yelling. Mackie can't think of the last time he heard Blue yell. Or if he's *ever* heard it.

Mackie gets hit again. The pain is a flattening curve. Adrenaline dulls everything. There is time to feel it later.

He's yanked off Joe and pushed back. Someone is directly behind him and has no qualms about shoving a dazed man. Mackie catches himself on one of the brick pillars holding up the awning of the bar and pushes himself upright. Everything spins for one sickening moment before settling into reality.

Joe has made it to his feet with the help of two of his friends. He's swollen and bleeding from his nose and mouth, and one eye will not open. The good one, he trains on Mackie instead of Blue. Which, in Mackie's opinion, is how it should be. Unlike Blue, he doesn't mind using his fists to get his point across.

Joe lunges. Mackie gets out of his way and elbows him in the ear. His victory is short-lived. Joe's friends come at him again. Their attack seems coordinated, and Mackie can't keep them all back, though he does his best, hitting one in the gut and the other sort of off-centre in the face, aiming for the temple and only getting his ear.

Then Mackie is sucker-punched in the face while at the same time the guy on the right jabs him in the liver, and it all goes downhill from there. Joe takes advantage of the situation and pushes his friends back so he can lock his hands around Mackie's throat and bully him to the ground.

Still dazed, Mackie has a hard time pushing Joe off, even though Joe is drunk, and Mackie is sober. They crash onto the gritty pavement harder than Mackie is prepared for.

Joe tightens his hands and strangles him.

Spots dance before Mackie's eyes. His head smacks against the ground time and again. This isn't a typical fistfight; he can feel it. He's never been throttled like this before; Mackie is positive that given the opportunity, Joe won't stop. He's possessed by something animalistic and revels in it.

Mackie's panic is dull but everywhere, like electricity humming through hydro wires. He needs to switch their advantage.

Somewhere behind him, Blue is cursing. Mackie sees a flash of black and pale skin and the hands around his throat disappear. He sucks in greedy breaths. That's when he realizes it's not his panic humming through his thoughts like the electricity in a transformer, it's the air.

Goosebumps run up and down Mackie's arms, and the hairs on the back of his neck stands on end. Unconsciously, he skitters to his feet and backs up, away from the source. Away from Blue. The air purrs around him, high voltage. The crowd moves away in much the same way, all except for Joe. His gaze is narrowed in on Mackie, and nothing, not Hell or high water, will break his focus, his scowl says.

Joe rushes Mackie, fists balled. Simultaneously, a strong gust of wind rockets across the courtyard. One of the picnic tables lifts off its feet. It whirls past Mackie's face, so close, he can feel the way the air disturbs around it, and then it collides with Joe and squashes him against the side of the building. The window behind him breaks and glass rains against the pavement deafeningly loud. The picnic table falls away, and Joe crumples to the ground.

People are screaming and fluttering. Mackie can't concentrate on that. He can only look at Blue. His skin is glowing, and his eyes look black. His chest heaves with each insufficient breath he takes, reminding Mackie of the night he stole him from the forest.

Blue blinks and faces Mackie. His eyes lighten back to brown. Tears have made his makeup smear down his cheeks in dark, muddy tracks, and blood stains his face.

"Are you okay?" Blue's voice is high-strung and thin.

Mackie doesn't know how to answer that. Thankfully, he doesn't have to lie. Professors and security guards fill the courtyard, eyes on Mackie and Blue, the only two that remain still in the chaos.

Hoping to earn some bonus points, Mackie lugs his body toward the security guards before he can be beckoned.

Chapter 3

Mackie's apartment is a dank cave at the end of what the townspeople have dubbed No Daddy Lane. It's low-income housing for students and families, and when he's not kept awake by his neighbour's raucous fucking, heard through the floor, it's children outside, disturbing his sleep by screaming in the bitter hours of the early morning.

Blue doesn't complain, though his room is right below the uncourteous neighbour's, and if Blue doesn't complain, Mackie won't, either.

For once, the building and all the property around it are quiet. Mackie throws himself down on his old-as-your-grandma couch and swallows three Tylenol and an Advil; he has a headache like an earthquake.

Blue chooses the arm next to Mackie's seat and balances gracefully on it. He smells of antiseptic and cologne. His expression is disapproving as he studies Mackie's discoloured face and neck. He presses a cloth full of ice against Mackie's lip.

"That hurts." Mackie winces and pulls away. Blue anticipates his movements and plants his legs over Mackie's, making a cage that traps him on the couch. He takes Mackie by the chin and holds him still.

"It'll only look worse if you don't ice it. You know that."

He does know it. Mackie sighs and goes limp. Feeling boisterous after that win, Blue adds scolding to his activities. "You shouldn't have gotten involved."

Mackie does a lot of stuff he shouldn't do, smoking, Carley Hunts, the occasional dose of LSD, and, of course, getting involved in fights that don't have too much to do with him. Knowing he shouldn't do something has never stopped him from doing it.

"Aren't you going to say something?" Blue asks.

His throat feels tight with disuse. He's grunted just a few words since stepping out of the security guard's office with a strict warning ringing in his ears: he's not to be seen on campus unless it's for his exams.

He's not the best student in the world with a 3.0 GPA, compared to Blue's 4.0. He's not a troublemaker, though, preferring to end fights rather than start them. His spare time finds him in his garage, fixing vintage muscle cars like his prized GTO. When he's not doing that, he sits quietly in the front of class doodling in the corner of his notebook dreaming about the autobody shop he's going to open next year, with a bit of luck and a hefty loan from the bank.

His record kept him from being expelled. Joe's broken ribs saved him from a similar fate. And Blue's exceptional grades granted him a crushed carpet to walk across. They were all lucky, in their own way.

Blue presses against Mackie's mouth with too much force, this time purposeful. "*Mackie.*"

"What?" Mackie barks.

Blue doesn't recoil, frightened of Mackie's sharp mood. They know each other too well for that. "Why did you do that?"

Mackie casts his gaze aside. "The same reason I ever do. Because he was wrong."

Blue shakes his head. "This was different. *You* were different."

If they're going to talk about *different,* Mackie has quite a few questions of his own. If he thinks about the charge in the air, he still gets goosebumps.

He's not ready to ask, though, and leads with ignorance. "I've gotten into fights before."

"You never looked glad before," Blue says. "You wanted to hit Joe."

Oh yes. He's wanted to hit Joe for quite some time now. "I hate Redding. I hate people *like* Redding."

Blue sighs and shifts. His knees press against Mackie's chest. His skin is warm through the material of his pants. Mackie tries to relax into the familiarity of their closeness. Sometimes, it feels as though they've been together always, and the night in the forest was all just a weird dream.

"Who was the guy?" Mackie asks, remembering the redhead leaning into Blue and laughing.

Blue turns his lips down in a frown. "Just someone that comes to the Alliance meetings."

Just someone. Blue is always pulling people into his orbit and then forgetting they're there. It's not malicious; it's just his nature. Mackie's always played the humanizer and easily falls into that role again. "He thinks you're great."

"Everyone thinks I'm great," Blue says. Beneath his cocky smile is an edge of dismissal and sadness. "Except you, maybe."

"Why would you say that?" Mackie narrows his eyes; the motion pulls on a cut over his eyebrow he doesn't remember getting; it threatens to split open again. He wonders if he should have it stitched. He declined a visit to the hospital when Blue offered. He doesn't want to explain the fight yet another time. People just kind of tilt their eyebrows like he's insane, and it's frustrating, thinking these fights are important to only himself.

"You're always rushing in to defend me," Blue says. He's looking at Mackie, and Mackie's looking at Blue's smeared lipstick. There's still some red caught in the corner of his mouth. He didn't even bother to take care of himself. How very like Blue.

"I didn't see you punch Joe in his stupid mouth," Mackie mutters.

Blue holds up his fingers indignantly. Beneath the tips of his fingers and his chipped black nail polish, his knuckles are blue and purple. "I did, actually; he just has an exceptionally hard head and didn't feel a thing."

Mackie laughs: it's the first thing that's felt normal since the fight.

Blue's returning smile doesn't reach his eyes. "I don't know what happened. After."

Mackie isn't sure he wants to talk about the table. "Micro storm." That's what everyone's saying. *Micro storm picked up the picnic table and threw it against Joe. Micro storm broke three of Joe's ribs.*

"Yeah," Blue agrees. "Micro storm."

Two days pass. Mackie's classmates, who have never been overly friendly, nor overly rude for that matter, give him a wide berth and study him nervously when he treks to class to write his final exam. It's his elective history, and he flies through the test without issue.

When it's time to go, he beats the rest of the class out of the room and stalks home to pack. On his way, he sees Carley sitting on the stone wing wall at the front of campus, smoking, and kicking her heels against the plaque commemorating Sir Barron Owensboro for his contributions to science.

Carley locks eyes with him. He braces for anything she might say. She seems to be choking on something. Stuttering. Heaving. Desperate to spit it out. In the end, she only seems capable of lifting her middle finger. Mackie's relieved. He doesn't know what he'd do if she harassed him. Or worse, came over and tried to act like nothing happened.

Blue is sitting on the other side of the wall at a picnic table with the redhead guy from the pub. Whatever they're talking about, the redhead is starry-eyed. His will be another broken heart to add to Blue's collection.

Blue cups the guy's face and pulls him in for a scorching kiss. *Just someone.*

Mackie hurries by.

In his apartment, Mackie leaves his bedroom window open as he packs, allowing the early spring air to rush in. It's getting heavier by the minute. Despite the sunny sky, rain is on its way.

Blue comes home an hour later and retreats into his room where he packs. He's not meticulous like Mackie is, folding his clothes neatly. He prefers to throw his stuff everywhere and shove it into his loud suitcases without reason. *If it fits, what's it matter*? is his favourite mantra.

Blue's never understood there's a place for everything.

It's been an entire hour sitting in the front seat, fielding skeptical glances from his mother. She's eyeing Mackie's split lip, the cut over his eyebrow, and black eye, probably reliving Mackie's youth. He was always getting into a fight in high school. At first, because he didn't appreciate the way people treated Blue, and then because he realized if he had a reputation as a scrapper, Blue would be shaded under that umbrella, too, and fewer people would bother him.

And it worked. By grade twelve, seven fights a year had whittled down to two.

The silence goes on. Mackie thinks he's free of Mom's questions, but when they're just pulling into the driveway, she gathers her courage and asks, "What happened to your face?"

"Bear fight," Mackie says spontaneously. It's meant to be a joke; she doesn't laugh.

"Mackie."

"They're rampant in Owensboro," he continues, looking out the window like it doesn't matter one way or another.

"You're not funny."

"I think he's hilarious," Blue leans forward between the seats to add. Mackie notes that he keeps his bruised knuckles out of Mom's line of sight. He follows Blue's lead and hides his own beneath his jeaned legs.

"Not you, too." Rachel King bunches her nose up and looks at Blue in the rear-view mirror; the expression makes the lines on her face more pronounced. Mackie doesn't know when she got so old-looking. In the three years he's been in college, she's aged seven.

The headlights wash over the house. Mackie drinks in its white brick, though he doesn't smile. Like most things in his life, he has a complicated relationship with this house.

"How's dad?" He's been afraid to ask, he realizes that now. There's no more running, he's home for the next four months.

"The nurse said he was sleeping."

Mom must know she's avoiding the question. Mackie doesn't push because there really is bliss in ignorance. As soon as he walks into the house, that blissfulness will be dashed, and he'll have to face reality again.

Well past its zenith, the moon hangs in the sky, a sleepy, blind eye staring down at Mackie through his leaded windows. He flicks through Instagram, uploading a picture of his residence and hashtagging it #anotheryeargone. He doesn't usually bother with things like social media. It's a lot of effort, and he's busy, but he's trying to ignore the quiet cries below his bedroom, happy to use anything as a distraction.

His father is having a bad day. According to his Aunt Priya, who came for dinner and left as soon as the dishes were done, *most* of Dad's days are bad now. Mackie is equal parts sad and annoyed, and annoyed that he's annoyed.

The cries go on for another twenty minutes before Mackie decides he can't take it anymore and shucks off his sheets. There's a flannel housecoat hanging on the hook behind his door. He throws it over himself so he's not walking around the house in just his boxers.

The air in the hallway is much warmer than in his room, where the window is open, though the floor is still cold on his bare feet. He takes the stairs two at a time.

The downstairs looks like one of those staged homes in those magazines women in their sixties buy from pharmacy-convenience store combinations, needing to either feel bad about themselves or to make themselves look cultured—*look at the life you* can *live!* The furniture is in good condition, the floor is brand-new, and the decorations Mom has thrown up are tasteful, if not this side of cheap. But everything's arranged nicely, so people around town can feel unironic when they say, *they were a nice family before all this tragedy.* Before Dad walked himself out in the middle of the night, naked, dick flapping in the wind, screaming about sacrificing himself to devils, and Mom chased him down. Before the following altercation because Dad didn't recognize her. Before the police, the doctors, and the medication that doesn't do anything to help.

Dad is in the living room, sitting on the couch with his blankets pulled up to his chin.

He barely recognized Mackie when he and Blue came in through the door that night. *Or didn't see us,* Mackie thinks, remembering the way his father's eyes glanced over them with hardly any acknowledgement. After Mom prodded him, he grunted something that might have been a greeting, but mostly, he ignored them, preferring to stare out the kitchen window into the forest with the same blank expression he usually wears when he looks that way. *Devils, devils, devils.*

Still, George King acts like Mackie isn't there. His eyes are fixed to the outside; his fist is in his mouth, and he worries his teeth on the wrinkled skin. He wears the same expression he used to wear when he was still well enough to look at the hydro bill.

Devils! Dad has never believed in devils.

They used to look a lot alike. Mackie gets his height from his dad, his fit, thin frame. The blue-grey eyes, the freckles, and high, thin cheekbones.

But now his father has lost so much weight, his skin looks translucent, and his shoulder bones press out like axe blades through his T-shirts. He hasn't shaved in months, and his beard is long and scraggly, like his hair.

Mackie pushes his own hair back from his face self-consciously, afraid he's looking in a mirror. His fingers meet the ends and break through in short order. The relief is minimal. He can't shake the fear that this will be his fate, too, as it was Grandpa Roy's, Great Grandpa Thom's, and probably every other male in his family. Alzheimer's, madness, obsession with beasts. Both Grandpa Roy and Great Grandpa Thom walked themselves into the forest, muttering about whatever it was their addled brains cooked up, and never came back.

Like it's a family curse or a twisted tradition, Mackie's gruesomely counting the days until Dad does it, and then he does, too. He hasn't told anyone about that thought. He's leery of it. Once in the forest was enough.

"Dad?" Mackie asks. His voice squeaks out too low; Dad doesn't hear him. He grips his blanket and tugs on the threads obsessively. He mutters. Mackie struggles to understand what he's saying.

"Wipe your eyes if they're bleary,

Watch Sorrow sleeping, weak and weary..."

"What is that rhyme?" Mackie asks, louder. He's never heard it before, and it gives him goosebumps.

George repeats it over again, then pauses while he tries to remember what comes next. Stiltedly,

"Crush your bones and take the heart

So they never have to be apart."

Another pause as he tries to recall. His mind fails him, and he starts from the top again.

It's dark outside the house. Shadows roll off the forest and meld together, one on top of the other. They seem to move. To *breathe*. To watch. To creep.

Something skitters at the treeline, small and twig-like. When Mackie's focus falls on it, it gets still, and Mackie can't see it anymore. Something else moves, though, on the opposite side of the yard, bigger, more ungainly.

It's the trees, he thinks abruptly. He hasn't thought of the living forest in a long time and is startled by the thought now. Not because of how ridiculous it sounds. But because of how *sure* he is that the oaks are uprooting themselves, one spindle root at a time and stepping closer.

Coming for Dad.

Once he thinks that, it's like someone holds a lantern beneath the canopy and he can see them more clearly. The trees part like a curtain and a tunnel appears, leading way down into the darkest part of the forest, like a throat. The new leaves shudder as one. Mackie feels their call. He wants to go to them. He wants to see what's at the end of the gullet. He presses his hand against the glass. He can feel the forest's heart beat on the opposite side. It's a limping thing, and sluggish. With a little help, it can be better... It just needs—

"You should get away from the window." The voice is cold water in Mackie's hot veins. He tears his eyes away from the trees and looks back at Blue. He's in a black and gold pajama set, and his feet are as bare as Mackie's. His blonde hair is dishevelled, and his face is clear of makeup. He's all pointed angles, his nose, his lips, his cheekbones. Stark. Blue has always been stark.

Mackie lets his hand fall. His skin burns with cold. The fog of his palmprint evaporates slowly.

"Come on." Blue takes Mackie's father by the hand. Unlike Mackie, he's not afraid of the way Dad is wasting away, a prisoner in his own body. He's gentle but firm, leading George down the hallway, back into his bedroom.

Despite Blue's warning, Mackie steals another peek outside. There is no more tunnel, and the trees appear still. Yet, the backyard looks wrong. *It's the shadows.* Though he hasn't been home in months, he knows how the moon draws dark lines on the grass, and almost none of these lines are familiar.

He concentrates on one particularly stout and malformed blob by the birdfeeder at the forest edge, and before his eyes, it comes to life. It darts as it moves from the shadow to the light. Scales bunch together and run down its short back; hoof-like feet dig into the grass. That's all Mackie sees before it launches into the forest and disappears.

The forest is full of devils.

"Mackie."

Mackie whips around. Blue stands on the bottom step of the stairs. His bare feet look pale against the dark floor.

"Come on." Blue waits patiently until Mackie pulls himself away from the window, drifts his way, and even follows him up the stairs and into his bedroom.

Mackie drops to his bed while Blue pulls the drapes to block out the moon. Suddenly, he feels very tired.

"I put your dad to bed." For as long as Blue's lived with them, he's always been careful to say *your dad, your mom,* or *Mister King,* and *Missus King*. He's never let this place become his completely. The thought makes Mackie sad.

"Thanks."

Blue's smile doesn't quite reach his eyes. "What's going on, Mackie? You've been weird since we got here."

Mackie's surprised to hear himself say, "Dad. He's dying." It's the first time he's spoken it aloud, though it's been a reality for six long months.

"We all are," Blue responds.

Not everyone forgets who they are as their body wastes around them.

"I hope I don't go like that." Which sounds pretty selfish once it's spoken aloud.

In Blue's responding silence, Mackie can hear the leaves beyond the window chattering again. "I think there's something in the forest."

"Trees and grass and leaves. Fungus, wolves, worms." Blue ticks them off on his fingers.

Ghosts. Witches. Devils.

Chapter 4

Mackie peels his eyes open one at a time the next morning. It feels like he hasn't slept for long at all. He's exhausted, right deep down into his bones. Under that is a sensation he doesn't know how to explain. When he breathes in, the air feels... Fresher.

Something's different.

He's alone in his room. He remembers Blue leading him upstairs and the way the moonlight shone on his hair and skin, the confession Mackie made aloud, inhibition momentarily crippled by fear of his own mortality. He doesn't remember Blue leaving.

Mackie drags on a pair of dark jeans before pulling aside the drapes.

The sun is just cresting the horizon. Its glow glazes the treetops and a narrow slice of grass in sticky orange sherbet.

The world has changed.

Their garden is in full bloom, though the snow's only been gone a week or two, and the forest is bright, flagrant green. The leaves, so stumpy and new when they arrived home last night, look lush and fresh and full of hope, unfurled on their branches, stretching for sunlight.

"What the hell?" Mackie murmurs. It's like waking up to the first snow of the year, a world slathered in makeup—fresh-faced, ready for a new day.

He pulls on a pair of socks and a plain grey T-shirt and takes the stairs two at a time. He can hear Mom's snoring and Dad's gentle breaths as he passes their room.

Mackie follows the stench of coffee into the kitchen where Blue stands overtop a simmering pot.

"Morning," Blue says without turning around.

"Did you see the forest?" Mackie is near breathless.

"What about it?"

Though Blue's tone is bland, Mackie has lived with him long enough—has studied him long enough—to know when Blue is uncomfortable. The muscles between his shoulders tighten minutely, and his hands, almost always in motion, still. Just like when Joe Redding stepped out of the pub.

Mackie banishes the memory of violence. "It's like summer came overnight."

Blue turns. He's already swiped eyeliner beneath his eyes and wriggled into tight black jeans, knees ripped, and a vibrant pink sweater. His socks are in the shape of sharks, snapping at his ankles. He holds his steaming coffee between his hands, smiling a little like it's all a big joke. "You're whacked."

"The garden is *flowering—*"

"Which is how it was when we got home. It's called climate change, Mackie."

Blue has an unprecedented ability to make Mackie see things his way. But not today. Something is different—about the weather, and about Blue, and Mackie won't let Blue sweep this under the rug. "No, that's not it, and you know it. *Maybe* there were sprouts last night, but this morning, the garden is in *full bloom.*" He can see the tulips from where he stands, their red and yellow faces wide open, full, flush leaves stretching up toward the sky like people in prayer.

Blue raises one perfectly sculpted brow. "It was dark when we pulled in, how would you know?"

"The light was on." And he'd spent an inordinate amount of time staring out into the garden after dark. Into the place where the forest had, for a moment, opened and invited him inside.

It chills him to the bone, wondering what would have happened if he'd walked out the door, and into the bars of trees.

"Do you want a coffee?" Blue asks.

"Thanks." Mackie takes Blue's rather than make his own but doesn't drink it yet. Its warmth chases away his deep unease. The forest is beautiful, yes. Beautiful things can also be dangerous. Spiders and scorpions. Snakes, storms.

Blue looks out the window and whatever he sees there makes him smile. He takes a five-dollar bill off the counter and goes to the door. Mackie waits at the kitchen table, hearing the hinges creak open. Cool spring air rushes into the house. It smells almost magical. He's always loved spring best.

"Hey, Kevin," Blue greets.

Mackie props his chair up on two legs and leans back to see beyond the kitchen wall. He spots Kevin Evans on the stoop in his *Lakeview Citizen* T-shirt. The matching baseball hat is crushed over his blonde hair. Behind him is a cart overflowing with newspapers, each tied neatly with twine. He's hit a growth spurt and is almost as tall as Blue's bicep.

"Hi, Blue!" When Kevin smiles, it nearly destroys the bags beneath his eyes, but Blue is astute.

"Were you up all night playing Animal Crossing?" Blue scolds lightly.

Mackie expects Kevin to drop his eyes sheepishly, or grin wider while he gushes about gameplay, not look ashamed.

"No. I just couldn't sleep last night," he says.

Blue sobers. "Why?"

"Mom and Derek were fighting," Kevin admits to the ground. "I went out on the roof to get away from it, and while I was up there, I thought..."

Blue gets intense. Though there's some distance between them, and he's not the focus of Blue's attention, Mackie wants to squirm beneath the strength of his glare. "Thought what?"

Kevin checks over his shoulder before he speaks. There's only the driveway, lolling behind him like a gravelly tongue, and trees crushing in to hear his words. "There was something in the forest in my backyard. It was kind of glowy. I thought it was a ghost." The last bit all runs together, making it difficult to understand. His whole neck is red, his cheeks.

Mackie watches Blue's shoulder muscles get tight all over again. "There isn't any such thing as ghosts."

"There could be."

"No, there can't."

"You didn't see it." Kevin drops his chin further as he speaks, defiant but ashamed. "It looked like a girl, but her eyes were black, and she wanted me to come into the forest."

"How do you know?"

"She told me."

Blue reaches for Kevin's shoulder and waits until Kevin lifts his eyes again. "Don't ever, ever do that, okay? No matter what she says. Stay away from the forest."

"I thought you said—"

"Just stay away."

Mackie's skin pricks and the hairs on his arms stand on end with the weight of Blue's words. It's not just his words, though. It's something else. *His magic,* Mackie thinks, and knows, though it's ridiculous, there's nothing else it can be called. It peels off Blue in layers, filling the air as it filled the courtyard those days ago, except this time, there is no violent intent behind it.

Blue releases Kevin a second later. Kevin's eyes are blank, and he blinks slowly.

"This is for you," Blue says like nothing happened between them and hands Kevin the five-dollar bill. "Don't spend it all in one place."

"Thanks, Blue," Kevin says and takes the crisp five hesitantly. He seems much less burdened now, just a little dazed. He looks at his cart of newspapers as though he can't remember all the steps it took to bring him up the driveway, to their front door.

"See ya, kid." Blue closes the door practically in his face and leans against it. He doesn't look at Mackie right away, pretending Mackie isn't still leaning as far out in his chair as he can to watch their conversation.

"What was that about?" Mackie asks anyway.

Blue pulls himself upright and comes back into the kitchen. "Nothing."

Nothing is always something. Mackie lets his chair smack back to the floor. "Something spooked you."

"He's just a weird kid is all," Blue says. "I worry about him and his mom. Derek's a bastard, and they fight a lot."

Which is true, Derek Merk is a douche that frequently cheats on Kevin's mom, and yells at Kevin for playing basketball, video games, and breathing, but that's not the whole truth.

"You saw what Kevin saw in the forest," Mackie guesses. "When? Last night? Is it the same thing that was in our backyard?"

"There wasn't anything in the backyard," Blue reiterates.

Mackie holds the coffee cup tight even though it burns his hands. "I know what I saw."

They've never come right out and talked about the forest, but they've never really avoided it, either. It's always been the festering wound in the backyard, full of huge spiders and dangerous predators and otherworldly things, like the twin-headed hawk they saw soaring above the canopy two winters ago, or the bald bear-sized beast with a coyote nose they spotted gorging itself on a deer while on their way to school the last day of grade twelve.

"It was dark, it could have been anything." Blue gives Mackie his back and makes himself a new cup of coffee, putting an abrupt end to their conversation.

Mackie sighs, sips the coffee he stole, and winces when it touches his still-raw cuts.

Though the sun blazes in the cloudless sky, its heat is spring-pale when it reaches the ground. It's still a big change from winter and feels warmer than it is, especially with trees enveloping him on three sides.

Mackie lets his bare toes graze over the grass in the backyard while he stares out into the forest, daring it to move as it had last night. His phone rests quietly beside him, ready with video only so he can prove to Blue that he saw what he saw, not because he thinks catching a devil on camera will make a difference.

A beer sweats in his hand. The taste lingers on his tongue, bitter and sweet, and only mildly distracting. His thoughts keep churning toward last night, the malevolence he felt staring out into the darkened backyard, the throat opening into the trees, inviting him inside, and the change that has overcome the land this morning.

Dad's rhyme.

It doesn't mean anything. He was just rambling.

But it's sticking in Mackie's head like gum to hot tarmac. And coupled with the change that's overcome the land overnight...

This morning, as he did that first day after he brought Blue home, Mackie waited with bated breath when his mother came down the stairs. Even had explanations primed, theories they could bounce back and forth. Yet, when he pulled the drapes back for her, she just glanced out the window and grunted non-committedly. Yes, the grass suddenly needs to be cut, maybe you can do that this afternoon, Mackie. Yeah, the trees now all have huge leaves.

Strange things happen in Lakeview Township. So what?

It's the way things always are.

He remembers the year all the newts crawled out from beneath the logs and baked to death beneath the July sun how eerie and quiet the town was before and after, and how shortly after that, a great swath of the forest died for no apparent reason. It's still dead today. He drives by it slowly sometimes, just to see if any of the trees have fallen over to make room for more life, but even the sedges at the edge of the forest are limp and rotten, with no new growth. That place could be a photo frozen in time.

That's how it feels now, wavering on an unknowable edge, ready to topple over and change.

Despite how long he watches it, the forest doesn't move. He feels it studying him back, though, as curious as he is, perhaps, and isn't that unsettling? What does the forest have to be curious about him for?

Mackie waits until noon to leave his property. He wants the sun to be at its highest point, making it impossible for it to cast wild shadows along the road. The dark has never scared him. What lies in it does. Some people—like Shawn McIntyre—might call him a wimp. He prefers the word *prudent.* He still dreams about the night he met Blue. The way the forest felt poised, ready to flay him alive if he lingered in its verdant depths. Rub him out. No one remembers Mackie King. It could do the same thing again, and will, given the opportunity.

Everywhere he goes is a riot of spring colour. Goodbye, dreary April, and hello June. No one cares what happened to May.

In scrubby lots slotted for development, children pick daisies and pluck the petals. He loves me, he loves me not, they chant. She loves me, she loves me not. He loves me, she loves me. Not. Not. Not. Squealing laughter and birds and the dull, mono-hum of insects.

Rebel Park is in the center of town and surrounded by the forest on two sides. The river loops to the north. East of that is the main road. West and south are wildland, the kind of place where fairies might live.

Mackie takes a wide berth around a few couples picnicking while their kids play on the playground. He heads directly for a casually scruffy man sitting on a sagging park bench, watching a German Shepherd chase a ball he's too old to catch.

Sam Chester has been flicking a lighter, trying to catch his cigarette. He pauses to look up at Mackie. "Hey, man." He has a rasping voice. He's no older than Mackie's twenty-three years, but he talks like a life-long smoker. Mackie asked him once how long it had been, and Sam told him he started at the ripe age of seven. After a few arguments about quitting that lasted into his early teens, Sam's family gave up and started buying him cartons of cigarettes for his birthdays and twenty-four packs of beer for Christmas.

Mackie eases onto the bench beside him and puts his head way back. The sun hits his face, and he shivers. The plants might think it's June, but the air still has a nasty nip to it.

"Done for the semester?" Sam asks. Despite his grades, Sam chose not to go to community college. He's never worried about it, though. His family are farmers by day and fortune-tellers by night. He's learning to take over.

"Yeah."

"And you couldn't walk out without busting up your face, huh?" Sam teases. He used to watch Mackie brawl, wincing every time someone got a hit on him, but never interrupted or cheered. He has a stoic personality that Mackie's come to lean on.

"What did you think of the daffodils this morning?" Mackie skirts his fight. It's hard explaining why he feels the need to get his hands bloody. Not because he thinks Sam won't understand. But because he *will.*

"What's to think?" Sam says. He's one of the only people in town who doesn't pretend the forest is a natural place. The year the newts crawled out to die, Sam made a line of drink umbrellas, trying to save them. In the 2017 flood, unnatural fish with round, human eyes, and human-like mouths that they used to scream in human-like ways, were regurgitated by the flooding river. Sam was out there at dawn with his hatchet, to put a bloody end to the lot of them with the efficiency of a farmer slicing the head off a chicken. He didn't like to see them suffer.

"Something's happening again," Mackie poses. *Something.* The forest. *Happening again.* Changing in new and mysterious ways.

With his cigarette lit and coiling smoke toward the sparse clouds, Sam throws the ball for his shepherd again. The dog lopes after it. Sam leans back, making his shoulders even with Mackie's. "Something's always happening."

"Actually?"

"That's what my Nan says." Sam's Nan, Isabela, is a lot like Sam: rough edges and shrewd glowers that can stop even the strangest peculiarities in their tracks. Sam's sister, Theodora, likes to say if a devil walked out of the forest with a bowler and a bad attitude, Nan could glare at them and make them see things *the Chester way,* which is to say, *the right way.*

"Just last week, she said she caught a ghost."

Mackie scrutinizes him. "You can't *catch* a ghost. If you can, what you have isn't a ghost."

Sam lifts a broad shoulder. "Whatever it was, it was nasty."

"You saw it?" Mackie asks, suddenly interested. He's only ever seen a forest thing from a distance. "What'd it look like?"

"Like a dead fish. Half my size. Kinda slippery and slimy. It was sniffing around the barn, scaring the goats. Woke Nan up in the middle of the night. She rushed out there with her salt and put an end to it."

Lakeview, for all its obstinate obliviousness, is a suspicious town if you know which dark corners to peer into. Isabela Chester fancies herself something of an exorcist, and she gets her exorcism salt from Father Callahan, who may see the beasts in the forest or may just have an overactive imagination and access to Amazon. It's hard to tell sometimes.

None of this is spoken of in polite conversation, however, and must be gleaned in bits and pieces.

"What happened to the body?" Mackie asks.

"Buried it in the front yard. Killed the apple tree once it was in the ground," Sam says sagely. His shepherd brings back his ball, panting, half-dead but still hungry for more. Mackie pats his head and tells him he's a good boy before wrestling the ball from his mouth and chucking it far across the park. As Mackie tracks its trajectory, he spots a familiar figure in the distance, dressed plainly in a pair of jeans and a sweater. He wouldn't know it was Blue if he didn't recognize Blue's familiar white-blonde hair. He's the only one in Lakeview with that electric shade.

Blue gazes into the forest with his hands planted on his hips, as though confronting it. Mackie can't see his face, but he knows Blue's expressions better than even his own and can imagine the way he's popping out his lip in what is almost surely annoyance. What Mackie can't imagine is why Kevin Evans is with him, staring off in the same direction. Both seem tense and reserved, in the park, and separate from it at the same time. If they're talking, they make no indication, both facing straight ahead, backs to the crowd.

Sam's voice brings Mackie back. "Nan's worried."

"About?"

"Like you said, these last few days, the forest has been more active than it's been in decades. She thinks maybe Sorrow is waking from her sleep."

Mackie curls his nose. "Sorrow is a myth."

"And summer doesn't come overnight," Sam responds.

"Touché."

Mackie leans forward and settles his chin in his hands. Sam's dog has returned with the ball, but he doesn't hand it off to Mackie again; he's finally submitted to the ground. His chest rises and falls, gulping in huge breaths.

"Maybe she's onto something. I thought I saw devils in my yard last night. That's weird, isn't it?" Mackie adds. They're never so bold.

Sam suggests, "Maybe they're attracted to you."

Mackie rolls his chin in his hands to glare. "Is that supposed to make me feel better?"

"It definitely wouldn't make me feel better."

Which only makes Mackie sigh.

"Do you want me to see if my Nan will give you a charm for protection?" Sam asks.

"If a witch rises from the dead, you think a charm's going to stop her?"

"Sorrow isn't dead," Sam corrects him. "She sealed herself away to preserve what little life she has left until a time when she can revive herself."

Mackie can believe in moving trees, devils, and a forest that spills bones out of its borders in neat piles, but those are things he's seen. Sorrow is a Halloween tale he's pretty sure the librarian, Miss Gregson, made up.

"Doesn't matter if you believe it or not," Sam finishes, "It's just a charm. Won't hurt either way, right?"

Mackie watches Blue come unglued from the forest edge and walk toward the Kings' red Civic parked haphazardly at the side of the road. He has to stretch his legs over the ditch to get into the driver's side. It peels out onto the tarmac and then is gone.

Kevin goes the opposite way, hacking it on foot.

Mackie opens his mouth to tell Sam it's fine, he doesn't need help. He hesitates under Sam's study. He came along after Blue, transferred from Lakeview's southern school, but just like he knows the forest is more than just a clump of trees, he can see Blue is different. Sam has asked Mackie *how* in a roundabout way, but Mackie has never come out and said he stole Blue from the forest. That might imply that one day, he must give him back.

"Fine. Ask her," Mackie says.

Chapter 5

Later that evening, Mackie follows the thrumming of techno music up the stairs. He pauses by Blue's room, the epicentre, and peers through the crack in the partially open door.

Blue's room is as boisterous as he is, painted pink and black and bedazzled with glittery things. Pictures cover every inch of wall, mostly of the Kings on various vacations, Mackie and Blue, arms around each other on beaches, and boardwalks, shooters pressed to their lips on fluorescently lit strips, and some are of Blue's friends. In most, Blue is staring straight-lipped at the camera—it's how he says he looks best (which is a matter of varying opinion)—but his eyes are dancing.

Blue is at his vanity, carefully applying a dark layer of eyeliner. He uses a brush to smear it, making himself look dramatic and tired.

His eyes meet Mackie's in the mirror. "You can come in."

Mackie pushes open the door and enters. The room smells of candles and cologne, the good stuff that Mom got Blue last Christmas. He rarely breaks into it.

"What's the occasion?" Mackie sits on the bed where he can watch Blue in profile. He used to like doing this when they were younger and is surprised the fascination hasn't waned. How many new people has Blue turned himself into with a few strokes of a brush? Does he like it? Or is he like Gloria Bell, Mackie's ex-girlfriend, who changed herself into a new person every day to forget the one she was without her makeup? And if that's the case, what's Blue hiding from?

Mackie doesn't have the nerve to ask him.

"There's a party tonight," Blue says. Once he's satisfied with the layers beneath his eyes, he uses a separate brush to smear his upper lids with an icy blue shadow.

"Where?"

Quickly, Blue says, "At Shawn's."

"Shawn Macintyre?" His name brings up memories of bruised ribs and split lips. Shawn was where the fighting began.

"He's not that bad anymore." Blue smudges black lipstick across his mouth, masking the pink tones beneath. He looks like he belongs in a rock concert. Something flamboyant and rough, *loud*.

"Are we talking about the same Shawn Macintyre?" Mackie asks. "Tall, kinda moose-like, bad fucking attitude?"

"His dad died last year," Blue says. He moves on to his hair, slicking the blonde locks back with a product that smells strongly of sandalwood.

"That doesn't make someone a good person."

"No, but it can change you."

Mackie scoffs. "Shawn Macintyre has all the personality of a cinder block. Nothing's changing him."

Blue doesn't laugh like Mackie's hoping—like he normally would. He turns his head this way and that in the mirror, then slides large beetle earrings through his ears, reminding Mackie fiercely of the night they met, when Blue was picking water beetles from the river and crushing them between what had seemed like sharp, white teeth. If he looks hard, he can almost see them under the glamour.

"Are you coming tonight or what?"

Immediately, Mackie says, "I don't want to stay home by myself." Not where he can watch his dad slowly husk out like corn in autumn. He doesn't look at Blue as he speaks, afraid of seeing the acknowledgement on Blue's face. It would crush Mackie if Blue decided he doesn't like the coward sickness turns him into. He can fight any fight for Blue, be brave in a hundred different ways, but take his childhood role model and strip him of his power, and it's too much to bear.

This house is a prison for Mackie. The bars get smaller each time he escapes and comes back. He always returns anyway.

Blue purposefully smudges some of his lipstick with the tip of his finger. He looks like he's spent hours kissing some unlucky soul. Mackie has seen it all: late-night poetry at Blue's window, lovelorn notes, sparkling, hopeful eyes. Blue never settles down, though. He's a drifter, and he likes it that way.

Blue checks himself over one more time then rises from his seat and comes to Mackie. He stands between Mackie's legs, close enough that Mackie can feel his body heat through his clothing. He dips his fingers into his hair product, warms it between his hands, and slides it through Mackie's hair. His fingers are long, and his movements are precise. Mackie's scalp tingles.

"Dying isn't supposed to be easy." Blue has a way of imparting little wisdoms like that. He's as blunt as a hammer and twice as decisive, the tough love you need without the barbs. But beneath his steadfast look is a gentle one. He understands about hard things, he's lived a hard life, after all.

Icy moonlight plays through the grass and lights the way down the abandoned dirt road. It's picturesque and spooky, like an empty glass castle. Dew beads on the thin ends of grass at the side of the road and soaks through the tops of Mackie's Converse. His socks and the bottoms of his jeans are soggy. Blue doesn't seem to notice. He's in a pair of boots tonight, heel square and modest compared to most of his other footwear. They're pleather and the shiniest things Mackie has ever seen. Blue has them zipped up over the legs of his tight pants. On top, he's in a white collared shirt that he's left open, showing off the collection of tattoos on his chest, and though it's night, he wears blue-lensed glasses.

The wind blows and it's cold. Despite his scarce attire, Blue doesn't shiver. Fashion over function, always. Mackie has no such qualms and nestles deeper into his leather jacket. "I can't wait until the GTO's running."

"How's it coming?" Blue asks. Mackie can never tell if he's terribly interested in or if he's just entertaining Mackie's fascination with the beat-up car he saved from the scrapyard once upon a time.

"I spent some time on it this morning," Mackie says. "Just need to replace the fuel pump and timing belt."

Blue laughs. "Remember your dad said it'd never run?"

"Yeah."

"Probably wouldn't if he were working on it, he's too impatient. Not like you," Blue says with surprising fondness. He tacks on, dreamy, "I love the way you love old things."

Mackie flushes for no reason he can name and rushes to change the subject. "Who's all going to be there tonight?" He can hear the party's deep bass already. It echoes off the trees and the gravel road, as glaring as a piece of glass shoved into your finger.

"Everyone," Blue answers over the sound of a twig breaking in the forest. He flicks his eyes toward the trees, making Mackie nervous, yet, when Mackie looks, too, he can see nothing but the faceless mask of conifers. "Everyone will be there."

Lakeview only has a small cohort. There were fifty people in Mackie's graduating class, and of those, approximately twenty have returned to town for the summer. "Bree?" Mackie ventures.

Blue distances himself from whatever's caught his attention in the trees. He cocks his head to the side and looks at Mackie from the edge of his sunglasses. "Is that a bad thing?"

It's not a *great* thing despite what Blue's smile suggests. Their relationship has been on and off since the first year of high school, and when it's on, it's glorious. Likewise, when it's off, it's spectacularly bad.

"I don't know," Mackie says and means it. It's been months since he's seen her. Probably, she wouldn't even talk to him. And that's good. The last time they split, she had quite a few deep-cutting things to say about the way Mackie was living his life. Or not living his life, as it were. "When we were together, she kept bugging me about not going out with her to things like this." Mackie makes a point of looking between him and Blue and Shawn's approaching house.

"It's not your scene."

"I know."

As an afterthought, Blue asks, "Do you want to go home?"

"I don't know. Not really."

"But kinda."

"Kinda," Mackie agrees.

Blue rolls his eyes. "No one's going to care if you show up tonight. Except me, and honestly, I'd rather you be comfortable than go to something you hate."

"Shouldn't you be encouraging me to be more social?" Mackie asks. It's the way it's always been. He had people he hung around, like the group that met outside the forest that summer night, grade six, with their bags of Pixy-Stix, but never any close friends that he'd bring home. Not like Blue.

"You should do what you want. We're not kids anymore, and I don't need to impress your mom, she already loves me."

Mom used to rejoice whenever Blue brought a new friend home. It meant, by proxy, Mackie had a friend, too. Only it didn't always work that way. By his own designs, admittedly. He didn't care for most people.

Even while Mackie was being included, he was the outsider at the edge of the circle, trying to figure out how to fit in and mostly not wanting to.

Mackie slows to light a cigarette. The wind keeps putting out the lighter. He's just about to give up when Blue stops in front of him and cups his hands around the flame. When it's burning evenly, he takes the cigarette from Mackie and puffs on it as payment, leaving a ring of black lipstick behind on the filter.

"Do you want me to spend the night with you?" Blue asks, handing back the cigarette. Mackie's stomach drops. It does that sometimes when Blue says things like that. Harmless things, but the words twist up in his head until he thinks maybe they aren't as harmless as they should be. It's possible, if he listened to what Bree said during their last argument, he doesn't *want* them to be, either.

That thought is a stray one, flitting in and out of his mind quickly; Mackie doesn't give himself time to register it before it's gone again. "I'm an adult," he says with a smile and an elbow in Blue's shoulder. "Pretty sure I can handle it."

Blue laughs it off and whatever awkward air between them, real or imaginary, is gone.

The Macintyres live on a farm set well off the beaten path. Its driveway is made of dirt and riddled with potholes and the occasional beer can. More lie in the field, winking in the moonlight. They are a pathway to the party, like the breadcrumbs in Hansel and Gretel, except instead of a nasty old witch waiting to put him in her oven, Mackie is faced with the peers of his past, glory-hungry enemies and indifferent 'friends'.

A massive fire roars in one of the abandoned horse paddocks. The Macintyres got rid of their horses when Shawn went on to college—full football scholarship. Shawn's never been very bright. In high school, Mackie had it on good authority he paid the A students for homework. It's one of those things people say won't pay off for them, but it always does. His family has money.

Even before his father died and left his mom a substantial life insurance policy, they had money, and money can buy a hell of a lot when you're willing to pay for it.

As they draw near, the oppressive heat of the fire hits Mackie like a dry, hot blanket. The property is crowded with bodies. When Blue said *everyone,* he meant it.

There are people of Mackie's age and some younger, even a few older, men with wizened faces and smiles that go on forever, drunk, stoned, happy, and women with cigarettes poking between their lips, trying to catch someone's eye.

Laughter and chatter fill the air to bursting. It lulls as people notice Blue and Mackie. A girl squeals, startling Mackie. She launches herself across the paddock into Blue's arms. "Blue!"

He lifts her up and spins her around. Graceful as a ballerino, he sets her down without stumbling or struggling. "Hi, Kristy."

Blue was Kristy Chow's tutor in Math class. Mackie thought she was half in love with him. Platonically. Kristy is unquestionably gay, and when they left for college, she had just come out to her parents with her girlfriend Mai. Back then, she idolized him and his blatant disregard for society's norms, and it's clear she still does.

"Come on! I want you to meet my new girlfriend," Kristy gushes.

Blue glances back once to Mackie and smiles toothily. Apologetically. Mackie waves him on. There is no reason they should both be miserable.

The party rages around him. He takes the flask from his pocket. He topped it with tequila before leaving, the good stuff Dad bought three years ago and hasn't touched since.

It burns his tongue gently and settles its warmth in his stomach.

"You surprise me, Mackie," says a familiar voice. Mackie spots Sam sitting with his legs slung between the boards of the cedar fence. He has a filthy baseball hat on backwards and wears a red flannel jacket and a pair of torn-up jeans. A red dixie cup hangs limply in his hand, empty. Judging by the half-cocked smile on his face, Mackie thinks the drink is not his first or even his second.

Mackie crosses the sandy ground and drops his weight beside Sam's. The fence boards bow and threaten to break. He holds up some of his weight on his legs. "What are you doing here?"

"That's my line," Sam says. "This isn't your crowd."

"Blue wanted to come." Mackie takes more tequila. It spreads through his limbs and burns away the anxiety that's been festering there. He can breathe. "Gave me some lines about Shawn changing since his dad died."

Sam rummages through his pocket for a package of cigarettes and knocks out a neatly rolled joint. He sparks it up and passes it to Mackie. "Anything's possible, I guess. But not fucking likely."

No, not really.

"So," Mackie says, looking into the crowd, "I'm here because I was guilted into coming. What are *you* doing here?"

Sam considers his response. "Just wanted a night to *not* think."

This is not the same Sam that Mackie met in the park. Layers Mackie didn't notice in the daylight have peeled back and he can see something is very wrong.

"What's going on?"

Sam sighs. "Dora's pregnant."

The news is a heavy, wet blanket hitting Mackie in the face. "Shit."

"Yeah, that's what I keep saying. Shit. She told me two days ago, and I *still* can't believe it." He twists his head and sets unfocused eyes on Mackie. "She doesn't want the rest of the family to know yet." He flicks the joint unnecessarily, looking for anything to do with his hands. "So, you know, don't say anything."

"Who's the lucky guy?"

Sam cocks one eyebrow. "She wouldn't tell me."

Probably because she's afraid Sam would kill him. Theodora's his baby sister, nineteen just this year. "James Darson?" Mackie guesses.

"They broke up."

"So?"

Sam has no response.

"If you want, I'll go scare the shit out of him and see if he'll confess," Mackie offers. "I think I saw him by the alfalfa field when we came in." He's only half-kidding.

Sam is a skeptic, and his doubt is written all over his face. "Your face is still beat up from the last time you scrapped. Maybe you should just take the fucking joint and try to stay out of trouble tonight."

Though Sam's mood only sours his own, Mackie takes back the offered spliff. Desperate to change the subject, he asks, "Do you think it's weird?"

"What's that, bud?" Sam takes the joint back from Mackie and breathes deep, deep, trying to fill himself with smoke in the hopes that when he breathes out, there won't be anything left in him, no worry, no pain. He's not usually this broody.

"This morning, the forest changed the landscape, and no one's talking about it. We're just all out here partying like nothing's happening."

Sam's face splits into a dopey smile. "Maybe they do see and they're just smart enough to ignore it."

"Not like us," Mackie mutters.

"Not." Sam takes a drag. "Like." And another. "Us." And one more still.

Near twelve, Mackie spies Bree laughing next to the keg. She hasn't changed much. His reaction to her hasn't, either. He gets still and quiet.

"She's been asking about you," Sam says. Even stoned, he's in tune with Mackie's thoughts.

"Yeah?" He's more interested than he should be. Then he would be if he were sober.

"Wanted to know if you were home yet."

Their eyes lock across the field. Bree's are still big, bottomlessly blue. Her smile cuts her face in half. It's short-lived, though, and she goes back to listening to whatever story Craig Goreing is telling her.

"Do you think her cronies help pour her into those jeans?" Sam asks idly.

"I used to help her, so yea." Then Mackie elbows him. "Stop looking."

Sam cackles. "Why?"

It's just an automatic response. He doesn't *want* Bree, not like he used to, but the familiarity they had... he craves that. Someone to fall into at the end of the night. To press their cold palms against his too-hot cheeks and sweaty brow. To shush him into peace when his mind is a drunk riot.

Usually, Bree was the one encouraging him to be drunk, though. He sees the toxicity. Tastes it. Wills it to be bitter even when it's sweet.

"She's dating a hockey star." Sam digs out another joint as he speaks and lights the end. Mackie's world is still spinning from the last one; he doesn't know how Sam is still sitting upright. "And that, my friend, is nothing but trouble."

That's Bree. Nothing but trouble.

Someone across the field sends up cries of a water fight. Splashes and squealing laughter follow. Mackie frowns. "What the hell are they swimming in?"

"Pond." Sam staggers to his feet. A hook of a smile makes him look five years younger. "Come on, King."

Mackie diligently gets to his feet and follows staggering Sam. Paddock fencing warps and warbles in his periphery and the sand does nothing for his balance.

Sounds of buoyant laughter lead them to a place where the firelight barely touches. A group of ten stand around a seething pond, while four people brave the cold and murky waters to wrestle.

One is Kristy Chow, on top of the shoulders of a reedy man Mackie doesn't recognize, against two other people from their graduating class. Nicole Burgess, and Henry Pike. Philip Ewing officiates the match from a perch on a sawed-down log at the pond's edge.

Already, Mackie can see Kristy and her partner have the advantage. Henry can't seem to find his balance and Nicole teeters dangerously on his shoulders. They clash together in fits of laughter and splashing, and in seconds, Kristy has Nicole crashing into the water.

There is some part of Mackie that expects she won't resurface. You don't go into any water that's not Yarrow Lake, certainly not this close to the forest.

She pops back up, sputtering, and grinning while Henry coughs and grumbles.

"This round goes to Kristy and Mike!" says Philip.

"Who's next?" Kristy lifts her voice above the laughter. "Who will challenge the reigning champion?"

Blue materializes beside Mackie. He has two Dixie cups in his hands and seems to be drinking them both. "One win doesn't make a reigning champion!"

"Throwing shade, Blue? Get in here and back up your challenge!" Kristy whips icy water in their direction. Mackie cringes when it touches him.

Blue turns to Sam and shoves the Dixie cups in his hands. "Hold my beers."

The crowd hollers, catcalls, and only gets louder as Blue strips his shirt and his boots and his jeans, right down to his underwear. He's thin, and his muscles spare. Tattoos cut dark marks on his skin. Mackie knows them by heart; he's sat beside Blue for every single one of them. He still stares as though it's his first time seeing them.

"You need a steed!" Kristy reminds Blue.

Blue makes a show of looking around the crowd, eyes lingering on Shawn, who stands across the pond with a bottle of whiskey in hand. He opens his mouth and Mackie knows at once, that as soon as Blue asks, Shawn will agree, regardless of their history.

Before that can happen, Mackie steps forward. He would never normally. All eyes that aren't fixated on Blue, are pinned to him. It makes him itchy. He's here, though. Nervous, but here.

His peers catcall louder as he strips his shirt, shoes, and pants. Cheer him on. Sexualize and diminish him in ways he's never been before. In a way, it reminds him of the night he stole Blue. People spurring him on. Taunting. The words and circumstances are different; the players are the same. They've all changed, gotten older, and more bitter, but the dare is still there.

Cold air bites into his naked chest and legs until everything shrinks away.

Blue seems as surprised as Mackie is to see him there. If he says anything, Mackie might slink away, shamed. But his eyes skate over Mackie's form once, then he looks back to Kristy with a wicked grin. "It's over for you now, Chow."

Mackie tells himself it's too late to back down. He's already mostly naked, and Blue is tugging him into the pond. Mud slips between his toes as the icy water bites into his ankles, shins, and thighs. Blue pushes on Mackie's shoulder, and Mackie drops obediently to his knees. He gasps as the water touches more tender areas. It's the kind of cold you won't get used to. He doesn't know how Kristy's partner is standing it. Mackie's teeth are chattering already, and they've only just begun.

More icy water sluices down Mackie's chest as Blue throws his legs over Mackie's shoulders one at a time and gets situated. He wiggles, bones pressing in. Mackie grips Blue's thighs.

"Rise, mighty steed!" Blue commands in an overtly baritone voice.

It takes some focus to get properly to his feet. The ground is soft and so is Mackie's understanding of balance. He's too high and has had too much tequila. They almost go down before they even begin, staggering dangerously close to the surface of the water. The crowd laughs. Mackie finds a spot of muck that's tougher than the others and gets upright. The laughter settles to the occasional chortle.

"We'll have a good, clean match!" Phil tells them over the residual noise. "On your mark! Get set! Go!"

Mackie digs his feet into the muck and lets Mike and Kristy come for them. They collide with a splash of startling water, and Blue and Kristy wrestle. Mike staggers around, trying to give his partner a better advantage. Mackie turns his feet only when necessary and occasionally jars his shoulder into Mike's to put them more off balance.

Blue's laughter fills the air. His skin is warm where it meets Mackie's and keeps the water from touching him. One hand he has clasped in Mackie's hair, the other trying desperately to dislodge Kristy from Mike's shoulders.

They spin around the pond, stumbling into deeper, murkier water. *Into the devils,* Mackie thinks without any source to back it up. Any panic he should feel is a long way off. There is only this.

Blue tightens his grip on Mackie's hair, his legs on his shoulders. Mackie's entire body feels scraped raw. He's aware of everything. Blue's breaths swelling his lungs, his muscles tightening, the warmth of his legs, his laughter, their closeness. *Everything.*

Blue leans forward. The heat of his body bleeds into Mackie's neck. There's not an inch of space between them. A dizzy spell almost makes Mackie lose his footing. They need to be done with this quickly. He needs some space between him and Blue. He needs to not think about how it feels to be under him and caught in this spell. How good his fingers feel in his hair, and how much his blood throbs every time Blue's muscles flex.

Gritting his teeth, Mackie lurches toward Mike, hooks Kristy's flailing leg around Blue's, and lifts with considerable force.

Kristy yelps, teeters, and then crashes into the water with Mike. Blue raises both hands into the air and cheers along with the crowd. His elation burns through Mackie, too, and he can't help the foolish grin on his face. Crouching, he lets Blue climb off his shoulders. Once he's gone, Mackie feels both free and empty.

He falls twice getting back to shore and thinks maybe he feels hands sliding across his ankles, trying to hold him underwater. They draw away before he can panic, and Sam pulls him out. Someone else shoves a towel at him, clean and dry. Mackie wraps it around his shoulders. His teeth chatter.

"I didn't expect to see you having any fun."

Bree, Mackie realizes. Bree handed him the towel. He blinks. She stands in front of him, looking at him with those same big blues, with the same expression he's never been able to decipher.

"Hey," he says lamely.

Blue exits on the other side of the pond, dangerously close to Shawn. Mackie watches them, expecting a confrontation. Shawn says something no one else seems to see or hear, their eyes on Bree and Mackie, and Blue nods with a little, secret smile. He heads toward the house, and a second later, Shawn turns and heads in the same direction.

He's changed, Blue said. What does that mean, though? Half of Mackie thinks he should chase them down, and half thinks whatever's going to happen, it's none of his business.

Mackie's still indecisive when Bree takes him by the hand and pulls him toward the still-blazing fire. Three steps in, Sam shoves Mackie's clothes into his hands.

Sam's expressions are more than easy to read. Don't get caught up in this shit.

Any warning from Sam shouldn't be taken lightly.

With that in mind, Mackie says to Bree, "I hear you have a boyfriend." Which is not the most tactful way Mackie has told Bree he doesn't want anything to happen.

He expects her to pause, to question why he's led with that statement. The only thing she says is, "We broke up."

"When?"

"A few hours ago."

He grinds his feet into the hillocky ground and pulls Bree to a stop. She turns back on him. Moonlight makes her look eerie, sharp, with terrible angles, long, filaments of blonde hair. Wicked. Wicked. Wicked. A gash of red for a mouth. Beautiful. A fairy from folklore.

"What's wrong?" Bree whispers.

"I can't do this again." Mackie doesn't know which creature has possessed his body and keeps taking control of these situations. He's not sure he likes it. This isn't how he stays out of sight. This isn't how he *goes with the flow.*

"You can't find an empty spot in the field and let me revenge fuck?"

Bree has always been a straight-A student. The captain of the cheerleaders in high school, head of the debate team, the good girl. Her lewdness seeps out at odd times, though, and is still as enticing today as it was in grade eleven when she would drag him into the weight room and give him blowjobs between English and Science.

Like a shark sensing blood in the water, she grabs him by the back of the head and pulls him in toward her mouth.

It feels like they're being watched. Mackie breaks her hold on him and looks beyond. The field stretches out around them, boulders, hillocks, the pond not too far away, where the group still lingers, two people in the pond, searching for challengers, the firepit blazing against the shadows. The farmhouse sits on the opposite end of the property and a light blazes from inside. And then there is the forest, the great looming presence, waiting for them to get too close so it may entice them into its belly.

"You don't want me anymore?" Bree breathes against his neck. She punctuates her words with a wet kiss. Goosebumps that don't have much to do with the cold dance down Mackie's arms.

He hesitates. Bree takes that as an invitation and grabs the place stiffening between his legs. He gasps at the sudden pressure. His underwear is cold. Bree's palm is warm.

"Come on, Mackie. This is what we're good at."

The light in the house goes off and doors close. From the forest, something chitters, soft, and for some reason, it makes Mackie think of Blue, which makes him think of the way Blue's eyes landed on Shawn first when he was choosing someone to be his wrestling partner.

Then, "Bree!"

Bree jolts. Mackie doesn't move, watching a huge guy cut through the party. He lingers around the bonfire and likely can't see past the blaze.

Mackie rasps, "Boyfriend?"

"Ex," she reiterates with a scowl.

"I'm not sure he feels the same way." Mackie pulls away from her, grateful for the excuse. Honestly. What was he thinking? "You should go talk to him. Maybe you can patch things up."

Bree shies away from the bonfire. "No fucking way."

"Bree!"

"Did he hurt you?" Mackie hunts her face for bruises. Carley had a boyfriend that would beat her. Leave her black and blue, head to foot. She left him just before second year. He still hunted for her until Mackie cracked his cheekbone one night, fourth semester. Though it broke two of his fingers and hindered him for weeks, he'll do the same for Bree. In a heartbeat. She's better than Carley. Better than almost everyone. The first nearly always is.

Violence isn't saving anyone, Blue said to him once. That said, Carley's ex never came back, so maybe he's wrong.

Bree sees something in Mackie that makes her hesitate. His righteous viciousness has always thrilled her in the past. Now, she looks at him with fear. She pulls away and shakes her head. "No one's hurt me, Mackie."

There's an instant where he thinks he wants a fight anyway. It's the tequila, he tells himself. It's the tequila and everything is fine.

Nothing is fine.

He's never felt so helpless.

Mackie reminds himself, *that's not Bree's problem.*

He breathes deep. Thinks of Blue. *Violence isn't saving anyone.* He lets his breath out. He's good. He's calm. He's dangerous, but he's calm. "Sorry."

"Mackie—" Bree reaches for his cheek.

Mackie pulls abruptly away. "Don't." He can't get sucked back down into the spiral. It's toxic, and he so desperately wants to bleed out the problematic toxicity. He needs to get out of here.

"Bree!" her ex yells again, the loudest yet.

"Over here!" Mackie cups his hands around his mouth to be heard.

"Are you out of your fucking mind?" Bree hisses. "He'll flatten you."

Flatten?

"Oh." Mackie remembers his state of undress and trips into his clothes. The boyfriend doesn't seem to know where *over here* is, giving Mackie plenty of time to wrestle his pants over his still-damp skin.

"You're an asshole, Mackie," Bree watches his body even as she insults him. He considers quipping back, thinks better of it, leaves her standing in the field seething and heads back toward the bonfire.

"That was fast, even for you," Sam greets from the same spot he occupied before.

Mackie throws himself down on the fence and rests his cheek against the wood. "Fuck off."

"Yes, sir." He lights another joint and offers it. Against Mackie's better judgement, he takes it and sucks on the end.

"Have you seen Blue?" he asks around his exhale.

"Since he disappeared with Shawn and no one seemed to notice, you mean?" Sam grins. It's a secret joke, made at the expense of all of Blue's lovers. Mackie can't bring himself to snicker at the magnetic pull Blue has over even the most horrible people. Sam sobers. "They came out of the house a few minutes ago. I don't know where they went from there."

Mackie starts to stand. Sam catches him by the elbow. "Remember when I said to chill?"

"You don't know Shawn."

Sam points to a scar just above his eyebrow where Shawn punched him in grade twelve. "I disagree."

"Then—"

"Just chill," Sam reiterates. "Smoke. Chill."

Mackie huffs and falls back into his seat with Sam's joint between his fingers.

It's late. When Mackie looks up, the moon is slumping drunk in the sky, stretching for the forest like it's going to fall in amongst the trees and be lost forever. Goodbye, night sky.

People are still laughing. The sounds are muted. In amongst the noise is the intermittent fighting of couples and friends. The night's fun has gone sour.

Sam is passed out with his face pressed against the fence. He moved to the ground because he complained the world was spinning too hard. Mackie sympathizes. His world is doing circles, as well. He wants to get up, though. He needs to pee, and it was bad twenty minutes ago when he first noticed. Now it's almost unbearable.

He musters his strength and wriggles out from between the boards. His feet sink into the sand and the splintered cedarwood fence digs into his hand, but he's up, and now that he's here, he doesn't feel nearly as detached from himself.

There's a rent-a-toilet by the barn. Mackie tries the door; it's locked. Figures. He moves on, spotting a bush beside the barn and down a little hill, toward the river. The forest looms ahead of him, a massive, breathing thing. Its many eyes pass him by. He's not afraid of it, not like he should be; he doesn't feel afraid of anything right now.

The bush is a rose bush, of course, and when he uses it to steady himself, he pricks his finger on the thorns. It aches very distantly. Crickets scream, an owl croons and a coyote howls, all the noises Mackie couldn't hear with the roaring of the fire in his ear and Sam yakking on about sending some of his goats to slaughter.

It's nice, the night.

He finishes up and starts to head back up the hill, deciding it is past time to pack it in. The hushed sound of nearby voices stalls him.

Mackie spots the cherry of a cigarette burning in the darkness. The moon's finally given up and has sunk below the treeline, and the stars are winking out one at a time as a storm gathers.

"I'm not gay or nothing," says the first voice.

"Definitely not." Just a hint of sarcasm.

"I'm serious."

"Okay."

"Like I said earlier. Just curious."

More sincerely, "I know."

A staccato breath. "I can trust you, right?"

"I never kiss and tell."

The sound of feet shuffling. "Just hurry up and do it already."

Mackie's eyes adjust to the night and the forms start coming out of the layers of darkness.

Blue's white shirt is pushed off his shoulders and hangs from one arm, a limp white flag. I surrender, it seems to say, do what you want. Blue prefers to spend the last part of any party at someone's mercy. Why the *fuck* is it Shawn Macintyre's, though?

Shawn is standing close enough to Blue, it's impossible to imagine their purpose can be misconstrued by anyone.

Blue cradles Shawn's face almost tentatively and kisses him. In seconds, it's torrid enough to make Mackie blush. It's clear he's been thinking about this moment for some time. Maybe for as long as they've known each other. What is it about fire and water? They can't seem to stay away.

Shawn gets his pants undone. His white underwear bulge lewdly with his erection. Blue's shorter than Shawn by just enough that he looks up at him through his lashes, gaze scalding. He touches Shawn's chest and starts to sink to his knees.

Mackie turns away, eager to get out of there and give them some privacy despite the warnings trilling in his head. It seems wrong to leave Blue alone with Shawn after all the years of torment and abuse, but it's like none of that matters right now. Shawn is just desperate to have Blue on his knees and Blue is happy to be there for him.

Mackie's heard it all before, the biggest homophobes are those that are gay themselves. He's never imagined the stereotype is true. That Shawn Macintyre might hate Blue so much because he *wants* him and hates himself for it.

Mackie steps on a twig. It breaks under his weight. He winces and comes to a complete halt.

"What was that?" Shawn's words come out as scalding as acid.

"Probably a cat or something." Contrarily, Blue's voice is heady and sweet, lust drunk. How easy he falls into the trap of infatuation. He forgets that once, Shawn broke his finger for no other reason than he didn't like that Blue wore nail polish. He would have broken the rest, but the teacher came to the sound of Blue's wailing and Mackie launching himself at Shawn from across the room.

There have been other incidents, numerous enough, they just blur into one another. Blue sweeps all his bad memories under the carpet, hoping never to look at them again. Mackie's constantly lifting the corners, desperate to do the opposite. It makes for good life lessons. He'll never be caught in the trees with someone that made his childhood a living nightmare.

Once again, Mackie hears the wet sounds of kissing. He stares resolutely ahead, visualizing his track back to the barn. A moment goes by, and something happens that makes Shawn's breath catch. Mackie makes a break for it, tiptoeing quietly until he's sure he's out of eyesight.

He keeps going past the paddock, leaving the party behind. A guy's retching at the side of the driveway. His girlfriend is complaining to him. *You always do this*. They're all slaves to their weaknesses, Mackie thinks.

Halfway home, a car passes and honks at him, though he's on the other side of the road. The back window rolls down. He catches sight of blonde hair before whoever is in there chucks their half-full dixie cup out at him. Though it doesn't reach, and the beer splats on the road, it pisses Mackie off anyway.

He swears loudly at the retreating car and picks up the garbage to recycle. He doesn't want to clean up after assholes. He wants to enrage the forest even less.

He thinks he can feel the forest's sigh of approval as a small gust of wind ruffles his hair. The pomade Blue applied for him is coming out, making him look washed up and worn out. He just wants to sleep.

The front light is on for him when he wobbles up the driveway. Mackie leaves it on for Blue, too.

The sky is grey-blue when Mackie hears rustling in the bathroom outside his door. The tap is running, and below the constant drum of water, he can hear sniffles. He opens his eyes. They're bleary and his head is full of cotton.

He's left his door open some, and when the bathroom finally opens, he can see Blue's silhouette. He's traded his party clothes for a ratty band T-shirt and a pair of track pants.

Mackie pushes himself up on his bed. Hearing squeaking bedsprings, Blue hesitates outside the door, peering in. It's not light enough that Mackie can read his expression. It's the slump of Blue's shoulders that makes something stick in his chest.

Mackie recycles Blue's line from the previous afternoon. "You can come in."

Blue does without further hesitation and closes the door behind him. He slides across the floor, as silent as a ghost.

Mackie's bed is a twin, barely big enough for him these days. He moves over as best he can and peels back the covers. Blue settles in beside him, curled up with his knees against Mackie's thighs.

"Are you okay?" Mackie asks as he settles back down.

"Just tired," Blue's voice cracks around the lie. Mackie gnaws his sore cheek, enraged by whatever's upset him. He doesn't want to scare him off, though, so he doesn't pursue it. Not yet. They haven't laid like this since grade nine. The first few years Blue lived with them, he had night terrors and wouldn't sleep unless he was beside someone.

Mackie pulls the blankets up over them both and closes his eyes again. He can feel Blue's breath breaking over his lips, sweet and laced with the scent of alcohol, and his hands, cold and bundled together, brushing Mackie's bicep. He falls into a deep sleep.

Chapter 6

It's well past noon when Mackie next opens his eyes. Blue is awake already, dark eyes boring into Mackie's. Sunlight struggles through the heavy drapes, making the room shadowed like the blanket forts Mackie used to make in the days when he still felt carefree enough to make them.

His mouth tastes like last night's tequila and smoke, and there's a headache pressing between his eyes. "What time is it?"

"Late," Blue answers. When he talks, it pulls on his newly split lip. He winces, though he tries to pretend it doesn't bother him. "What happened to Bree?"

"Her boyfriend showed up," Mackie says.

Blue doesn't even look surprised. "Was he pissed?"

"Dunno. Didn't stick around to find out."

Blue seems a little too relieved. He goes to gnaw on his lip and winces again when it hurts him.

"You should put saltwater on that."

Blue prods the wound with his tongue. "Thanks."

"Do you want to talk about it?"

"If I say no, will you drop it?"

"If it has nothing to do with you and Shawn last night."

Blue lets a noisy gust of breath out his nose.

"Hell, Blue."

"He's not used to the idea," Blue admits.

Mackie's rage simmers: he can feel it threatening to boil over. He tries to keep his voice calm, his tone inviting. He's someone Blue can talk to. "That's not an excuse."

"You don't know what it's like," Blue says. He's not fooled by Mackie's placating tone. He doesn't raise his voice, but Mackie feels the clapback like it was him that Shawn hit and not Blue. "His dad used to hit him with a horsewhip every time he'd do something his old man thought was gay." He throws the word like it's a live grenade and he must duck for cover. "He'd do it until he bled. To his own son. Because he wasn't attracted to the kind of people his old man thought he should be attracted to."

Mackie feels a small pang of sympathy. It evaporates while he watches Blue prod his lip once again.

"The world's a shitty place," Mackie says in the resounding silence. "But—"

"Thank you for worrying," Blue says, and it's clear the conversation is over. He crawls out from between the sheets and leaves Mackie's room, closing the door behind him. Mackie rolls forward into the spot Blue left. His warmth is already fading.

What little is left of the day, Mackie spends nursing a hangover in a disenchanted stupor. Blue won't look at him and finds ways to fill his time that doesn't involve Mackie. Mackie tries to do the same, but the only other person he wants to talk to is Sam, and the only person that seems to want to talk to him is Bree, with texts like *can we talk about last night?*

He ignores Bree, and Sam ignores him.

With nothing else to do, Mackie is forced to stay home. The air feels strained inside *and* outside the house. The forest seems to dance with static electricity every time Mackie gets brave enough to look at it. Contrarily, the inside of the house is stagnant and stale, thick with a terse silence that he can't even fill with the sound of music.

He chooses instead to go into the garage to work on his GTO. He's making great progress until Mom comes out and asks him almost sheepishly if he can make Dad lunch while she does some grocery shopping. He agrees only because he loves her more than he hates the thought of his father dying.

Once she leaves, the afternoon is rife with non-conversation and lots of news on repeat.

Around four, Dad goes for a nap, and Mackie finds himself in the backyard again, superstitiously looking at the forest and the huge slate of clouds hanging over top of it. It's raining in the trees; he can hear it. It's probably a peculiar thing for other places in the world to have such microclimates, but Sorrow's Forest seems to have an ecosystem of its own, like the Amazon, but colder, more remote, and mostly devoid of the screams of life. It's a place for the sad, as Mackie's grade school classmate, Heidi McGregor suggested on the balmy afternoon the bones of her grey tabby, Mister Sneed, turned up at the forest edge.

Mackie's phone trills at his side in the undulating siren of an Amber Alert. He's always hated that noise. It's eerie. It reminds him of air raid sirens, which reminds him of the fragility of life.

He reads the alert twice and still doesn't quite understand.

Thirteen-year-old Kevin Evans, missing. Last seen in Rebel Park, Saturday, April 7th. Five-foot-seven, one hundred and twenty pounds, blonde hair, fair skin. Last seen wearing a red hoodie and blue jeans.

The back door opens, and Blue is there. He's dressed more plainly than usual in a pair of jeans and a shiny gold hoodie. His lip looks even worse now, swollen and crusted with blood. He hasn't used the saltwater Mackie suggested, probably because Mackie suggested it.

"Did you see?" Blue asks unnecessarily; his gaze is settled on Mackie's phone in his hand, and just like that, the obdurate silence, the awkwardness between them is gone.

A bad feeling sets down its roots in Mackie's chest. He's not a fan of the manic look in Blue's eyes. As though the wind agrees with him, the air gets cold and whips around his feet. He shivers and watches as the flowers, bright in bloom just a few minutes ago, start to curl in on themselves for protection. If it gets much colder, they'll wither and die in no time.

"I saw him," says Mackie. "I saw him yesterday. And he was fine." *Fine.* Fine and then he wasn't. Fine and then *gone*. "You were with him."

"I know."

"His mom must be going crazy."

"I know."

"We should..." Should *what*? What can they possibly do? Then it hits Mackie and it's so obvious, he's embarrassed it took him the seconds it did to come to this conclusion. "We should look for him."

"No one finds the people that go missing in Lakeview," Blue says.

His words settle around them like a premonition. Mackie swipes at them with optimism. "Maybe today they do. Kevin is too young to be gone without a trace."

Blue knots his fingers together nervously but Mackie doesn't pay attention. His thoughts are already racing through the possibilities. "We can check the quarry first. And then the old drive-in. Kids love to hang out there... oh, and the park in the direction I saw him going last..."

"Wait," Blue says, and Mackie pauses in rising from his chair. Blue swallows. "Before we do that... I... I have something I should show you." The tremor in his voice has Mackie's heart sinking.

"What is it?"

"This way." He takes Mackie by the arm. His hand is as cold as ice, and Mackie shivers as he stands from the lawn chair and follows Blue around the side of the house to the dirt road.

Blue marches like he's on a mission. On either side of the road is the forest, split in two by some brave settler.

The presence of the trees is oppressive, almost in the same way an August humidity is, except the temperature just keeps dropping and dropping until Mackie wishes he were wearing his coat. Shortly after that thought strikes him, a stray piece of snow flutters through the air, carried out of the forest by the wicked wind. It melts when it hits the ground.

Blue doesn't talk, and when Mackie speculates aloud about where they're going and what they're doing (did Blue spot a body in the ditch? Did he see someone take off with Kevin?), Blue pegs him with a sharp look like, *shut up, the forest is listening, and her heart is still broken.*

It's hard being silent. Though Mackie's generally quiet, nervousness makes him blather. Blue slides his hand down Mackie's arm and lattices their fingers together in silent support. Mackie's head spins. He looks at their hands. In the back of his mind, he wonders what it means. If it means anything. The thoughts sink like sediment beneath the panic he feels for Kevin.

"How much further?" The green number at the end of the driveway is a speck in the gathering shadows. Mackie doesn't relish being before the forest at any given time, but especially at dusk, and especially on days like these when she feels bad-tempered and frustrated.

"Not much." Blue tightens his hold on Mackie's fingers like he thinks Mackie might bolt, and it's true. As the sky darkens and the temperature slumps, he thinks about stretching out his long legs and running away. It'll feel good to feel his feet slapping against the dirt road, and to have the cold air stinging his lungs, believing that the forest's devils are trailing behind him and will never catch up.

Mackie glances nervously at the bars of tree trunks.

The thing about the forest is this: you can't have a symbiotic relationship. The forest has a long memory, and whatever happened to it in its past has tainted it. But sometimes, *most times*, you can coexist by staying out of each other's way. When her devils leave the shade of the canopy, they die. And when some foolish person wanders under her canopy, they don't come back.

Still, he walks on. It's Blue. He muddles Mackie's reasoning.

Finally, two kilometres down the road, a pathway cuts into the trees. Mackie drags his feet. He's not as brave as he was when he was a kid, darting into the forest's cold embrace just to say he can. The night he stole Blue, he emerged a victor, but he still can't say why. Perhaps Sorrow took pity on him. Perhaps he was just incredibly lucky.

"We shouldn't go into the trees." It's suicide.

Blue pulls him on as though he doesn't hear Mackie. "Hurry. We don't have much time."

Much time for what? Mackie's too afraid to ask. His heart is banging into his ribcage, making a hollow thud each time it hits. He can barely breathe as first Blue steps over the narrow ditch and Mackie follows.

Trees bend over Mackie, furious, wrinkle-faced matriarchs, daring him to put a toe out of line. Their knotted eyes make him nervous when he looks at them too long. He doesn't want to go any further for fear of their wrath. Blue doesn't seem to care, and he pulls Mackie along with him, too. Punishment be damned.

Again, Mackie tries, "We shouldn't be here."

Breathlessly, Blue says, "We'll be okay in the forest for a while, just hurry."

He sounds confident enough, Mackie believes him.

He lengthens his steps, crushes dry leaves and soggy moss, and breaks small branches. He can hear the forest lamenting each time he unintentionally injures it, trees croaking together back and forth, as though instead of dried branches, Mackie's snapping arms at the elbow and the trees can feel pain. When he breaks one that's not quite dead, a branch comes out of nowhere and whips him under the eye and splits the skin in retribution. A thin runner of blood slides down his cheek. Mackie swipes it away with his sleeve. He tries to be more careful; the forest does as well.

It gets no-stars-in-the-sky dark, and the forest opens—not its canopy, that's just as far-reaching as ever, but the tree trunks bow out, and the ground sinks to create a dish in the earth. At its epicentre is a sparkling pool. Mackie hesitates to investigate what's below the surface just in case he sees something he doesn't want to see. Of course, its glittering surface is what Blue is most interested in.

He pulls Mackie on without regard for mundane concerns—a forest that eats people? So what? Uncharted territory in its gullet? Someone must discover it.

He generally looks at home everywhere he goes, Blue just has that kind of aura about him, but as he stands before the pool, shining in its eerie cold light, Mackie appreciates that Blue is a boy stolen from the trees. He doesn't fit in Mackie's world the way he fits in here. He's mystic and supernatural, and there are things about the forest that he knows that he shouldn't—like the pool. He knows it's special. Mackie does, too, but unlike Blue, he has no idea what to do with that knowledge. He might as well be an electrician looking at physics.

Blue strides to its edge, hesitates for just long enough to think about ruining his running shoes, and then walks into the water, soaking his pants. He lets out a little gasp of shock when the water rises past his thighs.

Last night when they both stood in Shawn's pond, they were laughing and holding onto each other desperately. There is no joy between them now. Tense silence. Lapping water. Fear. Mackie loosens his fingers and Blue's hand falls away from his.

All around, the night chitters. The water bounces from one end of the pool to the other, as if pushed by the tail of some beast below who maybe doesn't appreciate Blue sharing its space.

Blue reaches back again for Mackie.

"No, Blue." Mackie shakes his head. "Get out." So many things about this make him fearful. He doesn't belong in the forest. He's known that always. The day he stole Blue, he vowed never to return for fear of having him stolen back.

"Hurry," Blue pleads.

"Not until you tell me why we're here." Mackie stands stubbornly at the squelching shore with his hands shoved deep into his pockets to prevent him from reaching back out to Blue.

"We can find Kevin," Blue answers.

In a glittering pool? In the vicious forest?

It's impossible, he imagines saying. *This is stupid. Let's go home.*

Blue looks at him. Mackie can feel time slipping through his fingers, sand in an hourglass. Every second that goes by is a second further away from saving Kevin.

"Trust me."

Mackie sucks in a breath of charged air and wades into the bitterly cold water. He's never let Blue down before; fear of what comes next won't stop him now.

His feet sink into the mud, and he almost goes down until Blue takes his hand and steadies him.

"Deeper," Blue commands.

Mackie takes another few steps. Water rises past his thighs to his naval, and a weak protest leaves him. It's colder than Shawn's pond was. He struggles to draw in deep, calming breaths. *I'm okay. I'm not going to freeze to death here. I'm not going to be lost to the forest.*

Unlike everywhere else touched by the unending cold, the leaves in this part of the forest are bright and full as they sway in the wind, and the ground is a vibrant green. The water glows with July vibrancy. When he notices that, he also notices the air is changing. It's starting to feel warm.

A breeze snatches in and pushes Mackie's unkempt hair from the base of his neck and roughs the surface of the water. Laughter trills, far away and inhuman. He's all at once sure the forest is laughing at him specifically. He's been lulled into her belly, as foolish as all the other humans that grave in her grounds, deeply in love and deeply blind.

He has one advantage that everyone else she's eaten hasn't: he has Blue with him.

It's hard to continue holding Blue's hand. It's like holding onto a storm. His chest is rising and falling rapidly. Each breath he expels taints the air with something Mackie hasn't felt since the day Blue threw the picnic table at Joe—pure magic. It bleeds into his skin, too, pricking Mackie like pins and needles. Tonight, he can't be like the rest of the town and pretend it doesn't exist, it's here, and it's gnawing his skin raw.

"Hold tight. Don't let go. No matter what." Blue doesn't sound like himself. His voice carries a cadence of wonder and power-lust. He's been starving for this and didn't even know it.

Mackie can feel them approaching a line that there will be no coming back from. He wants to tell Blue to leave it. They can go home where they can drink a beer and play video games and not talk about this hollow in the woods.

Even if he knew how to say what he was feeling, he doesn't think Blue would agree. One look at his face, and Mackie knows he likes this feeling of power. He likes the way it's wild and unpredictable. Why wouldn't he? Blue loves *everything* even a little dangerous.

With one last glance at Mackie, Blue reaches into the water with his free hand and starts feeling around, just like crawfishing in Yarrow Lake when they were young.

For several long seconds, nothing happens. Mackie entertains the idea that maybe he misread the danger in the air. Then water burbles around his belly, turning from clear to grey, the change spiking his blood pressure.

His first instinct is to look away—that's what you do when your mind can't accept the images unfolding before it—but he feels like a gawker at one of his many fights defending Blue. He just can't tear his eyes from the bottom of the pool as it morphs from something dark and featureless into a window he can look through. On the other side is a grove, where a huge, bulbous tree reaches for the black sky. There, the grass is green, and hundreds of flowers poke up through the blades and dead leaves. It could be a peaceful place, but thorny vines stretch from one tree to the next, preventing anyone or anything from easily entering the thicket.

Blue's hand mars the image as he reaches *through* it. His face screws up in concentration. Magic saturates the air. It becomes difficult to breathe. Mackie gasps through his mouth. His skin pricks like he's getting a tattoo all over his body.

The feeling peaks as Blue grabs hold of something and starts tugging it through the pool. He lets out a gasp that's half pain and half joy when it slips through the portal and into the water on their side. Whatever it is, Mackie can feel it brush his leg. The muddy bottom holds his feet firmly in place and prevents him from recoiling.

Blue crows and raises his prize. It's not a giant Clearwater crayfish, but a sopping wet Kevin Evans.

At first, Mackie feels joy. Against all odds, they found him! But Kevin's eyes are open, large, rheumy, and unmistakably dead, and the feeling curdles in Mackie until it is small and rotted.

"Oh," is all Mackie can think to say. *No.*

It's Blue's turn to cringe. "Hell."

Before Mackie's eyes, Kevin's skin turns white and chalky and starts to break off in massive chunks that hit the water with disgusting splats. Mackie screams and steps back. His feet are still stuck in the mud, and he goes down into the cold depths.

Like he is the water, and the pond is filled instead with icy oil, Mackie sinks rapidly to the bottom, toward the glassy image of the forest on the other side. His feet touch the surface, dip through... He can't pull back from this downward spiral, no matter how he reaches for the surface. He's dropping into the place Kevin came from. His right leg is totally subsumed, he's folding—

Hands close on his shoulders and pull sharply upward. A suspended moment holds Mackie between worlds before the portal releases him and his head breaks the surface of the water. Blue. Blue's holding him.

Mackie takes in a ragged breath and another. He sputters and coughs.

"Fuck, Mackie. Are you okay?"

Mackie would laugh on any other given day; Blue doesn't generally swear. He can't now, though, he's shivering too badly.

"Out. We have to get out," Blue orders; he's already moving toward the edge of the pool and dragging Mackie that way. Fatty chunks of meat swirl in the disturbed water, and oils grease the surface. Hair, bits of bone... that might be an eye bobbing by the opposite bank.

Mackie rallies his strength and pulls his feet from the mud. It's reluctant to release him. He can feel his ankles popping with the force of it. Though it hurts, he doesn't give up and is eventually rewarded for his efforts. The pool lets him go all at once, and he almost goes down again—would have, had Blue not caught him.

Blue wraps his arm around Mackie's middle, practically carrying Mackie. His muscles strain and the tendons stick out on his neck. He looks narrowly-escaped-death scared, and it's that fear that jumpstarts Mackie's heart and makes all his thoughts come into line.

The forest has changed yet again. A shrill moaning drifts through the trees and grows louder by the second. *Devils,* Mackie thinks. They've woken up, and they're angry.

Blue reaches the edge of the water and trips. Mackie goes down, too, sprawling onto the forest floor. Roots slither like snakes and lash at his ankles. He jerks away from them with a cry of shock. It's a phenomenon to see the forest at a distance do things you know forests aren't meant to do, even when you know *your* forest does them, and another thing entirely to have them done to *you*.

Blue claws at the mud around the pool and pulls himself out of the water. Mackie struggles to his feet, too. His legs feel half-numb. He uses the half that's not to run. Blue tracks by his side, lithe, steps quickened by dread.

A thunderous rumble shakes the air. It grows louder and louder the closer they come to the road. Mackie chances a look over his shoulder. A shadow is chasing them. It engulfs the path they've taken and leaves a swath of trees in its wake dead and dry, just like the trees in the patch of forest on the southern border.

And if it reaches you...?

It can't.

If it does, Mackie is positive even Blue won't be able to save them from its rot.

He feels the shadows nipping at his heels, January cold. The wailing in his ears has peaked. It rattles his skull and makes his skin crawl. They won't make it out. How could they possibly?

Please, please, please.

As though his prayers have been answered, headlights shine through the trees just ahead. Mackie pours on a final bit of speed and is regurgitated onto the road. He has just enough time to note the gravel beneath his feet and then he's dodging wildly out of the way of a speeding car blaring its horn. He can feel the pressure from the passenger's mirror pass within inches of his elbow.

Blue crashes out a second later and falls into Mackie. They both go to their knees. Mackie spins around to ward off the forest's attack; gravel cuts into his palm.

There is nothing behind him, except for the ditch, the darkened pathway he and Blue took into the forest, and the forest itself. It seems quiet now, the branches have stopped swaying and the trees have stopped moaning. The only evidence of the chase is the band of dead stretching into the forest. It's expanded its reach to a patch of dwarf irises forest-side but no further.

Mackie forces air down the pinhole his throat has become and winces at the way it wheezes. He hasn't had an asthma attack since he was a kid, but he feels on the verge of one now.

"Breathe deep." Blue's fingers hover over Mackie's shoulder. Mackie pulls away from his touch. Any stimulus is apt to cast him over the edge. Hurt flicks across Blue's face.

"Just..." Mackie pants. "Just sit."

Blue settles down on the scrubby shoulder a few inches from Mackie and looks into the forest.

Bit by slow bit, Mackie's chest loosens.

Several minutes pass before an owl is brave enough to break the barrier of silence that followed their escape. Its hoot is tremulous and uncertain. When it's not cast down for making noise, it hoots again, sounding marginally braver, and then the world erupts in night sounds. Crickets, nighthawks trilling love songs, a raccoon resuming its nightly scavenger hunt, the owl again.

Mackie gulps another lungful of air and has enough energy to spit, "What the fuck was that?" *Whatthefuckwasthat.* That's how it sounds, all bound up and bunched together.

Blue's shoulders tremble into Mackie's once. A scornful noise rips from his chest. Mackie takes his eyes off the trap that is the forest and narrows his gaze on Blue. He's laughing, depreciative and bitter. Tears stream freely down his cheeks.

"Blue?"

"I thought..." Blue trails off.

"Thought *what?*" Mackie's too stricken to give Blue the quiet he wants. "Thought *what*, Blue?" He wants to grab him and shake him until the words tumble out.

Blue puts his head as far back as it can go and closes his eyes. The truth whispers out of him. "I thought I could save him."

The idea that Kevin Evans needs saving, that *Blue* could be the one to do it—that he would know *how*—is a puzzle with too many pieces; Mackie doesn't know which to stick together first. "How did you know where he was?"

Blue lifts a narrow shoulder. "I don't know."

The answer is totally inadequate, but other questions are lining up in Mackie's mind, and he pushes it aside to make room for them. "What happened?"

"I don't know," Blue says again.

"Did we kill him?"

Blue shakes his head. "He was gone before we found him."

Long dead. They merely facilitated his decomposition.

Mackie shudders once, remembering the bits that floated on the water's surface. All the little pieces that made Kevin whole, broken apart. "What are we going to tell everyone?"

"Nothing," Blue says after a beat.

"Nothing," Mackie repeats it just to feel the word in his mouth. This impalpable, ungainly word. *Nothing.* "What do you mean? We have to say something. His mom is looking for him. *Everyone* is looking for him."

"They'll stop once the bones appear." He's almost like a shell of himself. It makes Mackie want to scream.

"In a day? Two? A month?" Who can say? "How long are we going to make them suffer for?"

Blue's mouth gets flat. "What is telling them going to change? Either they'll come here with a vendetta, and more will die, or they'll laugh at us, and we'll be committed to a psych ward, and Kevin will still be gone. You know this."

Mackie's grown up knowing that the forest is lethal; that's not what his mind is struggling with. It's that he *knows* Kevin. He *knows* Kevin's mother, Stephanie, and now he knows invariably what fate's befallen Kevin. Doesn't he have an obligation to tell everyone? But maybe Blue is right, and it'll only cause more pain, more confusion.

The helpless feeling he's been courting ever since returning home raises up and crashes over him like a tsunami.

"Are you okay?" Blue asks. He looks at Mackie for the first time in several long minutes. Deep shadows ring beneath his eyes, and he must have knocked his split lip again because it's bleeding sluggishly down his chin from the swollen gash.

"I'm..." Fine is for liars. Mackie can't make himself say it.

"I'm glad you didn't go any deeper," Blue says when it becomes apparent Mackie won't finish his sentence. He again looks like he wants to touch Mackie. Mackie makes more room between them, still unsure if he's ready for the stimulus. He wants to shower the pool off himself. Scrape it off. *Burn* it off. Anything to get the feeling of the slimy water from his skin, and maybe after that, he'll feel like himself again.

"What's at the bottom?"

Blue rubs both hands over his face roughly. Mackie can hear the metal of the spider ring he sometimes wears butting up against the titanium of his eyebrow ring. "That's complicated."

"Like algebra complicated?"

"Like Schrodinger's cat complicated."

Like pulling a dead boy out of the water complicated. Like, finding cleaned bones at the edge of the forest complicated. Sorrow's Forest complicated.

Mackie pushes his hair back from his forehead. It's already started to dry.

Blue cuts a look his way. "Can I convince you to forget about it?"

"Not on your life."

He breathes deeply and starts. "It's kind of like a scrying pool. Kind of like a portal. Kind of like nothing else at all. Understand?"

"Not really."

"If you look, you can see things," Blue tries. "And even when you don't. And if you want it badly enough, you can reach the things you see." He grabs at an invisible boy. Kevin falls apart all over again in his hands. Blue visibly shudders.

Mackie thinks maybe he gets it. If he forgets about the real world, the laws of physics and time and space and *logic*. If he remembers that he lives in a place where the forest breathes and lives as temperamentally as a jock on hour fourteen of a forty-eight-hour fast, then yes, maybe he can wrap his mind around it.

"You wanted to see Kevin," Mackie ventures.

"Yeah."

"So, then you did. He was in the forest?"

"As best as I can tell."

"And that?" Mackie waves his hands in the forest's direction.

"I think the forest attacked us because it realized we'd taken him back before it was done."

"Done *what*, exactly?"

"Feeding. She's hungry."

His words crash together in Mackie's head. *Hungry. Feed. She.* Sorrow.

Suddenly, he doesn't want to sit here anymore. He stumbles to his feet and starts walking back toward the house, following the centre of the road. Blue hurries to catch up.

"Mackie..."

"I just need to think," Mackie says. As though this is the kind of thing that will resolve itself in his mind with just a little time to ponder.

Chapter 7

Mackie spends his night sleepless. He lies in his bed in the same spot Blue did last night, wishing he was still there but not feeling brave enough to knock on his door and ask him to come back, even though Mackie knows he would.

He stares at his ceiling until the sky gets bright. When he hears Mom shuffling around downstairs for work, he gives up and drags himself from his sheets. It's Monday. Which means he promised her he'd look after his father today. He would rather be doing anything else, but he can't go back on his promise. His only saving grace is that there's a nurse on their way. With them there, he has about a two-hour window where he's free to do what he wants.

Mackie fills the hours until the nurse arrives by going through his morning routine, showering again, shaving, brushing his teeth, dressing—normal things, though the hours leading up to them have been so abnormal.

His thoughts are grease in soapy water, scattering anytime he tries to focus. They always eventually come back to Blue and the pool. Kevin. His small body breaking apart into fatty, sinewy chunks and hitting the water. *Splat.* Dead. How can this be? What *happened*? Is that the fate of everyone that gets lost in the forest? Did it hurt? How long will they have to wait until his bones appear at the forest edge? And *will* they appear now that Kevin's body has been disturbed?

Mackie is just chugging down his second cup of coffee when he hears Blue shifting upstairs. The bathroom door closes. Something like dread coils in his stomach as he considers both seeing him and moving forward from last night's disaster. He keeps wondering, did they wake something up in the forest? Does it warrant acknowledgement? Blind ignorance? How do they go on?

The bathroom sink turns off, and the door opens. Mackie considers bolting right then and there, his father be damned. A knock on the front door stays his thundering heart. He hurries to answer it.

Dad's nurse is Becky Rebel—yes, of the same family that Rebel Park is named after. Her grandfather severed some of his six hundred acres and donated it to the town, now the Rebels are town celebrities, especially amongst the blue hairs.

Becky was in the year above Mackie in high school. She fast-tracked through there like she fast-tracked through nursing school. Now she runs her own practice, doing home visits for all the blue hairs that love her so much, and, of course, Mackie's dad.

She hasn't changed much—she's a bit on the round side and soft. She looks like the kind of girl that gives amazing hugs, and her skin is supermodel clear. Her dark hair is up in a high ponytail, and she's in a pair of lavender scrubs.

Becky has a hundred-watt smile primed. It gets immediately brighter when she recognizes him. "Mackie! You're home from school!"

Mackie can't summon up the same enthusiasm no matter how he tries. He feels bone-weary. "Hey, Becky."

Her smile drops in increments. Mackie can feel her gaze clinging to the circles beneath his eyes, the healing wounds Joe gave him, and the ashen complexion of his skin. "Are you okay?"

"Just tired," he dodges. He can hear Blue's feet on the stairs.

"What did you do to your cheek? It looks kind of bad." Her fingers hover over the gash the tree gave him last night. Concern grows in her eyes. "I have some antiseptic—"

Mackie squeezes between Becky and the door. "It's okay. Just scraped it." He accents the half-truth with a smile that's supposed to put her at ease. It probably looks how it feels—manic and fake. "Sorry to do this, but I have an important errand to run. I'll be back before you leave. For sure."

"Oookay," she draws out.

Before she can say anything else, Mackie closes the door after himself and long-legs it down the driveway. The forest is behind him, watching like an accomplice to murder.

You didn't kill Kevin, he reminds himself.

He's just not coming forward with the information.

Which is different.

It doesn't feel all that different in the sunlight.

Mackie follows the wet splashes his mother's tires made driving through the puddles at the end of the driveway onto the familiar landscape of the road. He walks in the centre despite the obvious danger of getting hit by a car. Getting too close to the edge where the forest presses in seems suicidal, and he only dares when he hikes it up one of the few blind hills. Trees creak in a breeze he can't feel, leaves rustling like laughter and whispers, roots groaning as they strain against the earth. It's always been an entity capable of complex emotions, but lately, the forest has started to feel malevolent. A sleeping giant waking from decades of slumber, and furious about it.

His heart raps into his ribs, and though he can barely hear a thing over his thundering pulse, Mackie forces himself not to run. The last thing he wants to do is make the forest think of him as prey.

A few minutes go by, then Mackie passes the spot he *thinks* he and Blue ducked into the forest—he can see the tire marks in the gravel from when the car jerked around him—but he can't see the pathway that was there last night. He stops for as long as he dares and scours instead for the blue flag flower. There. The small patch sits just on the other side of the ditch, crusty and dead.

It feels unnaturally cold here, a frost giant breathing from the shadows. Mackie flips up the fleece collar on his leather jacket. As hard as he tries, he can't convince his feet to go forward toward the forest, where he can look for Kevin's bones and bring them back to his mother. His body won't be tricked. Not in the sunlight. Not without Blue egging him on.

Mackie faces the road again and walks on.

Sam lives five kilometres down the same road as Mackie. His house is set *way* off the beaten path, up a driveway choked to death in tall reed grass. The ground is wet on either side of the raised driveway, and in the late spring and early summer, the mosquitos are so bad, you can't step outside for fear of being drained of all your blood.

They called it the Vampire House when they were kids. Mackie still secretly thinks of it that way, though he and Sam no longer joke about it, not when they know wicked things really walk this earth.

The Chester house is huge, two-storey and five-roomed—one of those massive century homes, once nice, before Time left her mark on it. Now, it bows in the middle in a lazy V, the faded blue siding is filthy, and the grey shingles curl. It was always too swampy to build here, and whoever cared to make the house never bothered building it up out of the mud. Seems like a waste of time to build an unsound house, but Lakeview is full of places like this, on the very brink of collapse, already half-decayed.

One side of the house is covered in creeping vines while the other looks out at the road. Its windows are dusty, and its porch is missing paint. The only thing on the property that looks great is Sam's dad's work truck. It glitters like new in the early morning light, bright white against the dark green of the forest behind it.

Mackie treks up the walk to the ancient porch. Before he figures out which boards are safe or if they're all rotten, the front door squeaks open, and Sam comes out. He's in a pair of dark green shorts and a long-sleeved white T-shirt. His hat is on backwards again. Dark hair curls out its sides.

"Hey, Mack..." Sam trails off the way Becky did and lifts his eyebrows.

"Didn't sleep," Mackie offers pre-emptively.

"No, no." Sam curls his nose. "You stink."

"Fuck you. I showered," Mackie says. "*Twice* in the last twelve hours."

"Not like sweat. Like magic." Sam whispers now. Speaking too loud about the things in the forest is taboo. It's difficult to hear him. "I can smell the forest all over you. What happened?"

Mackie runs his hand through his hair self-consciously and feels it all stand on end. What other mark has the forest left on him, and what does that *mean*? "That's a long story."

"Good thing I have no place to be."

Mackie shoves his hands deep into his pockets and watches a grub inch its way over one of Sam's deck boards. "Blue and I went into the forest. Looking for Kevin."

Colour drains from Sam's face. "Evans? Have you lost your mind?"

Well. Maybe. Mackie shrugs helplessly.

"Jesus, Mackie." Sam looks toward the sky in exasperation, which is very similar to how he appeared when he shoved Mackie's clothes in his hands the other night. He sighs. "Nan says you can have a charm. You'll need it now, I think."

Mackie snaps his gaze to Sam's. All his muscles feel suddenly tense. "What do you mean? Why would I need it?"

"Like calls to like," Sam answers, as though that explains everything, and maybe it does, to a Chester.

Mackie, who is not of Sam's blood, stares at him blankly.

"The forest's devils will follow you, smelling like that. A charm can protect you for a while, at least."

Panic throbs dully in his belly. The one good thing about being tired is that all his emotions feel leaden. He can glaze over them for later digestion. "Thanks."

One of Sam's goats wanders into the front yard and looks at Mackie with its strange yellow eyes.

"Damnit, Morris." Sam leaps off the deck. His sandals hit the ground with a wet *splat* that startles cold midges from their perch on top of grass blades. He snags the goat by the scruff of the neck before it can roam out to the road and leads it around the side of the house. Mackie tracks after him, wincing when cold swamp water leaches up into the sides of his shoes.

Sam's backyard was almost as extensive as the front, but over the years, the forest has crept into it and made it smaller. One day, it'll sneak up and swallow his house, too. His family won't cut it back, for fear of angering it.

To the left of the property is a small shed, lined by a wooden fence, where several goats make their home. The gate has been pushed open, and another goat, one of the females, is looking outside hopefully. When she spots Sam approaching with the captured male, Mackie can almost feel her exasperation. *Morris, you fool. The front yard is off-limits,* she seems to say with a shake of her head. *If you want to eat the good grass and not get caught, you have to stay in the back.*

Morris looks properly disrespected.

Sam jams the gate closed once Morris is secured and cuts across to the other side of the yard, where yet another shed leans crookedly on its meagre foundation.

Though it doesn't look like much, this is where all the Chester family skeletons lie. Its boards are sun-rotted, and it smells a bit like the Chester cat has been marking the corner.

Mackie hangs back, unease settling in his bones.

The first time he saw this shed was after he'd spent the night at Sam's and the two of them went adventuring in the morning. Back then, secluded away from the house, this place seemed like a jackpot—the kind of place that would hold awesome secrets and keep them out of the watchful eye of Sam's parents. The kind of place they could try smoking weed for the first time or talk about things they didn't want anyone else to hear, girls, boys, everyone, and everything between.

It was all those things and more. The first time he opened the door, Mackie was unprepared for the collection of macabre forest cast-offs and gruesome bits the Chesters had gathered from around town. (Or the second time, third, and every other time after, truthfully.) It's been years since he's stepped inside, but even to this day, he still thinks about it, this little nightmare place.

"Aren't you coming?" Sam pushes the door open on its squeaking hinges. His eyebrows are lifted. It used to be Sam was as wary of this place as Mackie. He's since grown into the Chester secrets, and this hut is familiar and safe for him.

Mackie has never told Sam about the lasting nightmares. He doesn't pride himself on being a macho guy or anything, that's just stupid. He does, however, believe in privacy. When no one knows what your worst fears are, no one can hold them over you. That was a hard and fast lesson, learned in grade one when Shawn Macintyre discovered Mackie didn't much like slugs. After the first week of torture, Mackie conquered his fear by seeking it out, lifting logs and rocks, letting slimy slug bodies slide over his skin, to make sure the next time Shawn thought he'd drop one down Mackie's shirt, he was well-equipped to handle it.

You can't do that for Sorrow's Forest and everything she gives. It'd drive you mad before you got used to it.

Mackie pushes on. Wet grass swishes and squeaks beneath his feet. There's a little walkway of sunken patio stones leading up to the door; he leaves his footprints on it beside Sam's.

A wedge of sunlight marks the dusty floor, and the air smells just as Mackie remembers—dust, carcass, and miscellaneous rot. It could be the support studs degrading. It could also be the dead cat hanging from the ceiling or the mice desiccating inside the walls. There are so many old and gruesome things here, it's hard to say.

Mackie tries not to look at the cat too closely. Lakeview's overrun with them, and he knows Sam only takes strays. He recognizes this one, though—he caught Mom feeding it the other morning. He prays (figuratively, he's never seen much use in praying to a God if that God supposedly *has a plan*) that Whiskas wasn't Ol' Stubtail's last meal.

Most of the things in the shed are that way—dead and hung to dry. Witchcraft, even the pure stuff, takes an awful lot of sacrifice, Sam told him once. Some things in the room are more mysterious. A small branch from a lilac tree lies on the ground, just choked with flowers. It's separated from the main tree, yet the flowers look as bright and plentiful as ever. They're thriving in the dark. Most things from the forest do. It's magical in some way that only the Chesters know. It fills Mackie with serenity to look at it. That feeling flees just as fast when he studies the next prize positioned on the table near it—a thin pale hand with fingernails long and needle-like, good for poking or pinching or clawing. Human-ish. Scales and teeth make up some of the other assorted objects, shiny mussel shells, bits of sand. Nothing is quite as gruesome as the hand Mackie's eyes keep coming back to.

"Where did you get this stuff from?"

Sam knows without turning what's captured Mackie's attention. "Dora found it."

"She goes into the forest?"

Sam shakes his head. "The forest gives to her."

What a fickle beast it is—stealing boys like Kevin while giving to girls like Dora.

Sam props his foot up on the narrow bench beside the hand. It quavers with the rickety table, threatening to topple over. Mackie eyes it suspiciously. It seems like the kind of thing that might pull itself across the floor to get away if given the opportunity. Or something that might hook itself around your throat and choke you to death.

"You look like you've seen a ghost, Mackie," Sam says. "What happened?"

Mackie frowns. "You have a severed hand in your shed."

Sam shakes his head. "Even before you saw whitey here, you looked sick. You come here stinking of magic, scared straight, claiming you went into the forest. Tell me what went down."

Mackie scratches the back of his neck, wondering how much to give away.

"You know I can keep a secret."

That's true. Next to Blue, there's no one in Lakeview Mackie trusts more. He's already tired under the weight of this secret and looses the dams. "Blue took me to this pool where he found Kevin and pulled him out. He was already dead, though..." He shudders with the memory.

Sam goes still. "You stole from Sorrow?"

Mackie's stomach flips. "Blue said we were safe."

"*Nowhere* is safe when you take from her." Sam curls his hands on the workbench, his knuckles white. "Goddamn. What happened?"

Mackie explains how Blue asked him to follow him into the forest. He explains about the pathway and the pool and even its space-defying water, tripping only when it comes time to talk about Kevin. He wrenches the words out, though, and it feels like pulling a stake from his gut, painful, splintery, and afterwards, like he has one gaping hole in his middle.

Sam's face is the same off-white as the clouds seen through the dirty windows. "I've heard of that place. You went to Sorrow's grotto. She must have found out and hunted you. You're lucky you escaped."

"Not this again," Mackie groans.

"Are you going to tell me again Sorrow doesn't exist?" Sam crosses his arms and slouches. He could be a quarterback waiting to deflect the hit.

"No," Mackie snaps back harder than he means. He's not foolish enough to disagree. "But if she's supposed to be sleeping, how did she chase us out?"

Sam's stance relaxes a bit. "I don't know." He rolls his lips together thoughtfully before shaking his head. "I don't know," he says again. "Maybe... maybe it's like Nan says and she's waking up." He looks up from his sandals. "You need to be careful."

"That's why I'm here," Mackie reminds him. He's more uncomfortable than he wants to admit.

Something groans outside the shed, sounding like the noise the forest made last night, watching him and Bree. A familiar needle of fear spikes his heart. "What is that?"

Sam waves him off as if that's not what's important. "How did Blue know about that place?"

How does Blue know about anything?

"He wouldn't say." Sam's expression turns puzzled, and Mackie adds the qualifier he didn't think he'd need to. "Don't tell anyone."

Sam looks like he might argue but changes his mind last-second. "You're right. It won't change the result; Kevin will still be dead."

Mackie trails his fingers over the only thing he dares to touch in the shed: a reedy oak sapling starving for nutrients in its little pot. "Blue said the forest is hungry."

"The forest is always hungry." Sam leans in and sweeps the sapling up by its trunk and thrusts it upon Mackie. "Take this and plant it in your backyard."

Mackie stares at the tree without accepting it. "What?"

"You wanted a charm, didn't you?"

"Like something I put around my neck or hang on my door?" Mackie suggests. "This is a *tree*."

"It's what you chose; I don't make the rules." He grabs Mackie's wrist and makes him take the oak. "Don't let anything happen to it, and it'll protect you."

Mackie believes in devils and ghosts and ghouls in the forest. He even believes in magic, the kind you stuff into bags and hang on your door, but he's not entirely sure what a tree is going to do. Who is he to argue with the closest thing Lakeview has to a shaman, though?

"Hurry up; it needs to get in the ground," Sam instructs and shoos him back outside.

The weather has turned rapidly. It's windy as hell, and the clouds have gone slate-grey and heavy with seasonal rain. It settles around him as soon as he's under the sky, drilling hard into the ground and making ephemeral streams, as though determined to wash him away, into the forest. (*She's hungry.)*

From across the yard, the goats bleat and run back and forth with their eyes rolling in their heads. One of their numbers is missing. The male, Morris. The gate's not open, though, and if Mackie isn't mistaken, that's blood staining the fence line closest to the forest, like something's reached out and snagged him.

The noise, Mackie thinks. It was the goat speared and hauled away. He can only imagine by what.

The ground turns muddy in a blink.

"Hurry!" Sam yells over the deafening storm. "Before you can't!"

Mackie begins to run, leaving Sam staring into the forest from the walls of his shed of oddities, daring it to come closer.

Chapter 8

Mackie is soaked. Rain pounds into his eyes and his mouth, trying to drown him. That's not the worst part, though. As he races down the road, he imagines something in the forest following his progress. The branches sway and crack, and the trees moan. If he doesn't look for red eyes or knotted fur and twisted claws, if he ignores everything around except for the gravel road and the slapping of his wet feet, and the small stitch forming in his right side, it really could be just a storm.

Ten meters from his house, the road is bisected by a washout flowing with opaque dirt-coloured water. Mackie leaps over it. He should be able to easily make the jump, but the washout widens on him just as he's about to land, and his foot sinks into the new gushing river.

For an *instant*, Mackie feels claw-like fingers closing on his ankle. He knows immediately that it's a forest devil, come for him.

He jerks out of the devil's grasp and scratches his way to safety. His fingernails and shins rip on the gravel.

Once he's up, he whips around to peer into the dirty brown water. A lime green tail slaps the surface in annoyance. Just like the night he took Blue when the fin severed the otherwise still water. Then it's gone, and he only has a cold gash on his leg to show for his troubles. It weeps freely into the top of his white sock.

An ambulance's siren wails far off in the distance, bringing Mackie back to the driving rain, his short breaths. His blood is rushing through his veins, making it hard to think. Each drop of water is boring into him; it hurts. The trees are bending so far forward, that it seems like they could reach out and pull him into the forest. Sam was right. She is angry.

Mackie takes two giant steps back from the impromptu river, and only then is he brave enough to turn around again. He's close to his driveway and hurries there before the forest makes off with his body.

All the lights are on inside the house, and it looks welcoming. Mackie hits the garage first. The man door has been pulled off its hinges by a large gust of wind and lays beaten in the yard. Rainwater pounds through gaps in the shingles and drips onto his GTO and the concrete ground. Mackie avoids the puddles and grabs the garden spade.

The rain feels even colder when he steps into it again. There could be hail in it.

He marches into the backyard and faces the forest with determination. It's never good to fuck with the forest. That said, the forest needs to understand it can't fuck with him, either.

The ground groans when he jams the tip of the shovel in. *Like an earthquake.* Again, he thinks of the night he pulled Blue from the trees.

He can only take out a few inches of soil; the ground won't give. It will have to do. He takes the sapling from its pot and shoves it into the gash, then covers its roots up again. Its top is broken off from his fall on the road and it looks more than a little bit scraggly, but he's done the best he can, and now he just has to have faith that Sam knows what he's talking about.

A water-blue car pulls into the driveway, and Blue climbs out of the passenger's seat. Mackie squints through the sheets of rain and spots Kristy Chow on the other side of the windshield with her long smooth hair pulled into a glossy side braid. The car pulls out again.

By the time Mackie makes it through the mud at the side of the house and puts the shovel back in the garage, Blue is waiting for him just inside the front door. He, too, is soaked, dripping on the carpet.

"Hey," Mackie says.

"Hi..." Blue pulls out his chirping phone. Mackie sees Shawn's face on the screen for just a second, then Blue swipes to decline the call.

"What was that?"

"Nothin.'" Decent lying has never been Blue's forte. He doesn't even try now, though. He's a million miles away. "The road's washed out. We had to go around."

Mackie's leg gives an impatient sting. He considers telling Blue about his bad luck. Blue hasn't yet asked Mackie about the shovel or his bloody leg, though, and he decides it's easier to let it go.

Blue holds out one of the two towels he took from the entry hall, and together, they head inside, out of the storm.

It's another hour before the storm even thinks of subsiding. While it rages, Mackie showers the chill from his bones and cleans the cut on his leg. Four ragged gouges cross his calf. He thought it was hands or claws when it was happening. Under closer inspection, it looks like a pair of jaws closed on him. It seems shallow enough that he can forgo stitches. What would he say anyway when the doctors inevitably asked what happened? Like Blue, he's not particularly good at lying, and no one in Lakeview talks about the things in the forest or acknowledges their existence, for that matter.

He throws on a sweater and some track pants and comes out into the hallway. His mother is there. She's ragged, aged ten years from that morning, and scrutinizing him like a boatman scrutinizes the day's catch he's about to gut.

"What is it?" Mackie asks warily. He can't remember the last time she looked at him like that. Maybe when, at five, he stole China from her sister, Aunt Anna, and gave it to her as a Christmas present. *Maybe.*

As it did back then, the hardness falls away from her. Suddenly, she's a paper bag left too long in a storm, sagging, and threatening to fall apart. "You went out today," she states.

"For a bit."

She walks to the window on the other side of the hallway. Mackie follows her and looks out into the backyard, too. He's expecting devils; they've taken up much of his thoughts lately.

It's only a baking pan face-up on the grass, collecting rain. Around it is unrecognizable lumps of char.

Unnecessarily, Mom adds, "Becky couldn't stay. She has other clients, and I couldn't leave work. Blue wasn't answering his phone, and neither were you."

Shame hits Mackie right in the throat. "I'll clean it up."

It seems she can no longer strum up a filthy look for him. "I'm going to bed." Though it's only six in the evening and the sun is still stubbornly pushing back against the horizon.

As she walks by, Mackie wants to apologize. He can't bear to have her shrug it off, though, so, he stays by the window long after he hears her door click closed, staring out in the backyard at the forest moving in eerie synchronicity. Parts of it look beaten down, trees that have rotted and fallen inward, forming holes into the forest depths that look a bit welcoming. Gaps a person could walk through with ease and get lost forever if they wanted. Gaps Mackie suddenly *wants* to explore. The feeling settles into his bones, and he can think about nothing else. He can't remember if he's ever felt this way before.

It's incontestable: something is absolutely changing in Sorrow's Forest.

Movement catches Mackie's eye. A pale creature flutters through the trees, moving in and out of view. He can only focus on it when it stops just at the edge and peers out. Grey scales the colour of sky wink out at him, sharp claws dig into the tree trunk, and teeth like polished silver glint. It seems bipedal. It seems *intelligent* when it meets Mackie's gaze and holds it. Like a hunter searching for its prey.

Mackie shivers, and the beast sinks back into the trees out of view.

There is a yard and a house between them and nothing to say the creature is hostile, but Mackie's heart is pounding as he searches for it again. Glints of red and gold, movement where there should be none, flashes of light like fireflies, a horrid screech that sets Mackie's neck hair standing. The minutes whittle into half an hour, though, and still, he stands at the window without a clear answer, and it becomes obvious none of the devils will brave the forest line again.

Finally, he grows frustrated and turns his back on the trees.

Mackie pushes back his bedroom door and is surprised to find Blue sitting on his bed. He is dressed much the same as Mackie, except his tracksuit is the same green as lime guts. His blonde hair is wet and slicked back against his scalp.

Mackie notes his tense expression and closes the door. "What's going on?"

Blue folds one leg beneath his body and leans back against the bed so he can see Mackie fully. "Things are changing in the forest."

Blue's ability to mimic Mackie's thoughts is unsettling. He wards the feeling away with sarcasm, muttering, "Oh, great. We're finally going to talk about this now."

Blue's chin points stubbornly straight. "There wasn't any point before."

"Before what? Before Kevin went missing or before he fell apart or is there something else I should know about?"

Blue is impervious to Mackie's sass. "I think more people are going to disappear."

"More kids are going to die," Mackie says plainly. He has this insufferable habit of having to say things as they are. If he's always looking at the facts, he can never delude himself. Dad is going to die. Mom is going crazy. Blue is not his. Something is rotting in the forest.

"Yes." Blue studies his feet for the space of two blinks. "I should go." Blue's shoulders sag with his proclamation while sadness drips out of him.

Go. He doesn't just mean leave Mackie's room. He wants to *leave.* Leave Lakeview. Leave the Kings. *Leave me.*

Mackie's heart seizes dead for the second time that day. "Go *where*? And why?"

Blue digs his toes into the carpet and his fingers into the bedspread. "Anywhere else. And because... I think it's after me."

Mackie joins him on the bed, trying to force him to lift his gaze. He does, for a second. "Why would you say that?"

Blue shrugs, coy to the end. "Just a feeling."

"A feeling," Mackie repeats.

"Yeah."

"Like when you were sure I was going to drown if I went swimming at the dam that day with Robbie Wick and James Holder?" He hadn't gone because Blue was hysterical about it, and at the end of the day, his phone lit up with James' texts. They opened the dam three weeks early that day and Robbie couldn't get out of the water. They found his body a day later, bloated, floating in Yarrow Lake.

"Kind of like that..." Blue drawls.

"You're hiding something." He's all at once sure of it.

Blue looks away.

"This is bullshit, Blue." Mackie doesn't know why he's suddenly mad. Blue looks up at him, startled. "If you have no proof the forest is after you, you have no reason to think it is. Unless, of course, you're keeping something from me." They don't keep secrets from each other. They never have. Or at least, they never used to.

"There is something in the forest," Blue says with more certainty. "And when I look into the trees, I feel it looking for me. It woke up the day you and Joe fought. I felt it."

Mackie remembers the table flying across the courtyard, the forest blooming like it's late May and not early April, the devil in Kevin's backyard, and the one in the washout that left its teeth in Mackie's leg. Hungry beasts, but beasts hungry for *any* flesh, not Blue's necessarily. "They could be after anyone."

"They're not." Blue's conviction is ironclad. And the hard truth is, he's never been wrong before, not about anything like this.

"Then we'll stop it."

"How?"

Mackie flounders. "We'll find a way to fight it."

"Your solution to everything is to fight." Blue's voice gets monotoned.

"Because it works."

"Not always." Blue gazes out the window, down to that damned forest.

Possessed, Mackie leaps up and crosses the room with three large steps and pulls the drapes closed, pitching them into almost absolute darkness, cutting out the forest, cutting off the watchful eyes of unseen devils.

Mackie can feel them studying the King house.

He can't think about what that means.

When Mackie returns to Blue, halting so they're toe-to-toe, he ensures his expression is moulded into something stubborn. "I saw Sam this afternoon."

Blue tilts his head back. His mouth twists almost minutely. "Yeah?"

"He gave me something to try. To protect us. So, we'll be okay. Safe until we find a way to stop whatever's happening." Kids stuff. Plant a tree in the yard for protection against a sleeping forest witch. Also kid stuff: sleeping forest witch. Not kid stuff: Kevin Evans *literally* falling apart in Blue's hands and then almost getting swallowed by the forest.

Blue's sadness pulls at his limbs, curbs his boisterousness, ruins every bright thing about him. "You're so loyal, Mackie. But what if I told you, you were tricked?"

Mackie furrows his brows. "What are you talking about?"

Blue draws a deep breath. "I'm not who you think I am. Or what you think I am..."

Oh. Is that all?

Mackie already has an answer primed; he's thought about this quite a lot in the years he and Blue have been together. "I knew you were different when I pulled you from the forest. Even when you pretended everything was normal and people acted like you'd always been part of their life. I knew you weren't really."

Surprise crosses Blue's face. He blinks.

A spike of pleasure pierces Mackie despite everything. For once, he has the advantage. "You belonged to the forest before I stole you."

Blue's eyes go almost comically wide. Seconds go by where he doesn't speak, only stares at Mackie in disbelief. "Why have you never said anything?"

"Because it doesn't matter. You're my friend."

Another unmoving moment, then Blue stands, and before Mackie knows what's happening, he has Mackie enveloped in such a tight hug, Mackie can hardly feel him shake.

They stay that way in the gloom, Blue's cheek on Mackie's shoulder and their arms locked around each other for long minutes. The rain tapers off, and the wind slows.

Mackie hears himself say, "It doesn't matter where you came from. You belong here."

Blue's grip tightens on his shirt minutely, and he doesn't immediately respond, taking his time choosing his words. "I want to stay."

Which isn't an agreement or a promise to stay out of the forest. Mackie diligently ignores the details. He focuses instead on the thin structure of Blue's shoulders beneath his hands, the rise and fall of his knife-like ribs, the warmth of his body, his cinnamon smell, and his breath against Mackie's neck.

Being close to Blue is always kind of hard. When his attention is on you, you feel special, like the only person in the world, and when he pulls away, there's a definite withdrawal that comes after. Mackie's prepared for it, but the sting is still there when Blue releases him and leans back. He looks different; he's alive with that same otherworldly glow he was when Mackie first found him. Eyes a little too black, hair a little bluer than blonde, skin a little too pale. He's beautiful in the way all Sorrow's devils are. That enticing way that makes you hope they're not dangerous, even when you know they are.

Mackie needs to say something to cut through his errant thoughts. The only thing that comes to mind is, "Good."

The pulsing green power light from Mackie's computer is the only thing that illuminates the room. It limns Blue's cutting cheeks and dark-lined eyes, his mouth, where the deep colour of his lipstick has stained his skin.

Blue wets his lips; his lashes flutter down. He studies Mackie's mouth; Mackie studies Blue's. He's still holding Blue around the back and can feel the staccato rise of Blue's chest, and the moment he catches his breath.

It's hard to say who is canting toward who, but somehow, they're only centimetres apart. Realizing this, heat flares in Mackie's cheeks. He swallows, breathes, releases Blue, too, and steps back.

Blue smiles as though aware of the faux pas and used to it. He's almost always inches from kissing boys. He draws away, too, until they're not touching at all. He doesn't let it get quiet, moving, speaking, putting distance in between that moment and this one until Mackie doesn't know if he's the only one that noticed their proximity. "You're a good friend, Mackie."

Mackie's voice is rusty. "I guess."

"We'll talk more in the morning?"

"Yeah."

"Goodnight."

Blue squeezes Mackie's hand, then drifts out and closes the door.

Quiet permeates the room, large and oppressive save for the pulse thudding loudly in Mackie's head. He drops to the bed and tries to just *think. The forest.* It's a problem that requires his undivided attention. His thoughts won't stay there, wandering unwelcomingly toward bodies brushing together and uneven breaths, shallow things that still manage to fill a person up and make them feel frantic. He thinks about if he didn't think about it at all and just let it happen, images spooling out in his head like a movie.

The fantasy is all mixed up with shame and confusion. Blue is his best friend. Blue is his best friend, and he would give *anything* just then to have him back in his room, so he can figure out what happens next.

Headlights saw through his curtains, distracting him. There shouldn't be anyone pulling into the driveway this late.

Blue's door opens. Mackie plants his elbows on his knees nervously, trying in vain to look casual and calm. Blue hurries by his door without pausing, down the stairs and outside, into the waiting green Camaro. Mackie can't see the colour for sure, of course, not in the dark, but he knows the pitch of the lights off by heart, and there's only one Camaro in all of Lakeview. It's dark green, and it belongs to Shawn Macintyre.

The passenger door slams. Mackie peers between the curtains just as they peel out of the driveway and the taillights blur in the night.

Mackie texts Blue's phone immediately, asking *where are you going*? and hears it buzzing on the nightstand in Blue's room.

He sighs and falls back onto his bed.

It's late when Mackie hears Blue come in. There is no car in the driveway. It's possible Shawn pulled out before Mackie woke, but he doesn't think so.

Mackie's alarm goes off at seven-thirty. He rises, showers, and heads downstairs. His mother is in the kitchen getting ready for work. The air smells of coffee and toast and perfume.

"Are you staying home today?" she asks without turning around.

"I plan on it."

She nods, half like she doesn't believe him, and grabs her grocery bag lunch off the counter. When she moves away from the window, allowing a clear view of the outside, Mackie stops in his tracks.

Looking out toward the forest, all he can see is the craggy bark of a massive tree that, as best as he can recall, was not there the night before.

"What the hell is that?"

"What the hell is what?" Mom asks, brows pinched with irritation.

Mackie opens his mouth to say, *that huge tree in our backyard that wasn't there yesterday*. The words fizzle out, as anticlimactic as wet fireworks. It's pointless. Lakeview is built on willful ignorance. If a gutted devil walked down Main Street, no one would notice. "Never mind."

She shakes her head, muttering about him wasting her time, and continues out the door.

Mackie starts on coffee and a bagel.

"That's supposed to be our protection?"

At the sound of Blue's voice, Mackie's heart leaps into his throat. He swallows it and turns as casually as possible. He can feel the heat of the coffee pot on his back and the warmth from the heated tiles coming up through his feet. Has the kitchen always been this small and stifling?

Blue stands in the doorway looking exhausted. He's dressed in ripped-up black jeans and a black T-shirt stenciled with a neon yellow skull, that hangs off his shoulders. He hasn't bothered with any makeup other than what could be last night's eyeliner. There's a bite mark on his neck, dark purple. The teeth are plain to see. His lips seem swollen to Mackie, yes, from the split in them, but also probably from kissing.

A feeling spills through Mackie, ugly and unfamiliar. He bludgeons it before it can be identified.

"I think so," Mackie is relieved he sounds normal. "Sam never really explained what it did." He casts another furtive glance at the tree, suddenly glad Mom doesn't seem inclined to notice it. Half her yard is taken up by this monstrosity. He's sure it's ruined the daylilies that were supposed to grow around it.

"I see." Blue is eyeing the coffee pot. Normally, Mackie would pour him some. Today, he shuffles out of the way and lets Blue do the work himself.

"Where did you go last night?" Mackie hears himself ask.

Blue presses his mouth into a narrow line. "I had some stuff I needed to check on."

"With Shawn."

When Blue doesn't deny it, questions press against Mackie's lips. He wants to ask where they went, what they did, and if Shawn was nice to Blue afterward. He can't seem to squeeze those words out. Not after that scene in his bedroom. Blue had to know what Mackie was feeling, he just ignored it. Which means Mackie should ignore it, too.

"I wasn't sure if you were going to come back." The real fear—that he'd disappear with Shawn and Mackie might get a letter from the south in the middle of next winter—Hi, I'm alive. Miss you—no devils in New Mexico.

Blue sips his coffee. His hair falls over one dark eye. "I told you I'd stay."

Not exactly. Maybe he meant to.

"I'm going out with Kristy today, if you want to come," Blue offers up, almost like an apology.

Yes, he thinks immediately. Mackie catches himself before he can open his mouth and go back on his promise to his mother. He said he'd be here today, and this is where he'll stay. "I can't."

"Okay," Blue says easily.

"Maybe you shouldn't go out either," Mackie tries. "If you think the forest isn't safe..."

"I thought that's why I have you to protect me?" Blue is an echo of his old self again, tongue in cheek, wry smile.

Mackie can't even joke about it. His leg is still throbbing from that devil yesterday and he has a few bruises from driving raindrops. "I can't do that if I'm here."

"Then..." Blue waves to the door.

Once again, Mackie feels his magnetic pull, and he wants to go, really. Would do anything not to be stuck in this silent house with his ill and dying father. But he's already bailed once and can't imagine facing Mom after doing it again. "I can't," he repeats.

"Then I guess I'll risk fending for myself." Blue snags a cigarette from the pack on the counter and waves goodbye. Mackie settles in for what he's sure will be a long and anxious day.

Chapter 9

While the house is quiet, Mackie tries to fill his morning with research on his next semester of Business School. He'll have to do his capstone project next year and isn't looking forward to it. He doesn't know what he'll do, and he hates that feeling. It's overwhelming when the project is looming over him, and he has no idea where to start and where to end. The only way to remedy the situation is to dive right in.

He realizes too late that stressing about school that's still four months away isn't the way to unwind. He turns on the TV and it's all about Kevin Evans. Even the channels that aren't news are playing the Amber Alert commercial.

Mackie thinks about calling Kevin's mother. Even has the phone in his hand. He doesn't know how to begin the conversation, though, and drops the receiver.

He turns off the TV and instead gets a notepad from the kitchen, and a pen. He sketches to take his mind off things like he used to as a kid. He ends up drawing the road from yesterday, its roaring river, and the iridescent tail slipping out of the brown water. Its edges look sharp enough to slice through skin, even on paper. He can almost *feel* it, sliding through his middle.

He folds the paper up into little pieces and puts it into the fireplace, where the small fire curls its edges and hides the evidence. Once consumed, it's almost like it was never there at all.

Dad hobbles down the stairs around eleven, looking as ashen as the cigarette between his fingers. He's working on Emphysema to go with his early-onset Alzheimer's. Just like Uncle Paul, it seems he wants to die in his bed, reaching for his pack of cigarettes, oxygen mask down around his throat.

He stops on the bottom stair and looks at Mackie through narrowed eyes. Mackie prepares himself for an outburst like the one they had this Christmas past when his father forgot completely who he was. He didn't have a son, he said, and demanded the stranger get out of his house. When Mom tried to correct him, he only got more irate and confused.

Mackie and Blue spent the night at Sam's, Mackie ignoring his mother's phone calls and demands to come home and Blue ignoring Mackie's ignoring. Dad was fine the next day.

Alzheimer's is like that, Mackie's told. One moment, you know who you are and what this life is you've built up around yourself, and the next you're setting fish sticks on fire and screaming because you don't remember you've had a son for the last twenty-three years of your life.

"Hi, Dad," Mackie says, half ready to flee if things get strange.

Dad takes the last step as gracefully as a cripple and throws himself down at the kitchen table. He snags the lighter by the ashtray and lights the first of many cigarettes.

"Hi." A soggy cough follows the word. Mackie can't find the right way to scold his father without inciting a riot. Mom agreed no one would smoke in the house when he and Blue were home. Though both smoke on occasion, neither like the way it clouds the room and makes it hard to breathe.

He opens the window instead.

Dad's glare follows his movements. "You trying to let the devils in?" he asks.

Mackie starts and looks at him from over his shoulder. Dad's never talked about devils before. "What do you mean?"

"Don't be daft, boy, and close the damned window," Dad snaps.

Mackie stares at him until his father gets up himself and slams the glass closed so hard that it rattles in its frame.

Dad leans forward into Mackie's space. His breath smells of sleep and nicotine. "They've got their eye on you, boy, and don't think planting a tree in the backyard is going to change that, not even a tree like that." He pokes his finger at the glass, jamming it back and turning his too-long nail white.

The only thing Mackie can think to say is, "You know about them?"

His father snorts smoke scornfully from his nose and returns to the table.

Mackie sits across from him. "Tell me. What do you know about them?"

"The only thing there is to know. They take what they think they're due."

Mackie remembers Dad's rhyme.

'Wipe your eyes if they're bleary,
Watch Sorrow sleeping, weak and weary...
Crush your bones and take the heart

So they never have to be apart.'

"Crush your bones and take the heart," Mackie repeats. "It means something, doesn't it?"

Dad hunches his shoulders and makes himself smaller. He looks like a gremlin, clutching his fingers, twisting his cigarette filter in his fist. He glances surreptitiously left and right. "Don't say that. Not here."

Mackie ignores his whispered warning. "What does it mean? Do you know about Queen Sorrow? Is she looking for hearts? How do you know?"

Dad blinks, and his expression runs blank. His line of thought has dissipated like his cigarette smoke.

"Dad?" Mackie tries again. "What does the rhyme mean? Crush your bones and take the heart? Is Queen Sorrow hunting people?" *Absurd,* his mind screams. His instincts say otherwise. Mackie doesn't know which direction to follow.

Dad's mouth opens and closes, and no sound comes out. Then he furrows his brow. "What are you talking about, boy?"

Mackie can feel his hope shrivelling in his gut. "Nothin'," he says. What's the point? "Do you want breakfast?"

"Pancakes?"

It's near dark when Mom returns home. She gives Mackie half of a smile of approval that Mackie can't even enjoy. His sinuses are burning after being trapped inside with Dad's smoke all day. He takes the first opportunity he can to get the hell out of the house. How did he live here when he was a kid, and why the hell did none of his parents' friends say anything?

He ventures out to the road and looks in the direction of yesterday's river. A road crew has come and filled the spot with gravel and sandbags, directing the still cloudy water downstream to a culvert. They must have worked fast; this is the only road out to the highway and into town.

Something glitters on the road as shiny as a diamond. Mackie searches in both directions before venturing further than his driveway. There are no cars and no people, and the forest feels as docile as a lamb, treetops swaying in a gentle spring breeze. When you look at it like this, it doesn't seem like the kind of place that steals children and turns out their bones.

Mackie's shoes squelch in the soggy gravel. His shadow gets long and lean. It falls over the object but doesn't dull its brilliance. The sky and treetops reflect on its surface.

At first, Mackie thinks he's holding a shard of glass. Then he lifts it to the dimming sunlight and can see it is, in fact, a scale, a quarter of the size of his palm. It's green, pink, and yellow and sparkles brightly.

The smart thing to do is throw it back into the forest. He folds it in his palm. Its edges don't give an inch. They're quite sharp, too, and cut into his skin. He reels back to throw just as a creature with thin white hair and grey tissue-paper skin bubbles out of the ditch water and fixes Mackie with rhinestone eyes. They're hard and glitter like silver.

"Are you sure you want to do that? That scale is worth quite a bit in the right crowds." Its hold on the language is better than Mackie suspected any devils' might be. Maybe that's just ignorance, though. The only forest creature he's ever tried to talk to is Blue.

Mackie can't tell its sex from where he's standing and where it's lurking, but by its voice, high pitched and stony, he thinks it's female.

According to Sam, certain rules will keep you safe when dealing with forest denizens: don't look them in the eye, (which Mackie has already failed at), don't keep anything they offer you (he drops the scale on the ground), don't talk to them (he feels his mouth opening and slams it closed), and, lastly, don't get too close.

Mackie slides his foot back, ready to bolt.

The creature's eyes sparkle with delight. "Will you run?" It tips back in the ditch and a shiny green tail breaks the water's surface and wriggles teasingly. "It's true I can't follow as others might, but that's no reason to think you can outpace me. I am the water. Every time you turn on your taps or step into the rain, a dip in the lake. And *splash,* I could be at your feet, down your throat, drowning you."

"What do you want?" Mackie asks, breaking the second rule.

Its mouth pulls back, revealing teeth, sharp like needles, good for poking into the bodies of wriggling fish and small mammals and swallowing them whole. "I would enjoy a good, hearty meal. It's been forever since I've tasted human entrails."

Mackie takes another unconscious step back.

The creature laughs at his fear, and he feels stupid. When it sobers, it says, "You're safe today, human. The regent requests an audience."

Mackie barely understands. "The regent?"

"Of Sorrow's Forest."

"Wants an audience with me."

"With you. Am I saying this correctly? It's been a while. Or have humans gone daft?"

Mackie chooses to ignore the dig. His palms are sweaty. "What could it possibly want with me?"

"*She*," the devil swipes its tail menacingly in the water. "*She* would like to speak to you. For what reason? I do not know. I would as soon as eat you. I told her; I did." Its face folds into a smile and its teeth blink in the light.

Now Mackie's entire body is sweaty. He shouldn't have come out here. He can't remember why he did.

"If you don't come now, she'll come for you later." It lifts its hand out of the water and wags webbed fingers in Mackie's direction. Long talons cut the air.

Mackie feels his body leaning in toward the beast. Its long tongue slides between its wormy lips. It's as grey as its skin and bristled with bone, good for licking off soft flesh.

Never go into the forest.

Mackie jerks away from the ditch and the beast and starts to run, its warnings be damned. It cackles behind him. He can hear it give chase, water splashing and sloshing up onto the road, and now it's beside him, swimming through the ditch. It's monsoon fast, cackling, rejoicing in the chase. How long has it been since it hunted humans? It seems there is no greater joy for this devil. Mackie feels foolish already. How can he outrun this beast? How can he escape? *I am the water.*

Water bulges by the culvert beneath his driveway, reaching for him, and it's so close, he can feel mist against his face. Mackie takes a shallow breath and braces for the cold assault. It never comes. There's a sound like a gasp, then, as though someone has pulled a drain plug in the ditch, all the water starts disappearing at an alarming rate, leaving the creature marooned and screaming in the open air.

Mackie can't help but stare at the exposed devil.

A long line of amber spines mars its body from head to hip. Gills slash across its torso. Its skin is decaying-worm grey, and pearlescent. Its bare breasts sag against its cage of ribs, skin so thin, Mackie thinks he can see its heart beating.

From the waist down, the devil is fish-like, with a thin and powerful-looking tail reminiscent of a shark's, plate after plate of hardened, sharp scales.

It flounders in the disappearing water, still screaming in shock until it manages to turn onto its stomach, where it uses its arms to pull itself back into deeper waters, and then splashes off into the forest.

A calmness follows the monster's cries. Mackie stares at where it's disappeared, at the red roots that droop from the ditch side. They seem to grow before his very eyes, inch by inch, bright, bright red.

He remains immobile, breathing hard, until his phone trills in his pocket. Mackie fumbles to get it out and nearly drops it in the now-empty ditch.

Another Amber Alert lights up the screen. This time, it's a boy named Austin Leek that's gone missing, last seen last night, skateboarding in town by the skating rink. He is a little bit older than Kevin Evans. Mackie dated his sister, Elis, in grade ten.

Austin is in the forest. Mackie knows it without having to be told. Another lost to her gluttonous depths. *But why*? He considers the devil and this regent that wants an audience. He could probably get answers if he went to her. The likelihood of returning from such a trip is minuscule.

Is that how the forest got Kevin and Austin? Mackie wonders. Would they be foolish enough to be led into the dark by a beast so ugly and strange, it was beautiful? Or did they go in, compelled without knowing why?

He'll go mad with all the conjecture. He needs to ask an expert. Lakeview doesn't really have one of those, though. The closest he has is Sam, and Sam will probably tell him the same thing Mackie can tell himself—stay the fuck away from the forest.

But if Austin's still alive...

He looks down the road to the spot he and Blue went into the trees. It's hard to see from so far away, but he doesn't think the rain's touched that area. It's sacred in some way.

He tries to convince his feet to move in that direction. Even with the possibility of finding Austin dangling before him, after his encounter with the devil, they're saying no damn way.

At least, not alone.

He needs Blue.

Mackie steps into his driveway to let a septic truck roll past and scrolls through his contacts. When he calls Blue, the phone goes to voicemail. He tries twice more with the same response. He texts instead, asking *where are you at?*

When he gets a *Read* receipt and no response, he uses social media to find Kristy and messages her through that.

We're having a bonfire in my backyard, she responds almost immediately. *You should comeeee!*

Mackie chews his cheek. *Can you just tell Blue to call me?*

It takes Kristy a moment to respond. Mackie imagines her looking over the sea of faces in her suburban backyard for Blue before finally texting back, *He's busy.*

Blue's never been too busy to talk to him before. It's more likely she can't find him. Mackie drums his fingers on his phone, thinking of the best course of action. He doesn't want to waste time going to Kristy's. He wants to go into the forest by himself even less. What good would he do Austin if he has no idea where to even start looking? Besides, is the pool the kind of thing that will work for anyone other than Blue?

"Fuck," Mackie curses aloud. "Fuckfuckfuckfuck."

The forest rustles as if in invitation. He turns his back on it.

The GTO isn't ready, and there's no way Mackie's walking tonight, not when it feels like the forest is waiting for him to wander off the beaten path, so he returns to the house for his mother's car and then sets out.

Most of Lakeview is sprawled out around the town hub. If you want groceries, you must drive twenty minutes to get them, and there is no mall. Its largest shopping centre is a strip mall with a Giant Tiger, behind which Mackie smoked his first cigarette, and made it to second base with Melissa Reinhardt on a sidewalk peppered with spent cigarette butts and chewing gum.

There are a lot of townhouses in the area that all look the same, new, and monolithic, bracketed by ratty bungalows as old as the town itself.

Kristy lives in one of the latter.

It's fine enough as far as houses go, pretty gardens and clean windows and siding patiently waiting to be pressure washed in mid-May, and then again in July and September, but if you look closely, you can see wear marks on it. Porch boards will sag under your feet and a fractured garage window threatens to break loose during windstorms. A corroding old pickup sits in the driveway. Judging by the leaf litter gathered in its bed, it hasn't moved in ten years. A single front tire is rolled up on a rusty red jack, a project half-started and then forgotten.

Mackie follows the sounds of voices and music coming from the backyard, on through a narrow walkway, then a creaky gate, and into what is, considering its location, a fair-sized lot.

He's expecting to see three or four people spread on the lawn, max, and is surprised to see there are at least twenty sprawled out, utilizing every available surface, lawn chairs, barbecue wings, all over the ground on the dry patio stones and the back porch. Most have red Dixie cups in their hands and glow with bright drunkenness. Mackie doesn't know half of them

"Hi, Mackie!" Kristy bounds over, pigtails flying as freely as chopper blades. "You made it!"

"I thought this was a bonfire, not a party," Mackie says with another appraising gaze about the property.

"Wasn't supposed to be but Shawn brought a bunch of his friends." She wrinkles her nose for just a second. "But we're having fun! Want some?" She pulls out a baggy with what looks like heart stickers inside. One has been cut in half.

"No, thanks." He's had a weird enough day without acid.

"Are you sure? I heard you *looove* it."

And he hates small towns. He doesn't know Kristy well, but she has more than enough information on him, and he's not quite sure how she's gotten it. Towns like Lakeview are like that. You can stub your toe in the privacy of your bedroom and the next morning, the whole block will know about it. "Just not feeling it, you know?" Mackie musters a smile to blanket his horror. He doesn't need the forest dancing weirdly in his thoughts when it does it readily all on its own. Besides, this doesn't feel like a safe space. It will undoubtedly be a bad trip.

"Oh, fine." The drugs disappear. Kristy's about to, also, deeming Mackie too boring for her buoyant buzz.

Desperately, Mackie asks, "Blue?"

"Playground." She hikes a thumb over her shoulder to the plastic yellow and red slides in the far corner of the lot. Firelight barely touches its ageing sun-bleached plastic.

"Thanks."

There are a lot of legs he must step over to get there. Some people yell his name exuberantly. Mackie smiles and waves, even at those he doesn't recognize.

The bonfire's roaring out of control, and its light keeps him from tripping on unsuspecting patrons. While most are glassy-eyed drunk, some are LSD manic, laughing and crying, sometimes all at once.

There seems to be a barrier between the crowded grass and the playground, a band where no one sits, and no one passes or even looks toward as if repulsed by some unseen force. As he approaches, the air changes and becomes humid and thick and sticky. It makes Mackie think of the day Blue threw the picnic table at Joe. It makes him think of the forest. Of magic he doesn't understand. He holds his hands out in front of him like a blind man and walks forward against the screaming nerves in his body, telling him to leave well enough alone. He has no business with things mystic. He should go home.

His fingers pass through the heat into cooler air, and the party gets quieter behind him. He can hear crickets leaping from one grass blade to another, hesitant breaths, and clothing rustling.

Then a hateful voice whispers, "Just admit you're a little fucking pervert." Pause. "Just admit it."

Immediately, Mackie's rage spikes. He hears soft choking noises, and his fear elevates with the tension. Sand spreads out around his feet; walking is difficult. He comes wide around the edge of a large yellow side and stops, at first confused by what he sees.

Blue is on his back, lying flat against the plastic at the end of the slide, held in place by one of Shawn's massive arms. Shawn is standing over him, hand on Blue's neck, squeezing. He holds his cock in his other hand, jerking away roughly beside Blue's face.

Mackie almost turns away. Shawn's expression makes him stall. It's too intense. Mean, though that seems too innocent a word to describe the outrage in his expression.

Mackie stays where he is, stunned by the sight, the violence wrapped up in sexuality; it's one of those things he can't turn his eyes from. Like the mermaid's grey flesh. Just a train wreck his brain needs to categorize and scribe, so it has something to terrorize him with when the lights get low.

Shawn gasps as he edges closer to orgasm. His muscles flex. Blue grabs his wrist and sputters. His eyes are wide and alarmed. If it was a game at first, it isn't any longer.

"You're a fucking faggot. You like seeing me this way? You like doing this to me?" Shawn arches forward and presses the head of his engorged cock against Blue's lips, but now Blue is fighting to get away. This only seems to enrage Shawn more, which only serves to pleasure him more. He groans animalistically, jarring Mackie from his immobile state.

"Get off him!" Mackie lunges and shoves Shawn with all his might. Caught off guard, Shawn sprawls in the sand, sputtering. Shock turns to fear. He's been caught with his cock in his hand, and he's afraid of what Mackie will say about *that*, not what he'll say about Blue, who, suddenly free, is coughing and trying to catch his breath.

Mackie can't even look at him. His anger bubbles up and over, blinding him to everything but this. He falls on Shawn with fists swinging, and it's unfair, he's not drunk like Shawn is, hasn't been blindsided, and his pants aren't down around his ass, distracting him from fighting back. Mackie doesn't care.

He hits Shawn again and again until someone physically pulls him back and shoves him off. One of Shawn's friends. Blue's magic must be broken. Mackie tries to go back for Shawn, feeling like a dog fighting in the street, but then arms lock around his middle and haul him back. He turns, and it's Blue holding him off.

"Let go." Mackie struggles, trips, and falls in the sand with Blue.

Shawn sits up. Blood is running out of his nose, and one of his eyes is swelling closed. "The fuck is your problem, King?"

Mackie's so enraged that he can't even form a proper sentence beyond a vicious, "Fuck you!" He punctuates his words with a fistful of sand that hits Shawn in the face but doesn't seem to harm him.

"You like protecting a fucking child killer, huh?" Shawn spouts. With Blue's spell broken, the party comes flooding in. Shawn has a small army gathering behind him. They seem to be ignoring Shawn pulling at and holding up his pants, staring instead at Blue.

Blue furrows his brows and rasps, "Child killer?"

Shawn seems to have found his proverbial footing, he's more confident now with his friends at his side. "I saw you last night with the Leek kid."

Mackie glares. "He was with *you* last night. I saw you pull out of the driveway."

Shawn goes the most glorious shade of red. Instead of denying it, he distracts. "Yeah, I picked him up. He asked. And then I dropped him off at the skate park with that kid and drove away. Now the kid's missing? I don't have to be an engineer to figure that one out."

Murmurs around the group.

Blue isn't saying anything, and that worries Mackie. His wiry muscles loosen on Mackie's chest. Mackie gets up. He's still tight with adrenaline. When he looks down at Shawn, he wants to beat him until he's an ugly red mass, but he wants to get Blue out of here even more. Before Lakeview's new adults get hit with the mob mentality.

"We don't have to listen to this shit. Come on." He grabs Blue's bicep and drags him up. He's almost bird-light.

Blue stumbles behind him. The partygoers make a pathway for them; every eye in town seems to follow their progress. Blue's chest is rising and falling too fast like it did that time when he broke his arm when they were kids and he cried for forty minutes straight. Mackie prays he keeps it together. Otherwise, he's going to turn right back around and beat on Shawn some more; consequences be damned.

As if reading Mackie's mind, Blue swallows, and his shoulders stop quaking. Mackie pushes open the property gate with his burning knuckles. The air feels cooler on the other side, beyond the party and into the street; he breathes deep.

The car is parked crookedly in front of the house; a sedan needs to take a wide berth around it. Blue is silent as he fumbles for the door when normally, he would scold Mackie for parking so carelessly. Mackie waits until he's inside before coming around the front of the car and getting into the driver's seat. He starts driving immediately. He wants to be as far away from Kristy Chow's as possible.

It takes two minutes to cross town by car. Mackie does it in a minute-ten, coming back to his senses only when he pulls up to a red stoplight and a police car is waiting on the other side of the intersection.

"You didn't have to do that," Blue says finally. Gold lipstick is smeared across his mouth. It glitters by the red traffic light when he speaks.

Mackie squeezes the steering wheel tight. "He was choking you."

"I asked him to."

A hot flush crawls up his neck, and he wonders if he misread the situation completely. He plays it rapidly through his mind again.

No.

No, there is no mistaking the violence in Shawn.

"Maybe he was playing at first," Mackie says more confidently. "Then it changed."

Shame taints Blue's face.

"He's hit you before. Why do you keep going back to him?" Mackie turns and demands. He's never been good at keeping the peace or not speaking his mind because it's the *polite thing to do*. Why start now?

Blue slides his fingers over the dusty dash and avoids Mackie's eyes.

"Tell me," Mackie says.

Blue sighs and makes his voice small. "Because he wants me."

Shocked by the response, Mackie doesn't move forward when the light turns green. "What do you mean *because he wants me*? There are *lots* of people that want you."

Blue lifts one shoulder. "It's different."

"Because he's been awful to you for his whole life?" Mackie wields the words like a slap. Blue doesn't flinch.

"I guess so."

"Do you hear yourself?"

Blue sighs and puts his head back against the headrest. "I know, okay? It's fucked up. After he hit me the first time, I told him to get lost. He kept texting me, saying he was sorry."

"So that's it? He says he's sorry and you go right back to him?" It's not like Blue at all. At least, not the Blue Mackie knows.

"No," he says, which is a bit of a relief until he adds, "But I just wanted to get out last night, and he kept texting me. So, I took the opportunity."

Mackie feels hot right from his head to his toes thinking about the small space in his room and the non-existent space between their bodies, Blue's arms locked around Mackie and Mackie's around Blue.

"It doesn't matter who is treating you that way or what they say. You don't let them get away with it. You used to know that." Blue has been an anonymous ear for LGBTQ2S+ issues for as long as Mackie can remember him being open about his sexuality. Which is *forever.* Blue's never hidden behind lies and the status quo, has never normalized sexual violence and hate or pretended to be something he's not. Why the games now?

"Okay. Yeah. But he hasn't had the same support I have," Blue adds. "His father was terrible; his friends still are... He asked for my help, and I said I would. I knew it was going to be hard."

Mackie's eyes are bone dry, but he feels like he could cry.

Tapping on the window jerks Mackie away from the spot where he doesn't know how to feel or what to say. He squints against the darkness. The police officer that was across the intersection has turned around, parked behind them, and is now standing outside Mackie's window with his flashlight raised. Mackie rolls the window down a few inches.

"Is everything alright, gentlemen?" the officer asks.

"Fine," Mackie says. "I just..." He scrabbles for a lie on the spot. Blue has his phone out and Mackie improvises. "I was trying to find my way to Evergreen Glen. Sorry. I know we're not supposed to stop here, but there wasn't anyone behind me..."

The cop stares into his eyes. "Have you been imbibing this evening?"

He's so, so happy he didn't take Kristy up on her offer of LSD. "No, sir."

The officer leans in and lifts his nose to catch a whiff of Mackie's breath. The only thing he smells on it is coffee and Oreos. He almost looks disappointed. "If you need to look at your map, you need to pull off the road," he warns, then walks back to his cruiser.

Mackie puts on his right-hand signal and turns, though it's the opposite way from his house.

"Why did you come tonight?" Blue asks once he's sure the police's headlights are a distant memory.

He's been so concerned with Blue, he's forgotten about the devil and the boy he was desperate to save. He breathes out. "I saw a devil from the forest."

Blue fumbles his phone. "What?"

"It swam out to the ditch and asked me to come into the trees."

"And?" Blue's eyes are as wide as planets.

"I'm not stupid," Mackie says crossly. "I didn't go. But Austin Leek's gone missing, and we're the only ones that know where to look for him."

Blue's already shaking his head before Mackie's finished speaking. "Absolutely not."

"You said you could save them."

"I said maybe, and I couldn't," Blue reminds him unnecessarily. Mackie still sees Kevin when he closes his eyes. Maybe always will.

"This time might be different."

"I don't see how. The forest knows what we did, and it's watching us."

Mackie tries, "Austin's innocent."

"We're *all* innocent, Mackie, until we're not," Blue bites.

They get quiet. Mackie drives the car white-knuckled and still too fast back to the house. He parks it in the driveway, and it's only then that Blue speaks again.

"I won't go at night. It'll have to be once the sun rises."

"Thanks." It's not the quick action he wants, but it's something. They'll be the only people in Lakeview looking for Austin in the right place. He has a chance now.

"If he's still alive," Blue mutters. He gets out and closes the door so hard, that the sound reverberates in Mackie's ears.

Chapter 10

The next morning, Mackie is woken by a heavy pounding on the front door rather than his alarm. Blearily, he dresses in a pair of light jeans and the first sweater he can find—a ratty Tragically Hip band shirt he's had for as long as he can remember—and hobbles downstairs.

Thud, thud, thud, falls in time with his footfalls.

When he gets to the bottom of the stairs, Mom leans out around the kitchen wall, dressed for work, hollow-eyed and grey with exhaustion. "Answer the door, Mackie?"

"Yeah," Mackie grunts, too tired, too irritated, to form a proper response or even a question like, *why can't you?*

His irritation cools quickly once he pulls the door back and sees two blue-uniformed officers waiting on the other side. One, a man at the cusp of retirement, is turned away from the door and watching the distance, as though it doesn't matter to him if Mackie answers or not. His partner, a woman in her late thirties, has her steady gaze affixed to the door, as though she hasn't done anything more important in her life.

The man's not particularly tall or wide, or unique in any way. He's so average, that Mackie thinks if he saw him in a lineup the next day, he wouldn't be able to spot him. The woman's short and stocky and looks like she could bench press a cow if she wanted. She's pretty; smooth-faced.

"Morning," the male officer addresses the door again. He's annoyingly bright for... Mackie checks the clock over the stove. Seven fifteen. "I'm Officer Soria, and this is Officer Adams."

"Can I help you?" Mackie asks. He tries not to be nervous, to act naturally. In his limited experience, police are a bit like dogs in that they can smell the discomfort on you.

The woman says, flat-toned, "We're looking for Blue King. This is listed as his permanent residence."

Mackie hears the upper floor creak, then feels Blue's presence like thumbs pressing against his back.

"I'm Blue," he calls from the top of the stairs. His voice is still raspy with sleep. He's tugged on yesterday's black jeans and has paired them with a tight-fitting soft pink long-sleeved T-shirt. His hair is still unkempt. Mackie watches him descend the rest of the stairs with caution, smiling small at the police, a little confused.

Mackie searches Blue's neck for the bands of bruising Shawn's fingers should have left but can't see the evidence. He doesn't let himself think it wasn't as bad as he thought it was, Blue smells of makeup and he will not, not for anything, look Mackie's way. It doesn't matter if he's carefully covered the bruising, however. After closer inspection, Mackie can see he's still swollen.

Mackie's eye twitches with rage. He's never had that happen before; he thought it was just something authors say in books.

"Can we come in?" Soria asks, oblivious to the tension.

"Yes," Mom says from the kitchen. Mackie forgot she was there. She's in a business suit, her dark hair is curled, and she has a cigarette in her hand. "Please, sit. Do you want a coffee?"

"No, thanks," Adams says. She glares at Mom's cigarette. She waits until Blue is seated in their little kitchen and then sits beside him. Her partner chooses the seat across. Adams can do the pressing, and Soria can monitor Blue's body language for lies. The whole situation is incredibly bizarre. Why are they here? Is it about last night's fight? No way Shawn went to the police, though, and even if he did, why are they questioning Blue? He didn't throw any punches.

Mackie leans in the doorframe where he can look out the window to the massive oak. Its bark looks as dark as wet dirt. If he's unwelcomed in this meeting, no one acknowledges him.

Adams scribbles a few notes on a small notepad, then jumps right into it. "Do you know Austin Leek?"

Austin's name is a splinter shoved under a nail bed. Everyone tenses to hear it.

Blue holds the detective's gaze, very nonaggressive, still confused, but compliant. "I know he's the boy that went missing... but other than that, not really. I knew Elis a bit, though. Austin's sister. Mackie dated her a little in high school, after Bree. Or before Bree. Or both." Because back then, everything was about Bree. He glances back at Mackie, then faces forward again. "We never hung out, though."

"Are you sure about that, Blue?" Adams pushes.

"Yes. Austin started high school a year after we graduated. We saw each other around town, and I knew who he was, but that's it."

Mackie cuts a glance at Blue. When he gets nervous, he wiggles his toes. They're going like crazy now. The rest of his body remains still, though. The officers won't see. He hopes it stays that way.

"We have an eyewitness that puts you with Austin the night he disappeared, likely within minutes of his disappearance," Adams continues. "You could be the last person to see him."

The words are right but what she really means is, *you could have been the person to kill him.*

Mackie's sweating enough for him *and* Blue and immediately regrets his presence here. Last night, he didn't ask Blue if there was any credence to Shawn's accusations. He tells himself it's because he forgot and not because he didn't want to push, not to where the answers might get ugly.

What are you thinking? He accosts himself for the dark thoughts. *You know Blue. What's he going to do with a kid like Austin Leek? Give him to the forest?*

Give him to the forest?

He shivers, remembering Kevin falling apart around him.

Taking. Blue was taking him from the forest.

Blue, who belongs to the forest.

"That's impossible," Mackie's mother steps in where Mackie falters; again, he forgot she was there. "The three of us went for dinner and a movie that night. To celebrate the boys passing all their exams." She casts a glance around the room, completely honest, as though she believes what she's saying wholeheartedly.

Mackie's too shocked to object. *Look at how smoothly the lie comes from Mom's lips.* What else has she told flagrant lies about? He then realizes he's gawking and returns his gaze to the oak where it's safest. There might be bald spots on its trunk. He can't tell for sure. The light is weird this morning, both grey and gold, shimmering and soft, encapsulating everything in its magnetic glow. He can't focus on anything it touches, including the things it can reach through the window. Like Mom. She's a soft-edged blur.

"Do you have proof of this?" Soria asks.

"Well, no, I paid cash and didn't take my receipt..." Mom's voice sounds almost dreamy.

What is happening? Mackie wonders. Something. Something is fogging his thoughts. Everyone around the kitchen blinks slowly. Except for Blue. He seems just fine. A little edgy, but otherwise okay.

"Tansy Carling was working the window at the cinema that night," Blue chimes in. "We talked. She can vouch for us."

Whatever game he's playing, Mackie isn't following. He knows he's the weakest link, though, as the second-least affected by this strange spell, so he keeps his mouth shut.

"We'll talk to her." Adams takes out one of her cards and hands it to Blue. Her movements are slow. "If you *do* remember seeing Austin, contact me, please. His mother is very worried."

"I will," Blue lies. "Thank you for everything you do. We're lucky to have such dedicated officers working for our missing persons."

The officers stand, and Mackie's mother shows them out. She returns a moment later. "I'm late for work." She hands what's left of her stubby cigarette to Mackie and gets her lunch off the counter. "Stay out of trouble," she warns them both, and then she's gone.

Mackie jams the cigarette out in the ashtray and asks without looking up, "What did you do?"

"What do you mean?" Blue watches the last of the smoke coil from the ashtray before it dissipates and is gone.

"You weren't *at* the theatre the other night," he says. "None of us were."

Blue falters before collecting himself again. "As far as everyone else will be concerned, I was."

"How?"

Blue won't budge. "Drop it, Mackie. I did what I had to do." He has his head in his phone and is scrolling through Instagram.

Mackie has the sudden urge to grab Blue's phone and throw it across the room. This is *serious.* People are accusing him of murder. Or child abduction. Or if not, they will be soon. "I don't know what you did here to make Mom say those things, but Tansy won't lie for you." Not straight-A good-girl Tansy.

"She will." He finds what he's looking for: one of Tansy's selfies. She's dark-skinned and beautiful. A flyer for the Lakeview Nighthawks cheer squad. Her dark eyes twinkle out from the phone screen. "She just won't know she's lying." The air around him bristles ominously with magic. Mackie's skin pricks.

"What are you doing?"

Blue's gaze catches Mackie's. "Do you trust me?"

"I just think—" This is dangerous. Neither of them knows what they're doing.

Blue repeats, "Do you trust me?"

"Yeah." Of course. Better than he trusts himself, certainly.

"Then, shhh." Blue looks like a man choosing which bomb wires to cut. His eyes close and his mouth gets flat. Mackie obediently quiets. In the space where his words would have been, he hears the glasses in the cupboards begin to rattle and shake, and then the cutlery follows. Pipes groan in the sink and beyond the window, at the birdfeeder, mourning doves and grackles flutter their wings as if warding against a chill.

A ringing starts in Mackie's ears, low at first. It quickly gets louder. The air is turning electric, just like it did when the picnic table flew at Joe Redding. He presses his hands against his ears when even the wind chime above the sink starts going, then slams his eyes closed just as the glass begins to break. It starts with the crystal wear in the China cabinets and moves like a shockwave onto the plates until Mackie's sure every dish in the house is broken.

As quick as it began, the destruction ceases. Shortly after, the feeling of distress disappears and all that's left is a cobwebby softness that fills his mind. Mackie breathes deep. The air has a dense ozone stench to it. He squints at Blue, who's luminous, as he was in the courtyard. He's beautiful, the same way obsidian is, hard and cold.

"Fuck." The kitchen is a mess of broken glass. Spilled lima beans and coffee beans, and breadcrumbs that were all in glass jars press against the cupboard doors, labouring to be let out.

Blue looks around at it all, blank, a stranger. Then he blinks, and he's Blue again. "We'll clean after. Let's go to the forest."

"Dad—"

"Everything will be fine," Blue promises. The air stings with magic again, soothing Mackie's worries.

Poisoned light spills from the clouds, getting darker and meaner the further down the road they travel and the closer they draw to the spot they entered the forest that last time. Every time Mackie moves from the shadow of a tree into the light of the sun, it feels like thousands of insects are crawling over him, and the only way to fix it is to move faster, to get further away from the house. It's like the forest is herding him in. When he checks over his shoulder, he almost expects to see wolves nipping at his feet. There is only him and Blue.

While Blue looks straight ahead, Mackie lets his gaze linger on his friend, attempting to discover if Blue feels the same way. His jaw is straight, his dark eyes heavy-lidded. Mackie can't read anything past the stiffness he feels in his lip—he keeps touching the inflamed gouge with his tongue and wincing.

The road curves up slightly, then down slightly. They pass where the mermaid devil spotted Mackie. He looks but doesn't see her, or even feel her presence in the trees. He's not foolish enough to think he's not being watched, though. His watchers are just clever and sneaky.

"Can we talk about why you were talking to Kevin *and* Austin just before they went missing?" Mackie asks. Mostly just to distract himself. He'll go insane if he winds himself up too tight, so he's examining every dark nook for red eyes.

Blue stops poking his lip. "Who says I was?"

His answer isn't surprising as much as it is disappointing. Mackie thinks they should be past evasion games. "I *saw* you and Kevin. I'm sure Shawn saw you and Austin, too."

Blue eyes him from the edge of his vision; Mackie still can't read his expression.

"Are you going to concentrate over a picture of me, too, and fuck with my memories?" Mackie asks. He doesn't usually get irritated with Blue in this way. It bubbles out of somewhere, though, and froths over.

Blue's first response isn't to fight; it never is. His shoulders drop, and sulkily, he says, "Probably wouldn't work anyway."

"You've tried?" Mackie spits.

"I mean, when I first came to live with you, yeah," Blue says with a shrug. "I just didn't know it didn't work until you told me the other night."

Mackie feels himself shying away even though he tells himself not to.

At his side, Blue's fingers twitch as if he might reach for Mackie and take his hand. He seems to think better of it and lets his fingers go still. "I didn't *do* anything to Kevin or Austin," he says. "Not really."

"Then why were you with them?"

Blue surveys the area around them, ensuring they are as alone as they can possibly be, before admitting, "I keep seeing ghouls. Which isn't very unusual, they're everywhere if you know where and how to look. Just usually, I'm the only one that knows where and how to see them." His tone is petulant. Blue is used to being special, now one of the things that made him that way he thinks is becoming commonplace.

"The day in the park, when Kevin was staring into the forest?" Mackie asks. His voice is just a creak above a whisper; it almost gets lost in the sound of their footsteps, and honestly, even that's too loud for a conversation such as this. He wishes Sam had given him some portable charm to ensure their safety away from the house. "There was a ghoul there?"

"It lit up all the trees around it with this soft glow. Kind of like a lightbulb. It was pretty," Blue says just as softly. "I saw it beckoning. I thought it was to me."

"You didn't try to approach it, did you?" Mackie's scandalized. Never approach the forest, that's rule zero. Blue *knows* that.

Blue shrugs. "They've never tried to interact with me before, I was curious. But then Kevin dropped his football and started approaching it, and I realized it wasn't looking at me, it was looking at *him*.

"I stopped him before he got too far and told him again to never, ever, go near the forest." Blue balls his hands into fists so tight, Mackie can hear his bones creak. His heart is almost always on his sleeve. The deep circles below his eyes are sleepless hours thinking about Kevin and how he should have done more.

Blue says, "He said okay. He said he was fine. He *seemed fine*. I don't understand what happened..." He trails off. Mackie counts ten footsteps before Blue speaks again. "It was the same with Austin. We were driving by, and I saw this white glow in the trees, and I knew the same devil was at it again. I got Shawn to pull over and leave me there."

"Why did you make him drive off?" Mackie has no delusions about Shawn. He's no one's saviour. If he'd been there, though, he could have vouched for Blue.

Don't be stupid, Mackie thinks immediately after. The only thing Shawn's interested in is Shawn. He wouldn't speak up for Blue because he's too ashamed to even be *seen* with him.

Predictably, Blue waves him off. "Shawn wouldn't understand. If he *could* see the devils, he'd probably just try to hurt them, and if he couldn't, that's just more ammunition to call me a freak and a weirdo."

Mackie again remembers the devil in the ditch, sharp nails and scales and teeth. Anything that calls the forest home is more than capable of defending itself against Shawn

"Do you know why the devil approached Austin?"

Blue shakes his head. "I tried asking, but she wouldn't answer me. Like... didn't even see me. It was so strange."

Mackie worries his lip. "So, you see a devil talking to Austin, you pull over and tell him not to talk to strangers." Blue shoots him a plaintive look for his glibness that Mackie ignores. *One* of them needs to be pragmatic. "And then?"

Blue kicks dollar-sized gravel down the road. It bounces into the ditch and gets lost in the grass. "Then I walked him home and came back to the house."

"Before you left, you watched him go inside?"

"Jesus, Mackie, of course." Frustration slips into Blue's voice.

"I'm just trying to figure it out," Mackie says by way of apology, but he's not very sorry. "Why is the forest suddenly taking these kids?"

"It used to *always* take kids," Blue says, as though this hiatus is a gift, and maybe they should let it go because if that's the way it's always been, then who are they to say differently? "If you go back through the town records, there were a lot of missing persons every year, kids, and adults, right up to 1997. Then it all stops."

1997, the year Mackie stole Blue from the forest. Mackie bunches his nose up. "Why were you researching that?"

"Grade twelve law," he says with a shrug.

"You almost failed that class."

"I was doing pretty well until I chose that as my culminating," Blue says with all the gusto of a conspiracy theorist. He gets more serious. "Maybe if we figure out *why* it was taking people in the first place, we can figure out why it's taking them again."

Mackie has lived with the forest all his life, *known* that people who go into it rarely come out alive, and those that do are never the same. Yet, to imagine that it's actively hunting is insane.

Or just frightening.

The closer they get to the pathway, the quieter the birds, frogs and wind become, until they're surrounded by complete silence. It gets ten degrees colder. Once more, the air's electrified. Mackie doesn't know how much more magic he can handle in a day.

For Austin, he thinks, staring at the dead blue flag. But he's stopped at the side of the road and doesn't move.

"Come on," Blue says expectantly. He's already in the ditch, waiting for Mackie. His skin is once more luminous except for the birthmark across his cheek. Usually, it's so pale, Mackie almost doesn't notice it. Something is happening, though, and now, it's a black smear across his eye. "This was your idea."

"Wouldn't be if you never showed this place to me," Mackie mutters as he steps off the road and into the ditch.

Grass squelches beneath his feet and cold, muddy water soaks into his running shoes. They were brand new two weeks ago but are going to be ruined before this spring is over.

The grass shivers around him as if shucking off a disguise, and the forest opens on the same pathway that took them to the pool. Mackie stares down at the dead grass and trees and vines. It looked healthy the first time they came, but now he can see the forest is diseased. Each time it blooms, it gets closer to death.

Blue says, "Are you afraid?"

"Aren't you?" he counters, sotto voce.

Blue looks at the cage of branches, the crusted grass. "It's dead here, it can't hurt us. Not anymore."

His words are meant to soothe, yet all Mackie can think is, that means they were in imminent danger of being caught in the disease the other night. How narrowly had they escaped with their lives?

Mackie lets out his nerves with one huge breath and steps under the trees. They croak in a breeze he can't feel, a reminder that they could snap closed around him if they choose.

"Blue?"

"Yeah?" he asks, distracted.

"Do you remember anything from before?" Mackie's voice echoes off the dead tree stumps and is thrown back at them.

"What do you mean, before?"

"Like, before I found you." They've never talked about that night, and not only is it strange to be talking about it now, but it's also strange to feel so nervous talking about it with Blue. He's usually the person Mackie finds easy to accost with all the bizarre things in his head, but this topic feels very personal.

"No," Blue says shortly, leaving Mackie to think he's not being entirely truthful.

Dead grass crunches underfoot, and vine husks droop lifelessly from petrified tree limbs. Mackie runs the pads of his fingers over one particularly rotten tree. "Why do you think this keeps happening?"

Blue returns, "Why does any forest die?"

Mackie considers his answer. "Lack of nutrients. Sunlight, phosphorus, nitrogen." He steps over a dull puddle. "Water."

"Or your way of up taking nutrients is damaged," Blue adds, pointing at a tree that's toppled over, taproot broken.

"So, the forest is one huge organism and either it's not getting enough nutrients, or it's lost its ability to intake them?"

"That's my working theory," Blue says.

"And the kids?" *Don't say it. Don't say it.* Even though he's the one who's asked.

"Food. It's trying to keep going."

Mackie shivers. He loves the forest. He hates the forest. He doesn't know what he'd ever do if it all got dry and dead like this swath.

Then Kevin falls apart in front of his eyes again, and he shames himself for the romanticism.

Ahead, the path widens, and the clearing appears, pool at its centre. Water that should be blue as crystal, is hibiscus red. The red of watered-down blood. He stops.

"That's new."

"Yeah." Blue marches forth.

"Wait," Mackie pleads. Blue stops with his feet at the water's edge. He raises his brows in question.

A hot flush crawls over Mackie's skin, and his heart flutters in his chest. He struggles to voice his thoughts. In the end, he blurts, "I can't go in there like I did last time." Kevin's bones haven't returned to the town, they're probably still here, stuck in the mud. He can't bear to find them under his feet.

Blue nods once, expecting Mackie's answer. "I'll do it alone. It's probably for the best anyway."

He pokes his toes into the water.

"Wait," Mackie says again. He's so nervous, his head is swimming. His thoughts are clouded with visions of the last time he was submerged in the pool when he almost fell into the place beyond.

"What is it?" Now Blue sounds exasperated. The forest hasn't ever scared him the way it's scared Mackie.

The best Mackie can come up with is, "Maybe you shouldn't."

Blue shakes his head. His blonde hair glints with blue. "Just keep watch."

Mackie feels another protest climbing up his throat, trying to gag him. He coughs on it until it's settled down again, quiet.

Blue steps into the red waters in his boots and sinks in up to his shins. The next step, he's at his thighs. The air is doing that prickly thing again. The water ripples gently, spilling red on the banks. Small ferns curl when it touches their leaves and die.

Mackie's supposed to be watching the area for dangers yet finds himself half closing his eyes and praying Blue will be okay.

Blue starts to glow pale white, and his words come back to Mackie. *It lit up all the trees around it with this soft glow. Kind of like a lightbulb. It was pretty.*

It *is* pretty.

And Blue is a ghoul. He's a wraith. He's a devil.

None of those words seem to fit him just right. He *is* otherworldly and beautiful. He *is* the forest's. Or he was.

The magic reaches an intangible precipice.

Blue plunges his hands into the water just as something solid swoops down from one of the dead branches and digs its talons into Mackie's shoulders. He feels himself getting lifted off the ground by two large and powerful wings, then a jarring pain on the top of his head brings blackness.

Chapter 11

"It doesn't smell magicked any longer," screeches a voice from within the black. "Human." Said with no small amount of disgust.

"But we smelled the magic. Maybe it was tricking us?" answers another.

"I heard they were tricky."

Quiet.

"Why doesn't it wake?"

"I pecked it hard," pipes in the first voice again. "Perhaps its soft human head made this soft human dead."

"Only their bodies are soft, their heads are hard with bone, stupid."

"*Stone*, it's said."

"Yes. Right. Stone. They're hard with stone." A pause. "Do you think it's truly dead?"

"Let's poke it and see."

Mackie feels something sharp jar into his side. It doesn't occur to him to play dead. His eyes fly open. He's on his back looking at the sky. Trees tower overhead, green, and lush. And above those, puffy white-grey clouds roar by in an unfelt wind. Distantly, Mackie's shoulders ache. He knows his shirt is wet on the back and on the front. He's feverishly cold and can't stop shivering.

A pale face moves above him, blocking his view of the sky. He knows at once it's a devil, though he's never seen its like before.

Like the mermaid, it's mostly inhuman. It has a mouth like Mackie's, wide and full-lipped, but its nose is elongated into what can only be described as a beak, though there is no way for it to open. Shiny and black, it curls just enough that Mackie thinks if they were standing face-to-face, he wouldn't be able to see its mouth.

Two stick-like arms push out of its torso. Behind them, sickly-looking wings trail the ground, bone pale and missing a few feathers. Further down, huge, sharp claws dig into the ground from eagle-ish feet. It stands ridiculously tall as it peers over him with red-rimmed eyes the same colour amber as liquid honey.

"I told you. It's too ugly to die," it proclaims victoriously.

"*I* was the one who said that." Another creature jostles beside the first. They look almost identical, except the rim around the other's eyes is sunshine yellow instead of red. Both are dressed in shawls made of young twigs and leaves. The creatures make no indication that they're scratchy or uncomfortable despite their appearance.

Something wriggles under Mackie's hand. He stands up with a jolt. The devils scatter like startled starlings, squawking and jeering as though Mackie is the thing to be afraid of. Mackie temporarily ignores them, desperately hunting for the thing that touched him. It felt like a snake, and while he's not afraid of snakes (unless one has snuck up on him), he would very much enjoy knowing what *kind* of snake is trying to steal his body warmth. Garters are fine. He had one as a kid. Rattlers, not so much.

But when he looks down, all he can see is his body print in a bed of moss and some vines.

Then the vines start to wriggle, and the moss, too, shaking Mackie's shape from their soft leaves. For a split second, he feels dizzy enough to faint.

Have to get out.

He spins a circle, trying to see if there's anything he recognizes. It's green on green on green with no definitive features. He's in the heart of the forest. *Just like Kevin probably was. Hell, this might be his resting place exactly before Blue pulled him away.*

He's going to be eaten in the heart of the forest, and no one will know what happened.

Blue?

Mackie turns another circle. He doesn't see him. He didn't think he would, really. If Blue knew where he was, he wouldn't still be here. Or at least, not here alone.

"I think it's going to *fall*," proclaims the devil with yellow around its eyes.

"I think it's going to *die*," says the devil with red around its eyes.

Both are almost salivating. They rub their hands together and stomp closer with their clawed feet.

"Should we try to stop it?"

"I prefer my meals wriggling."

"Yes," says Yellow, "but Her Grace prefers them dead and sizzling."

"Are we going to take it to her?"

"Of course."

"But it's not even the right one, I think."

"So?"

"It's been..." the red-eyed devil counts on its fingers. "Four! Four decades since my last meal."

"You're so *dramatic.* You stole a frog during the solstice celebration *just last year.*"

"And you stole a dog!"

They start bickering; it's hard for Mackie to tell if it's over his fate or over the last thing they stole and ate. Not that it matters. They're distracted.

Mackie chooses a direction and starts sliding in it as quietly as possible. The last thing he needs is to become someone's meal.

He's a good seven metres away when they finally realize he's escaping. They squawk in unison, feathers ruffling, and the chase begins.

This part of the forest is unfamiliar to Mackie, and he's unfamiliar to this part of the forest. As he moves through her brush, she doesn't hinder him, exactly, but she doesn't make his escape easy, either. Branches whip him, one even brushing past his already cut face, enticing it to bleed again, and mud tries to suck his shoes off and hold him still. He's the intruder, after all, and intruders are meals.

He tries remembering what he did when he was a kid, running through the trees. How did he and Blue escape the closing forest? Not only that, but how did they do it so *easily*?

The sad truth is, he didn't play any tricks back then. He just knew he had to save Blue. He had to get out of there, for both their sakes.

He holds Blue's image in his mind now in case he's the ticket. It's hard to say for certain, but maybe the branches spread a little further apart, and maybe the ground gets a bit drier.

"Stop it, hurry, before it escapes!" squeals one of the devils, Mackie can't see which one and he's reluctant to give up his mild advantage by checking.

"Hurry!" chimes the other. "Before he crosses the Waste!"

Before he crosses the Waste, the forest echoes back in the voice of the wind.

Then, smaller than that, *cross the Waste.*

Mackie doesn't know what the Waste is, or even how to identify it. He pours on the speed, though, and pumps his arms, pushes off tree trunks and slides below gnarly branches. He runs hard, barely breathing, barely thinking beyond *I don't want to be eaten*.

"Quickly! It's almost there!"

Mackie feels a vine closing around his foot, and something bony shoots up from a puddle of mud. He dodges both, barely, hops a narrow stream, and then the air shimmers in front of him like a barrier. Sure this is the divide into the Waste where the devils are hesitant to go, he dives in without thought.

There's a moment where he's suspended, a fly caught in a spider's web, then the forest gasps open. Without the resistance of the branches to fight against, he stumbles forward onto the mossy ground and lands on his hands and knees. The air feels cleaner here.

Mackie's at a disadvantage on the ground. He spins around, hands planted behind his hips, to try to see his pursuers. If he's going to die, he wants to fight, even if he can't win.

No one has followed him past the barrier, and he can no longer see the bird things, only thick trees that hang like curtains between this place and the last.

A butterfly flutters past his nose on big white wings, though it's much too cold for such things. Chasing it is a lightning bug, and a hundred others after that. Flowers grow between the gaps in the moss. Most Mackie's never seen before—purple and yellow, blue, and red—all mixed. Their leaves are serrated like knife blades. Their roots slither over the ground. If that's not peculiar enough, they lift their heads and fold open their petals. Mackie sees *eyes* surrounding their pistils, hundreds of them dotted on the part of the petals closest to the stem. They're small and black and beady, just like a spider's.

All the better to see you with, my dear.

They fold open again, and they have toothy mouths.

All the better to eat *you with, my dear.*

A scream is tearing its way out of his chest. It's horrible to be in their sights, to recognize that they have sight, to begin with. But then as one, the flowers speak, and the coming noise gets jammed in his throat.

"You shouldn't be here."

Flower voices are difficult to explain. They're wispy and weak, like a summer breeze on a humid day—there, yet faint enough, they're easily forgotten.

"Do you understand?" The flower closest to Mackie bends in. Desperation bleeds in its voice. "The queen can't know you. Once she knows you, she'll know him. And that is a very dangerous thing."

"I didn't mean to come," Mackie stammers. "I was just—there's a boy—he's missing—"

"Dead. They're all dead. Don't hunt for them."

Them? The way it's spoken implies more than just the two he knows of. His heart drops. "Blue—"

"Don't say that name here." Their voices turn tar-mac hot. His ears burn with them. "Never come back to this part of the forest."

He doesn't even know where *this part* is! He opens his mouth to plead this. The ground bubbles up under him and starts corralling him in a different direction, destroying his chance.

"Go now."

"But—"

The trees shiver and bend menacingly. Their bark croaks, rocks tremble and Mackie feels another presence sweeping the forest. He knows at once, a swath of death is racing through the trees, coming for him, trying to consume him in one hungry gulp, and it won't be long before it arrives.

"Now!"

Earth lifts into a hill, getting him to his feet, and Mackie is made to either run or fall.

Mackie, who is built for such things, chooses to run.

When Mackie crashes from the forest, he's winded and scared. The death rot has been following at his heels all the way, and just stops at the forest's edge. Something from within the trees screeches. The sound crawls down Mackie's neck, and his chest tightens. He has an absurd notion that he's escaped the forest only to fall dead at her borders with his heart exploded in his chest.

Cars buzz by. People are gawking at the sweaty and filthy man panting on the roadside with his hands on his knees. Mackie can't find it within himself to care.

Another screech pierces the air. Trees shake and break. Dead limbs drop to the ground as something moves from branch to branch high up in the canopy, like a cat trapped by a cage, but when Mackie looks, he can't locate whatever beast watches him with barely contained frustration. He feels like he's narrowly avoided something catastrophic, and the forest is very displeased.

Summoning every bit of mettle he has, Mackie turns his back on the trees and takes stock of his surroundings. A Walmart and McDonald's stand shoulder-to-shoulder on the opposite side of the road.

"Damnit," Mackie mutters when he recognizes his predicament. He's on the other side of town and it will take him an hour to get back on foot.

Twenty-five minutes into his walk home, he puts out his thumb to flag down a passing car. People look over his greasy, mud-stained clothes and his sopping wet shoes and press down on the accelerator every time. No hope there.

He sighs and takes off his shoes, wincing as the backs slide over his blistered heels. It's less painful to walk on the sidewalk in his socks.

Clouds reach for the ground with their heavy and dark bodies. It starts misting first, and as the hour elongates, the rain becomes harder. Soon, Mackie is soaked and cold and worried. What happened to Blue? Is he wondering the same thing right now?

Police sirens pierce the air; it's difficult to pinpoint their location and even harder to determine their purpose when he's so far away from the source, but like the noise of the Amber Alert, they set him on edge.

Mackie pushes himself to walk faster despite the cold sweat slicking his skin. He frequently looks over his shoulder in case he's being followed or spied on. Though the forest is a cold front throbbing against the side of town, threatening to swallow it up, it's unmoving. For now.

Eventually, the ragtag city falls away, and he cuts through Jackson's farm field and onto the dirt road leading to his house. To keep up appearances, he waves hello to Mister Jackson watching the storm from his porch, as he leaps over the ditch and onto the dirt road. From there, he's only a few hundred metres from home, and he walks with at least three-quarters of his attention to the forest. He can't handle another dealing with a devil. It was dumb luck to come out on top the first two times, and Mackie doesn't like to gamble.

In his driveway, at last, he can see the top of the oak leaning high above the house. Its leaves, which were green and healthy just this morning, have started to turn yellow and red. It's much too early in the year for fall colours; Mackie must assume it's dying. *No nutrients,* he thinks. *A tree without its tap-root.*

He swerves around the front door and heads to the back of the house to assess the damage. A tree that size will cut the house in half if it falls. It'll have to come down soon.

That's where he finds Blue. He's standing in front of the forest line with his feet shoulder-width apart like a linebacker. He's wearing the same clothes he was that morning, and his blonde hair is limp on his forehead. He looks like he's getting ready to do something unsavoury. His hands open and close at his sides, and his back heaves with deep, erratic breaths.

"What are you doing?" Mackie announces before Blue can make a break for it. He has the air of someone who will not stop once he gets going. Mackie knows he'll follow him into the trees if he has to; he just very much does not want to have to.

Blue whips around. He looks saw-ghosts-in-the-dark scared. "Mackie?"

"Come away from the forest." *Step away from the ledge, Blue.*

At once, Blue begins to shake. "Is that you? God, I thought... I don't know what I thought. You were there, and then you weren't—Where did you go? I was *looking* for you." As he talks, Blue's mood shifts as fast as summer weather. He's happy, then he's angrier than a badger. Then he just seems frustrated. "What happened?" He scrutinizes Mackie in the dying light. "And *why* are you covered in blood?"

Oh.

For the first time since waking in the forest, Mackie remembers his panging shoulders. When he pulls his shirt aside, he can see deep gouges in his flesh. They're bird-claw-shaped. The area around it is bruising, too. Perhaps that's why no one would stop for him. He must have looked raving mad on the side of the road, waving down cars.

Blue swears. He's so discomfited with his hair plastered to his forehead and his eyeliner, now a day and a half old, smeared down his cheeks. His clothing clings to him as much as Mackie's, and he's shaking with cold.

"I'm okay," Mackie says lamely.

His assurance only seems to annoy Blue more. "Glory."

All around, the air gets electric. Mackie can physically watch the grass perk up; the oak's leaves unwrinkle. He prepares himself for another one of Blue's outbursts, like the flying picnic table or the breaking glass in the kitchen. Blue's magic dissolves without any ill effect that he can sense, everything's just a bit greener.

Blue stomps over to the oak and takes a pocketknife from his pants.

Mackie stands over his shoulder. "I didn't know you carried a knife."

"It's yours," Blue says distractedly.

So it is.

"What were you doing with it?" It's out of place in Blue's hands.

"It was the only thing I could find that might be intimidating if it needs to be but safe enough to carry," he admits.

"You were going to go into the forest armed with a pocketknife."

"So?"

Mackie lifts his eyebrows. Blue doesn't bother glimpsing his disbelief. He digs the tip of the blade into the oak. It's sharp and easily slides into the bark. Mackie considers asking him what he's doing, but Blue is so irritable, he doesn't want to disturb him.

Sap starts pouring out of the wound. Blue fumbles on the ground for one of Mom's flowerpots and comes up with a clay one with a big, happy sunflower face on its front. Its insides are dusted with dirt. He uses it to catch the sap. The bits that don't end up in the pot trundle down the front of the tree, reminding Mackie of a great beast with its throat slit.

"Let's go."

Blue marches into the house first; Mackie follows. The TV is on in the living room, though the couch in front is unoccupied and seems like it has been for some time. Cold cigarettes heap in the ashtray, and coffee sits on the table, milk curdling on top, reminding Mackie he was supposed to keep an eye on Dad today. The good news is, he didn't burn down the house. Bad news, Mom is going to be furious again. He finds his phone on the scuffed table. There are a few missed calls: one from Sam, two from Mom, and a text from her saying, *I picked your father up for an appointment. We need to have a conversation when I get home.*

Already, he can tell it's not going to be one he's going to enjoy. He doesn't remember why he thought it was a good idea to leave the house.

The news plays on the TV, and the camera is trained on a segment of forest near Rebel Park. Mackie recognizes the *Easter Resort and Spa* sign on the side of the road, tagged last year with huge rabbit ears that have never been cleaned.

The camera zooms into a boulder at the tree border where a naked skeleton sits upright while looking out on the town. Northern blue flag flowers poke up through the ground around it. They remind Mackie of the eyed flowers in the forest, and their little mouths with their sharp little teeth. *They're dead. They're all dead.*

Police officers move in and out of the frame until finally, one spots the news crew and approaches. His face is weathered like a ship that's spent most of its life at sea. "This is a closed police investigation," he says sharply. "You need to be behind the line."

"Any comments, Officer?" pumps the journalist in a desperate way.

"Yeah, get the hell out of here and let us work." An impatient swipe at the camera and the lens moves away. It feels unreal, watching this. A body at the forest edge, police, reporters... Mackie's never seen the like. Usually, only whispers follow the discovery of a body. For what feels like the first time ever, people *see* this.

What any of it means, though, Mackie can't tell.

Up the stairs, a door opens. Mackie draws his eyes from the TV and follows the sound to the top of the loft, where Blue is waiting for him outside of his room. Mackie leaves the TV trilling in the living room and slowly mounts the stairs.

In Mackie's bedroom, shadows encroach, spilling in from the outside in the seconds before Blue turns on the bedside lamp and chases them out. The curtains flutter, still closed on the forest but not keeping it out completely.

"Take your shirt off," Blue instructs.

Mackie works stiffly, sliding his arm out of his sleeve and then getting the material over his head. The pain has gotten worse as time has progressed.

Finally, he's free. Blue looks him over, and his expression is shocked and concerned. "Holy damn. How did this happen?" he asks again.

Mackie sighs and drops into his wooden desk chair; it's the only safe place to sit where he won't get rainwater and blood in any fabric. "Devils."

Blue staggers with his suspicions confirmed. "I didn't see them, Mackie." He stammers. He never stammers. "I didn't... I was looking in the water, and then I heard this thing, like air moving through the branches, and when I looked, you were gone. I tried following."

"I know."

"Really," Blue presses, though Mackie believes him, heart, and soul. "I tried pushing through the trees, but they wouldn't let me. I got turned around for hours until the forest finally spat me out on the road right by the house. Every time I tried to go back in, the trees would close and keep me out."

Because it wanted to eat me. He clears his head of residual fear. He's not in the forest anymore. It can't touch him here. Sam's tree protects him. "Everything worked out."

Blue doesn't seem the least bit consoled. He combs his fingers through his flat hair, flinging cold raindrops when he does. "But now they know you." He bites his lip hard; it goes white and presses on the scabbed cut there. "They can find you again." Just like Sam said. "This was a bad idea."

"Which part?" Because from where he's sitting, a lot of things are shaping up to be bad ideas.

"We never should have gone into the forest again," Blue clarifies.

"You said it was safe."

"It was. And then it died."

"You said it couldn't hurt us if it was dead."

"Well, I was wrong!" Blue pants in the wake of his outburst. His cheeks are high with colour, and his grip is tight on the flowerpot, stretching the skin on his knobby knuckles.

"I'm okay," Mackie says again.

Blue skewers him with a powerful glare. It extends into long seconds. "What did they want? And how did you get away?"

"I don't know what they wanted," Mackie lies. Blue is a simmering fire and telling him that he was almost chow for devils will be pouring lighter fuel on the flames. "They were bickering when I woke up, and I ran."

Blue shakes his head and dips his fingers into the sap then smears it across Mackie's left shoulder. It burns at first, then the air electrifies, and the sap gets cool. The next time Blue rubs his fingers across the area, Mackie can't feel the hurt at all. He spares it a look and isn't entirely surprised that Sam's oak has healing properties, especially in Blue's hands. Already, the wounds have diminished to white scars, divoted in his skin, the bruising gone.

Blue moves on to the other side to the same effect. Mackie touches his shoulder. It tingles like the nerves have been asleep and are just waking up. Other than that, there's no pain.

"Where did you learn to do that?"

Blue shrugs. "I just knew."

"Do all devils *just know*?"

Blue is close enough, almost between Mackie's legs, and Mackie is studying his face so carefully, he catches the moment Blue flinches. He covers it up with a step toward the dresser. "I wouldn't know."

"I don't actually think you're a devil. At least not how they're normally portrayed," Mackie says. "I was just a kid. I didn't know what to call you. And then it just kind of stuck."

"I know." He looks at the ground. "It's not that."

Mackie longs to reach for him. "Then what is it?"

"It's..."

"You can trust me."

Blue leans against the dresser and lifts his gaze to hold Mackie's. His thoughts tumble behind his eyes. "It's not about titles or lying or trust. Not really. I just don't remember much, and no one ever told me what I am."

Mackie hunches forward in his chair and pushes a clump of damp hair off his forehead. "But you remember some." It's sort of strange and sort of relieving to hear Blue talk about the forest this way, no longer pretending as though he's not part of it.

"Little things. The grotto, for one," Blue concedes. "And which plants are good for eating, and which are good for healing."

"That's amazing." He can't quite sell his proclamation. As much as he loves the forest, he will always fear it a little bit more, and it shows.

Blue gets still and looks at the place next to Mackie's ear. "Mostly, I remember to stay away from the forest. It's dangerous." He repeats, "We shouldn't have gone in."

"I know." As much as he doesn't like to admit it. Austin deserved a better hero than Mackenzie King. Gruesome curiosity drives him to ask, "Did you see anything in the pond? Before, I mean?"

Blue rubs his face with both hands, smearing his eyeliner even more. He looks at the floor between his fingers. Gravity pulls his next words out of his mouth. "I couldn't find Austin. I mean," he laughs dully, "I didn't even really look. Once I realized you were gone, I gave up. When the forest spit me out, I came back to the house hoping you were just playing around, but mostly knowing that you weren't. That's when I got the knife. I was coming in for you."

The truth is grim. "Are those Austin's bones on the TV?"

"Likely." His guilt simmers at his feet, ready to pounce and overtake him.

"I don't think there was anything you could have done anyway," Mackie says soothingly. *He's dead*, the forest said. *They're all dead. Gone.*

"Probably." Then he exhales and looks up at Mackie. "I'm not even sure I cared, to be honest. I was just thinking about you."

There is truth to his statement, Mackie can see, but there is also more to it than Blue lets on. He *did* care about Austin, just not enough. It's very human of him, Mackie thinks. In times of crisis, there is only so much room available in a person to care about others of less importance to them. It's a survival mechanism, bred-in-the-bone, but Mackie can see Blue hates himself for it.

Mackie stands. Thanks to the tree sap, he feels better than he has in perhaps his entire life. Nothing hurts as he gathers Blue in for a tight hug, pressing his cheek against his shoulder. His skin is warm through his T-shirt. He smells of wet cotton and stale hair products.

"It's okay."

Blue nods silently; his chin jars Mackie's shoulder. "I know." His ribs heave in contradiction and his arms cinch around Mackie's back.

"It's not your fault."

"I know."

"It's not anyone's fault."

"I know."

"And I'm okay."

Blue doesn't vocalize this time. He doesn't need to. His fears are tangible and real. The forest knows Mackie now. The forest can find him. *Will find him*. It finds and keeps everyone it means to. Always.

Dully panicked, Mackie tries to lean back. He doesn't know what he'll do—race out to challenge the forest? Scream at it until it shrinks away like a mildly hungry bear deciding he isn't worth the trouble? Pack what he can and run for it? Can he drag Blue with him?

Blue secures his hold around Mackie's ribs. "Can we just stay this way for a second?"

Thoughts of fleeing evaporate. Without any fight at all, Mackie relaxes into Blue again. "Yeah."

Wordless minutes go by. Blue shivers minutely and won't take his eyes from the window. Mackie wonders if they're both cobbling each other's pieces together and have been for a long time. Mostly, he doesn't mind. Likes it even, being the one person Blue always comes back to. There's a small part, though, that's afraid one day, he won't come back. The Blue that talked of disappearing after they found Kevin lingers in his thoughts, very real and very boisterous.

He doesn't want him to go. Can't imagine life without him. Can't wrap his mind around what it means to be consumed with these thoughts.

"Still okay?" Blue wonders. Mackie realizes he's almost stopped breathing, each exhale careful and slow.

His mind is whirling into places it's never dared before. Places that both rub him raw and feel somehow comfortable, too.

Stay this way.

He wants this and is almost paralyzed with the knowledge.

Stay this way.

"'Mackie?" Blue shifts in his arms, warm, real.

With a rusty throat, Mackie says, "Yeah. I'm good."

But it's not true. He can't stop thinking. Can't stop feeling everything in this small space between them.

"I know when you're lying."

He always does.

Mackie turns his cheek on Blue's shoulder and lets his lips hover over his pulse point. Blue stills; even his breath catches. Goosebumps roll all over his skin.

Mackie's heart hammers with this subtle intimacy, and then harder when Blue moves his hand up Mackie's back and presses his cool fingers against the back of Mackie's head, encouraging him to make contact. Mackie does, gently closing his lips in an almost-chaste kiss.

Oh.

Blue's breath breaks on Mackie's shoulder, hot.

Time crawls to a stop. Lingers sweetly on this moment, elongating it, before picking up her things and moving on again.

Blue moves, too, but it's not away like Mackie expects. He clutches Mackie's hair with a bit more force and presses more firmly on his back, encouraging the contact to evolve. Mackie uses his tongue, tastes Blue's skin—salt and iron. Can hardly believe he's doing it.

Blue sighs quietly, tightens his hold again, and presses against Mackie. Mackie can feel he's excited, stiff in his pants, and his body responds without his permission. He imprints another kiss over the bruises on Blue's neck, open-mouthed, humid, gentle. He thinks about leaning back and finding Blue's mouth, and what will happen after. Kissing and petting and then? Summer fling, and then? Because there's always an expiry date on Blue's relations.

Who cares? spits the vocal half of Mackie's brain.

I do, croons the sensible other half.

In the end, Mackie is too paralyzed to do anything. It's Blue that has to move. He pulls back slightly and slides his cheek across Mackie's. His hand is still so tight in Mackie's hair, and he still presses hard into Mackie's middle.

He's going to kiss me, Mackie thinks. His stomach tumbles nervously. They're close enough, he can smell the iron from the split in Blue's lip and feel his staccato breaths on his cheek.

Headlights slash through the drapes and cut across Mackie's eyes. Blue pulls back and the moment is broken. "Someone's here."

Mackie breathes out, half thankful for the distraction. "Mom, probably."

Blue doesn't seem convinced. He cocks his ear and listens intently. Mackie does the same and hears it, too. Unhinged laughter tinted with a bit of rage.

Mackie follows the sound into the hallway to the front of the house and pushes aside a curtain.

In the driveway is Shawn's Camaro. Shadows move around the hood and dart up onto the porch. A bad feeling takes to seed a millisecond before Mackie hears a hissing noise.

"What's going on?" Blue asks over his shoulder. His voice wavers, and he hangs back a few feet, withdrawn.

"I don't know. Stay here," Mackie instructs, though of course, as soon as he starts down the stairs, Blue is there with him.

The Kings have a baseball bat by the door for *just in case* moments. None of them like to talk about *just in case of what*, but it's been there since they were robbed when Mackie was a kid. It's been a long time since it's moved. Cobwebs run from the handle to the wall. They break apart into dust when Mackie grabs it and tears back the door.

Three people stand on his porch. First, he identifies Bobby Vie. He's tall and skinny and wears an inflated baseball hat that makes his head look bigger than it is (it's quite small, lengthwise, if you take the hat away). Behind Bobby is Nate Holloway, a career football player who looks thick like a seal but is actually thick like a brick shit house.

Naturally, Mackie knows who's leading the pack. It still enrages him to find Shawn on his porch with a spray can of black paint in hand, using the headlights of his Camaro to see by.

Shawn stops scrawling his huge, shaky letters to grin at Mackie and sneer at Blue. He doesn't even have the decency to look ashamed or out of place. "Hey, child killer."

Without thought, Mackie lifts his baseball bat and swings blindly. Shawn is expecting his rebellion and dodges out of the way. His swing goes wide and almost takes out the window. There's a porcelain owl on the porch that's not so lucky. Bits of fractured porcelain scatter everywhere. The men laugh. Mackie reels back and tries again. He hits Shawn in the thigh, and he stops laughing.

Mackie feels sick with triumph. It flees immediately when Nate grabs him up around the middle and squeezes him hard. Mackie's ribs protest. He kicks his feet out at Shawn and Nate. He hits Nate in the shins and Shawn in the gut. Both men let out an *oof*.

Taking charge of his brief opportunity, Mackie reaches back over his shoulder, bat forgotten, and claws at Nate's face. It might be unsavoury, but so is hefting someone into the air like a child.

Nate hollers and drops him. Mackie scrabbles toward his baseball bat again. There is blood and sweat on his palm and the bat tries to slip through his grip.

Nate buckles around the blow to his ribs. Mackie swings around and catches a charging Shawn in the hand. He can hear his fingers breaking. Shawn screams wild profanities that brush by Mackie's ears without sinking in.

Whipping around, he hunts for Bobby and Blue, finding the former in the front yard, running, while Blue remains by the door. The air is charged around him, and he looks like a devil, glowing and inhumanly beautiful, with black eyes, and white-blue hair sticking up in a static storm.

Bobby reaches the end of the driveway, where the ditch water runs through the culvert. There's a huge *splash*. He disappears without ever getting the chance to scream. It could be the mermaid, but it could just as easily not. There is no shortage of devils skirting the edge of the forest.

"What is *wrong* with you, you fucking freak?" Shawn blurts at Blue. "What the fuck? What. The. *Fuck*?"

More electricity pops in the air. Both headlights burst, casting them in darkness if not for the moon. There's just enough light to see honest fear flash through Shawn and Nate.

"*Leave. Now.*" Blue barely sounds like himself.

In his eagerness to get away, Nate plants his hands firmly on Mackie's shoulders and pushes him back, hard. Mackie falls against the house, dropping his bat and knocking his head on the wall. Blackness momentarily fills his vision.

The Camaro revs and peels out of the driveway, spitting stones and dirt out from its wheels.

Blue heaves in breaths in the doorway. The light is fading from his skin in dramatic ways, leaving him grey and exhausted looking. Surrounding the property, the forest shudders. Mackie watches the grass grow and flowers bloom under the quarter moon. Something else is happening within the trees, and he doesn't like the way it feels. Things are growing, but they're seeping malice, the way a raspberry bush does when it needs to bear its thorns.

"We should get inside," Mackie says. He needs Blue's help to get off the ground and up the stairs, too. His ribs ache. He doesn't remember getting hit, but he must have.

It's not long after Shawn and Nate leave that Mackie's parents return home. He's showered and dressed by this point, has cleaned the kitchen as best he can of the broken glass, has slathered Polysporin on his cut face and slapped a bandage on it.

He waits at the top of the stairs to field questions about his earlier absence, the paint, the shattered owl, and the blood on the porch. Other than a long, cold look from his mother before she helps herself to the liquor cabinet, neither of his parents acknowledges he's there. The guilt is so bad, that Mackie considers apologizing. He can't bring himself to shatter the strained silence, though.

He returns to his room. Blue is sitting on his bed in his pajamas, still looking exhausted. Mackie closes the door, shuts out the light, and crawls into his bed, choosing the spot by the wall. Without discussion, Blue climbs in, too. He faces Mackie and looks ghostly.

"I didn't murder that boy."

"I know," Mackie says. Not Austin, at least. Neither are so sure about Bobby.

Chapter 12

Word travels like wildfire in a town as small as Lakeview. Mackie can only guess at what's being whispered as he goes into the hardware store and waits impatiently for the robust woman behind the paint counter to mix up his can of paint. Almost every eye is on him, and patrons whisper behind his back. He's used to people glancing at him in the periphery—Blue draws attention wherever he goes, and by proxy, this means Mackie does as well. But these stares feel different. They're heavier. Their judgement is palpable.

He gets fed up on his way out to his mother's Civic and has a stare-down with a man in his forties walking into the hardware store, holding his daughter's hand.

"What?" Mackie barks.

The man says simply, "I'll kill him if he comes around my family. Tell him that."

Mackie's *almost* taken aback, but he can't deny the capacity people have for cruelty, especially when they're scared. He forgoes responding—there's no point, nothing will change a person's mind if it doesn't want to be changed—and tears open the driver's door.

He drives too fast on his way home. It doesn't make him feel better. It's only when he's slathering white paint on the pale brick, covering up the K I L L E R Q U E E R, that he starts to feel a little bit human.

He hasn't seen Blue since that morning, just before Blue left for Westchester, a small city forty minutes west, for a job interview. Now the sun is high in the sky. Mackie texted him once around eleven-thirty to make sure he wasn't splitting town. Blue responded with a picture of a sushi spread with the hashtag *selfcare.*

They hadn't talked about last night when they woke nearly in each other's arms, not about the almost kiss or the fighting, not about the riot of colour that was the front lawn as flowers bloomed and spread, or the wallet Mackie found at the end of the driveway, splattered with red.

Blue simply rose, left for his room, and returned an hour later in a light blue three-quarter sleeved coat that showed off some of his innumerable tattoos, and a pair of dark slacks. The cut on his lip was somehow a distant memory, wished away by the same magic that wished away Mackie's injuries, and other than mascara, there was no makeup on his face.

"I'll be back later today," Blue said, then tagged on, a bit unnecessarily, Mackie felt, "Stay away from the forest."

Then he was gone.

Mackie smears paint over the last R and then moves on to his next task. Getting rid of the evidence that might tie them to Bobby. He feels a bit like he's covering up a murder as he retreats into the backyard and stands in the shadow of the dying oak. Half its leaves are on the ground, and huge false morel mushrooms with their bulbous cauliflower heads grow out of its decaying roots.

Mackie takes Bobby's wallet out of his pocket and flips through it quickly. His driver's license, an unnamed number, credit cards, a bank card, and a card for the same speech specialist Mackie used when he was a kid because like Mackie, Bobby always had issues with stuttering.

All the ways Bobby has made his mark on the world, Mackie needs to erase them.

He reels back and throws the wallet as hard as he can into the woods. He watches it soar through the branches and get lost in the leaves. He doesn't hear it land. Mackie steps closer and squints into the forest. Is it caught on a tree limb? If so, he'll need to fix it before winter comes, the leaves drop, and it becomes visible.

Movement. Mackie holds still as something distant drifts closer to the edge of the swollen river, twenty meters inside the trees. The mermaid devil, simmering in a shallow pool.

She smiles with closed lips. "Simply throwing him away won't work, will it? At least, not in my experience. If you want, we can make it like he was never here at all." Idly, she uses a long fingerbone to clean around her polished teeth. "Would you enjoy that, Caretaker?"

Any questions about the new pet name are sure to evolve into more games that Mackie doesn't want to play. "Is that his?"

She pulls the bone out of her mouth and looks puzzled. "Does it offend you?"

It does. Bobby was an asshole, but this is sick, seeing fragments of his body being used this way.

"Oh! It does! It does!" She spins in the water, thrilled. Her ghostly hair fans out around her like tentacles. "Humans *can* be delightful when they're alive."

"What do you want?" Mackie asks. He folds his arms over his chest and is careful to keep his expression blank. Any ammunition is too much for a creature like this.

The devil stops spinning and fixes Mackie with her yellowed eyes. "Before our queen's assassin finds you, I'm tasked with bringing you to the regent," she poses again. "Step into the forest, little Mackie. Step under her branches." Crooning, teasing, lilting, almost. Mackie can feel the pull of her voice. It takes all his willpower to resist. He steps back and feels the soggy trunk of the oak on his spine; his head clears.

"Forget it. I was almost a meal last time."

Her eyes spark like flint. "If you do not come peacefully, I will take you by force."

Mackie lifts his chin and hopes she can't hear his pounding heart. "You can't leave the water." He thinks. He hopes.

She's intrigued by his challenge. "I will make the rain drudge from the sky day and night. It will soak into the ground, where it will rot the roots of your tree, it will soak into the foundation of your home, into the basement, and then I will slip in, and I will drag you into the forest. Best come now, Caregiver, and save yourself some pain."

With the tree at his back, Mackie feels brave enough to lift his middle finger to the devil. "Fuck yourself."

She locks eyes with him. It's uncomfortable staring into her dead pupils. Mackie can't look away. The air sparks with the same electricity it does when Blue makes magic happen, and she surges forward in a gush of water. It carries her lightning-fast almost to his feet. Milliseconds before she's on him, the oak's branches bend in a non-existent wind, a weathered ballerina reaching for the ground, pushing back the devil.

She surfaces several feet away in a shallow puddle just outside the forest. Angry welts burn down the side of her face. She seethes.

"I warned you," Mackie says, and he sounds so much bolder than he feels.

The devil believes the front. "You'll pay for that, Mackie King." She wriggles her tail, splashing fetid water all over Mackie's front, and slips back into the deeper waters protected by the forest.

Oak leaves drift down in front of his eyes at an alarming rate, one after the other, destroying any relief Mackie might have felt. Soon, the tree will be bare, and he'll have lost his protection.

He whittles the rest of his day away in the garage, trying to replace the timing belt in his GTO to keep his mind off the forest, though it's an overbearing parent, looming just out of sight. Anytime he hears a noise, his heart gallops Loonie Toons style, threatening to beat right out of his chest.

Shortly before four, he gets a Missing Person's alert on his phone. Bobby's face is on the screen. Half an hour after that, the police pull into his driveway, Soria, and Adams again.

They ask him about last night, and Mackie tells them everything he can. Yes, he saw them, yes, they were on his property. Yes, they vandalized his house. No, he did not see where Bobby ran to after he raced down his driveway. The police diligently take notes.

"Is Blue home?" Adams asks. She leans against the duel-coloured hood of Mackie's car and lets her fingers play over the exposed steel and the flaking original paint. It needs to be sandblasted and repainted.

"Job interview in Westchester."

"I see. And last night?"

"He was by my side all night," Mackie replies. He holds his chin higher still and meets her eyes, challenging her to ask for clarification, not wanting to give any more detail but willing to if it'll exonerate Blue.

Adams scribbles some more things on her notepad before looking up and smiling, practiced, fake. "Thanks for your time, Mackenzie."

Mackie returns the smile, though, like Adams, he doesn't feel the emotion behind it. "I hope you find him."

"I'm sure he'll turn up, one way or another," she says.

Cops like Adams don't care about people like Bobby. Everyone knows it but no one says it. It's still a blow to the chest to see the way Adams pulls herself together. She draws down her mask of forced concern but lurking beneath is annoyance. She must look for Bobby, whom she believes has hit the road with his friends; it's her job. She wants to spend her time looking for kids like Kevin Evans and Austin Leek, though. Kids she believes are in trouble, and not on day three of a ten-day binge.

Mackie watches until they pull out of the driveway, past where Bobby was dragged into the water. Then he goes back to his GTO.

Mackie's covered in grease and the sun is low when Blue finally returns. He has takeout Thai food and four bottles of Singha.

He strips down to his T-shirt, hangs his sports coat on a hook by the door and pulls up two of the work stools, one for him and one for Mackie. "It's from Little Bangkok," he says, offering chopsticks. It's the best Thai restaurant in Westchester.

"Amazing." As soon as the scent of food hits his nose, Mackie realizes he's starving. The last thing he ate must have been breakfast.

Blue watches Mackie eat his spring roll and drink his beer without touching his own food.

Mackie chews and swallows. "What is it?"

"They're looking for Bobby."

"I got the update, too," Mackie says.

"Yeah." Blue looks at his food.

There's a lot of hesitation packed into that simple word, prompting Mackie to ask, "How do you know they're looking for him?"

Blue fiddles with his chopsticks. "The update."

Mackie echoes Blue's words from last night. "I know you're lying to me."

Blue rolls his eyes. "Yes. Sort of. I saw the update. But Shawn's been texting me, too."

Anger licks through Mackie. "Haven't you blocked him yet?"

"I did. He took Nate's phone and texted me through there." He holds up his phone for Mackie's inspection.

Child killer

The cops r going 2 know what u did

Their going 2 find his body
Ur not going 2 get away with it
Did u think u would?
Freak
Ur going to rot in jail with all the other faggots

It's Mackie's turn to lift his eyebrows. "You think he knows the difference between their and they're?" *Child killer. Faggot. Freak.* None of it means anything. Shawn is a monster in a man's skin. *He* was the one trying to choke Blue at Kristy's bonfire.

"He texts with the number two. No." Blue smiles, and it's a good front, but Mackie can see he's bothered.

"Bobby is gone, and he's not coming back. And even if he does, they can't pin anything on you. You didn't touch him," Mackie assures. He was the one fighting, Blue was just watching, and Mackie didn't touch Bobby.

"You're right," Blue says eventually. "It's probably fine." He changes the subject. "What did you get up to today?"

Devils flash through his mind, bloody wallets, dying trees, police officers. "Just worked on the GTO."

"Is it up and running?"

"Maybe. I fixed the ignition and timing belt," Mackie says. "If it starts, no more misfires, hopefully."

"We should take it for a test drive."

"Now?"

Blue's smile becomes real. "Why not?"

Blue's fever is catching. Mackie finishes the last few bites of his meal and fishes his keys off the keyring holder by the door. A miniature cast of a cherry red 1951 Bel Air swings from the chain, a gift from his father back in the days when he still remembered and cared about birthdays.

Blue slides into the passenger's seat, filling the car with the scent of his cologne. That and the roar of the engine turning over is intoxicating in the same way edging towards the brink of a cliff is, no safety harness.

The motor catches and revs. Blue cheers. "*Finally.*"

Yes. Finally. Mackie shows his teeth off in a grin that Blue returns.

"Let's get going."

Mackie straps on his seatbelt, warding away the untethered feeling. Blue leaves his off. He's never had a problem with edges or falling.

Mackie pulls out of the driveway and onto the road and guns the engine. The car leaps forward as seamlessly as a shark in the water. The RPMs jump and the forest whizzes by, all its little oddities and monsters, its ghosts, its secrets. They're otherworldly and full of magic, but the GTO has a magic of its own, and while he's in it, the forest can't catch him.

Blue rolls down his window to allow cool wind to rush into the cabin. He's glowing again, almost like he was last night as Bobby ran to the edge of the driveway.

"This is amazing," Blue gushes. He takes his eyes off the forest to look over at Mackie. "Remember when you brought this car home?"

"I didn't know if I could fix it." It was in bad shape. Dad had helped him tow it from the scrapyard on his seventeenth birthday. Blue spent countless hours in the garage with him, watching him work by spotlight into the wee hours of the morning. Those are some of Mackie's best memories.

It's been six years in the making, but finally, it runs, and part of Mackie is sad about that. He has no more excuses for late nights in the confines of the garage. He has no more reason to talk to Blue for hours over the sound of Led Zeppelin on the radio.

Blue looks at him in a radiant way that makes Mackie feel special. Like he's something. Some*one.* Someone special with Blue's attention on him. *Just like one of the boys Blue pulls into his orbit.*

"Want to go to Rebel?" Blue asks.

Mackie's deprecating thoughts are overpowered by Blue's offer. Maybe they don't need the excuse of the GTO.

Mackie makes a sharp turn onto the highway and guns it down the paved road. There are no cars out; it's a ghost town this late in the evening.

People are afraid.

People are going missing. First, just kids, but now Bobby is gone, too. There is no limit on what the forest will take, and when they're not in the eye of the public, people are spooked.

Mackie drives faster to outpace the thought. Blue beams in the passenger's seat, oblivious to Mackie's turmoil. He's built for doing dangerous things, and this is the closest he's come in a long, long time, his expression says.

Mackie fishtails into the empty parking lot at Rebel Park, following Blue's pointing finger up the narrow service road to the pier, where it looks out over Yarrow Lake. He parks as close to the edge as he can manage without nosing the steel guardrail and cuts the engine. The radio runs quietly in the background.

"This is better." Blue unrolls the window completely. Wild things sneak in—the smell of the cold lake below, fresh running sap from the forest behind them. They're miles away from where the ugliness with Bobby happened, and it seems like that's good enough for Blue, as though one part of the forest isn't as soiled as the next. Mackie can't differentiate the way he seems to; all the forest is malicious to him. He feels it like a weight on his chest. It wants to crush him but it's not quite strong enough yet.

They sit in silence for a few minutes, Blue listening to the waves crashing below and Mackie listening to the wind playing through the branches, on edge and pretending he's not.

"How did your job interview go?" Mackie eventually asks.

Blue says, "I think I'm in the running."

"What's it for?" He didn't even bother to ask earlier, and Blue hadn't told him, either.

"Promoting local bands." Blue puts his seat back. Mackie opens the sunroof, then mimics him. The sun is setting on the horizon, just under the heavy hand of an incoming storm.

"You don't sound very excited about it."

Blue locks his hands behind his head. His elbow is almost touching Mackie's ear. He doesn't look at Mackie as he admits, "It's hard. Being away from Lakeview. I mean, it's always been kind of hard."

"Like, homesickness?"

"Not really..." Blue trails off. Mackie thinks that might be it. Then, dreamily, he adds, "More like being on the moon when you belong on earth."

"That's..." Crazy? Different? Mackie isn't sure which to choose.

Blue draws in a breath to speak. It gets hung up. He lets it out and tries again with more success. "When we left for college, I felt like I couldn't breathe at first. It got better, eventually. But since we came back, if I leave, or even *think* of leaving, it feels like a missing tooth. Or a cracked rib."

Blue belongs to the forest, and the forest belongs to him. His confession makes it seem like Blue's slipping through Mackie's fingers. He would hold on tighter if he thought it would make it better.

"The forest scares me," Blue continues in that same dreamy voice. "I can't live without it, though."

"I know how you feel," slips out of Mackie's lips, too full of heavy meaning for the glibness Mackie longs to hide behind.

Blue turns on his side in his seat and peers at Mackie with his dark, dark eyes. He's forest-wild again and so painfully beautiful, Mackie can't look away. "Do I scare you?"

"Sometimes." He must consciously whittle the waver from his voice.

Others might be hurt or worried. Not Blue. He looks pleased. He reaches between them and pushes Mackie's hair off his forehead. The touch is jarring and electric and totally different from every other time they've brushed shoulders or elbows or anything else innocent and uninteresting. At least for Mackie. Blue's eyes are dark and impenetrable, and Mackie has no idea of the thoughts going on inside his head.

Blue states in a barely recognizable voice, "But you don't want me to go away."

"No." It feels like it's the answer to something illicit. With that one word, he's admitting something he's never spoken aloud, or even let himself believe, before. Blue hears it too, Mackie's sure, because his lashes flutter down for a moment, alighting on his cheek, and he looks like a person savouring something rare and rich. Mackie King wants something he shouldn't. Mackie King has put words to it, spoken it aloud, for only Blue to hear.

As if in a dream, Mackie watches Blue wet his lips and then lean in. He's not sure if he meets him halfway or if Blue has to close the entire distance by himself, but, as gradual as polarizing magnets being drawn toward each other, their lips are inches apart.

Blue's breath smells of cinnamon gum and comes out staccato. Mackie barely breathes at all. Barely thinks beyond the glowing light of the dash limning Blue's jutting cheekbones and skating his over-long lashes. Beyond how he doesn't look human. Beyond how he's too beautiful.

When Blue bridges the last of the distance and places his mouth on Mackie's, it steals Mackie's breath and the last of his reason. His thoughts cloud, everything falls away, and there's just Blue, his seeking tongue, silken, and his hand, closing in Mackie's hair, holding him steady. He's reminded of the way Blue gripped him last night as they tangled together in his room.

The kiss is torrid and outlasts any Mackie has shared before now. Both seem reluctant to break apart and rejoin reality. Music plays quietly in the background, something twangy and soft. Johnny Cash, maybe, or The Turtles, Mackie isn't sure. The only thing he can listen to right now is Blue's breaths and the creak of leather as he tries to get closer, the scrape of his rings on the gearshift, and then the crush of fabric in his hand as he takes Mackie by the lapel and draws him in, until the only room between them is what the awkwardness of the car demands.

Because he's so extraordinary, Blue makes people feel extraordinary just by association. Mackie has seen it time and again, boys in high school, college, and the spaces between, summer vacations spent at the cottage, where Blue would attract a gang of boys that wanted to be special. And he'd look at them, or hold their hand, kiss them in the shadows, and they'd leave smiling and dopy. Mackie feels like that now. Someone else, someone new. Someone he didn't know he could be. It's funny how something as small as a kiss might change you.

Blue expels a muffled moan and gently sinks his teeth into Mackie's lip. A dark thrill skitters through Mackie and entices him to lift his hips into nothing, desperately wanting to feel more of Blue's body on his but afraid to ask with words. The world seems to stop when Blue obliges and moves his hand from Mackie's lapel down his chest, touching achingly slow, palm flat, fingers seeking. He lingers where Mackie's shirt meets his pants, teasing a small, exposed slice of skin.

Blue breaks away. "It's okay?"

"Yes," Mackie says without hesitation.

Blue squeezes Mackie's shirt, and the skin beneath, and kisses him again. His hands are hot, the trails they leave like burns. It hurts, and the only way to make it feel better is more touch. But Blue lingers on Mackie's stomach, and he won't go any further, fingers sliding back and forth, following the leather band of his belt, tantalizing. Even his kiss has gotten as slow as syrup. Mackie waits patiently for the coming question.

"You're sure?" Blue's breath is hot on Mackie's wet lips.

"Of course." Another fast response.

Blue pulls back enough to lock eyes with him. "Mackie..."

Mackie speaks before Blue can ruin it. "Yes. I'm sure." He tries to make himself sound convincing and confident. This might ruin their friendship forever, he *knows* it. Even that threat doesn't make him want to stop. He does want this. He wants it as much as he's ever wanted anything. *More.*

Blue still doesn't move. His expression is a puzzle that Mackie isn't smart enough to solve. That could be longing in his eyes. It could be sadness. It could be a mix of both. It could be nothing at all.

Mackie rests his hand on Blue's face. Gentle blonde stubble pushes against Mackie's skin. He waits until Blue is looking at him and it feels like there are no veils between them. "Yes. I'm sure. I want this."

Outside, the sun has set, and the night is coming alive. Fireflies and moths flutter at the seam of the forest, watching the moon climb the horizon and glitter off the lake. The pier is abandoned. Below, on the other side of the lake, the town is lit up like a Vegas strip, bright but remote.

This time, Mackie leads the kiss, open-mouthed, sighing breath. He pulls Blue's hand back to the exposed skin at his stomach, decisive. This is what he wants.

Blue skates the tips of his fingers along Mackie's waistline and entices Mackie to buck his hips again. His cock pushes valiantly against the material of his pants. It aches in not an entirely pleasant way. He kisses Blue harder and wills him to go further. It feels like he's won a prize when Blue obliges. He makes his palm flat, rubbing teasingly over Mackie's sensitive parts, and then down the inside of his leg to his knee. Twice more, then he grabs Mackie's cock and squeezes until he hears Mackie moan.

As though in someone else's body, Mackie watches Blue undo his belt and slide his fingers in beneath Mackie's underwear. His touch is rhythmic and precise. He studies Mackie hungrily for his reaction and smiles when he gets the response he wants: overwhelmed pleasure.

Mackie isn't nearly as collected as Blue as he fumbles Blue's T-shirt out from the waistband of his pants and grips his side. He knows the tattoo under his hand off by heart, it's a blue jay crushing a butterfly beneath its foot and sizing it up to eat. The one beside it is a sun and a moon, and beside that is a coyote head, sly and mischievous.

Blue's skin is warm and soft under the press of Mackie's fingers. He feels Blue's hip bones as they dip into his pants, and the line of his underwear tight against his skin. He undoes Blue's pants and reaches in. His thoughts turn way down, get slow and sticky as he finds Blue's erection, new clinging to the old. This is his Blue. This is not his Blue. Just like he is Blue's Mackie, and he is not.

Blue breaks away before Mackie can pull him out completely. The tip of his cock strains against the band of his underwear. Mackie stares. Then Blue leans across the gearshift, and he closes his eyes as Blue's mouth seals around him. Needing something to hold onto and wanting desperately for it to be Blue, Mackie clutches his hair with both hands.

He doesn't last long, caught in the soft give of Blue's mouth. Blue feels him straining and takes Mackie deeper, allowing him to spill on his tongue and down the back of his throat. He holds there and prolongs the moment afterward, working to swallow. Lipstick is smeared across his mouth when he pulls back. He cleans it with his fingertips.

Mackie is at once nervous again. He's never done this before, and it's his turn.

Blue holds back Mackie's fumbling hands. "Just watch."

There's something in his voice that makes Mackie obey.

Blue pulls the band of his underwear down and his cock pops out. He's so excited, the tip is purple and wet. Blue slides his finger through the slickness, then takes hold of his shaft and pumps slowly. His shoulders press back against the GTO's seat and his hips arch.

Mackie stares at his profile, Blue hooking his thumb in his underwear and pulling the band down while he works. He thinks he's too afraid to participate, but as Blue draws nearer to climax, he makes a noise that obliterates Mackie's fears. He leans over the gearshift, and Blue turns his face to make their lips meet. That seems to do the trick. Blue gasps as he spills across his exposed belly.

Mackie peeks at the mess from the corner of his eye and feels powerful.

They do not speak. Mackie hands Blue a roll of shop towels, and Blue cleans himself up. The crooked smile never leaves his mouth. He's not shy or awkward, and his ease puts Mackie at ease, too.

The artist changes on the radio. Mackie thinks at first it's the music making the screeching noise. Then he feels a thud against his feet and realizes something is sliding across the GTO's undercarriage. Everything grinds to a halt, except Mackie's heart, which jackhammers in his chest so badly that it's even more difficult to draw breath than before.

He looks away from Blue to the outside world. It's changed. Vines creep from the forest across the ground and scrape the underside of the car. Something sleek and powerful prowls the forest edge, its eyes peering out, two globes of red. Moths and fireflies flit at the border as though banished from the forest to make way for something sinister.

The forest has gone from peaceful to violent in the span of a breath, and he didn't notice.

Blue seems to be blind to the change. He's still wearing that dreamy lustful expression.

"Something's happening."

Blue blinks. The fever bleeds out of him, and he takes in their surroundings. Seething, the forest presses against its boundaries, ravenous with rage.

The colour drains from Blue's face. "Drive."

Mackie fumbles with the ignition. The car revs to life with a satisfying roar, but when he throws the gear shifter into reverse, the tires spin and they go nowhere. Metal creaks. Then the weight of the car shifts, and they're being dragged inward, toward the trees by thick woody vines.

"Mackie!" Blue says, but it's not a command, and it's not a suggestion, and his name falls flat without any instruction behind it.

Mackie revs the engine and feels his tires grab the ground for an instant. They tear some of the vines and jerk back only to come to a complete stop again. The engine redlines, and the smell of burning rubber invades the cab.

Trees scrape the car's paint. Mackie lets off the gas before jamming down on it again, hoping that the sudden stop and start will tear them free. More vines solidify their hold on the undercarriage, and they go nowhere.

Blue fumbles for the door handle and stumbles out of the smoking car. Horrified, Mackie crawls out as well, and into the world stinging with magic and fear.

The forest seems huge. It's grown in the time they've been sitting in the car. Its trees jab toward the sky, and its vines are a tangled, writhing mass. A creature scowls out from the protection of the branches, starved to get to them, leaping back and forth from branch to branch, unable to cross from the safety of the trees into the open. Its yowl is familiar. This is the same beast that chased Mackie from the trees yesterday. The mermaid's words come back to him:

The queen's assassin.

It only has eyes for Mackie.

Blue's magic billows around him and turns the air almost unbreathable. It ruffles Mackie's hair and pricks his skin. The vines recoil from it, turning back from Blue and the GTO and Mackie.

"Leave us alone!" Blue commands.

The creature doesn't hear him nor even seems to see him. The presence of Blue's magic only makes it more rabid. It snarls and creeps as close to the forest edge as it can. Moonlight touches it. It's feline, large, predatory, with luminous red eyes and a mouth crowded with sharp teeth. It's not right, though. It has no skin, no fur, on its face. It's only raw sinew and creaking muscles holding its jaw in place. It looks as though someone has skinned a great cat, then left its bones to be picked clean and whiten in the sun, but it isn't quite dead.

Distracted by its grotesque image, Mackie doesn't notice the vines redoubling their efforts until they curl around his leg and yank him to the ground. For the second time in twelve hours, he hits his head, this time on the side of the GTO and sees stars. Gravel and sand bite into his shoulder blades and arms. For one terrifying second, he loses feeling in his foot as the vines tighten beyond what's safe.

Blue yells incomprehensibly, and the world gets white-hot and bright. Mackie protects his eyes from the sudden glow and his ears from the unbearable scream of the devil.

It's over in an instant, and silence follows. Mackie peeks out from behind his arm and squints.

Any forest that bordered the point has turned to ash. Most of the trees are gone. What remains cradles the body of the devil and protects it from the worst of the blaze. It's no longer cat-like. Now it is a woman, and she's tall and beautiful, head smooth of hair, eyes moss green. Despite her nudity, her body is not a lewd thing. It's more of a dangerous thing. A weapon. Spare. Sharp.

"Seedling, you have no life beyond the forest." Like the mermaid, this devil speaks startlingly clear. Her focus is still on Mackie. "There is no sense fighting. Come."

You should be dead, is all Mackie can think. The forest surrounding it is in tatters, and by rights, it should be, too. But it stands amongst the ruined trunks and peers down at him like a god.

"She will make it painless, but you must return to her," promises the devil.

Mackie is paralyzed when the thing takes a step out from the trees. Whatever was keeping it beneath the canopy is gone, and now it can venture into the open world. It reaches for him, fingers splayed.

Movement behind the devil draws Mackie's fleeting attention. Blue has positioned himself over its shoulder. Like a cellist striking their bow across their strings, Blue makes an erratic slashing motion with his hand. It happens quickly, and even after it's over and Mackie is bathed in stinking red blood, it takes him long seconds to understand.

Blue grips the devil by the head, and in his free hand is Mackie's pocketknife. The steel has a sinister glow bathed in blood.

The devil opens its sharp-toothed mouth in a silent scream. Its eyes bulge, and the gap in its throat gurgles. When it collapses, it falls on top of Mackie with its full weight. Its body might be made of cinders, it's so hot. Mackie gasps and writhes and manages to get out from beneath it.

Blue is still standing over him and breathing heavily, staring at the devil, waiting for it to move again.

It won't, aside from some muted death throes, where its limbs twitch and its throat gurgles. Its eyes alight for the first time on Blue and go wide before they get dull.

Blue shakes badly; he drops the knife.

Mackie clambers to his feet. He feels ill. The scent of iron is everywhere. His clothing is rapidly cooling, and he shivers in the early spring air.

"I didn't..." Blue trails off and doesn't start again.

Mackie swallows a lump in his throat and subsequently the bile that tries to overtake him. He can't. He rips off his shirt and drops it where he stands.

North, the swath of dead forest goes on for almost a hundred metres before it becomes lively again. Whatever Blue did to it, it looks very similar to the death that chased them out of the scrying pool.

The thought chills Mackie to his core.

Blue gathers enough breath to ask, "Are you okay?"

Mackie isn't sure how to answer that.

Headlights burst through the trees on the other side of the park. Squinting across the distance, Mackie makes out the bulbous shape of a police SUV. Of course they're patrolling. People are going missing. Why wouldn't they check out the parks?

He looks down at the mess at his feet wondering what they'll do when the police eventually crest the hill. How will they explain...

Almost as if spurred by his thoughts, the corpse of the devil is surrounded by burned vines, and though the plants should be dead, he watches them coil around the devil's prone body and slowly, inch by slow inch, they drag her back toward the forest.

An inexplicable knowledge falls over Mackie—there is evidence left on that corpse. Evidence of him and Blue. Once the forest has it, it will be closer to having Blue back.

Mackie lunges for the corpse. Its skin is slick and has the consistency of a rotting orange, and when he grabs it too tight, his hands simply slip off again. The forest withdrawals faster, a lolling tongue retreating to the safety of its mouth. Mackie stumbles to give chase. Blue catches him by the bicep and holds him tight enough to leave finger marks.

"Don't," he warns.

This is trouble, Mackie thinks. *If we don't...*

He's not sure what will happen, but he's sure he won't enjoy it.

"Let's go before the police see us." Blue gently but firmly directs Mackie to the car.

The police have pushed their patrol out to the far side of the park, giving Blue and Mackie a small window of opportunity. If they go fast and silently, they can get out without ever being seen.

Mackie feels drunk stumbling to the car. It's loud as a tiger when he starts it. He shuts off the lights immediately; there's no silencing the engine, though, even when he puts it in neutral and lets it roll back down the road. In the passenger's seat, Blue's eyes are closed, and the same pricking sensation that overcame them in the kitchen the other morning rapidly fills the cab. Mackie isn't sure what magic Blue is casting, but he is afraid of interrupting, even when it raises the pressure in the cab and makes the windows rattle and the radio stops working.

The night and forest press in from every side. The overhanging trees don't feel safe, and Mackie doesn't trust the road not to swerve and roll them into its grasp. He watches the shadows for devils. He watches the parking lot for the police. He watches Blue for the same intemperance that led him to slice the devil's throat open.

Blue is not violent by nature. But he's learning to be.

Thankfully, the house is dark and desolate when Mackie eases the GTO into the open garage.

Blue follows Mackie wordlessly inside, upstairs, and then into the bathroom. Mackie doesn't even consider if he should feel awkward stripping down in front of Blue and stepping into the shower.

Blue sits on the closed toilet lid, silent, staring at his bloodstained hands. Mackie can see him through the gap in the curtain, though he can't tell what Blue's thinking.

Minutes go by with only the sound of Mackie's furious scrubbing. He still feels sticky. Maybe it's because Blue is still bloody.

"Wash your hands," Mackie commands him. He can't stand looking at the red.

Blue lurches to his feet and turns on the sink. The shower runs cold. Mackie is done anyway and cranks off the water. He wraps a towel around his waist before stepping out into the stinging air.

Blue keeps his hands under the water, though steam curls up from the sink and his hands are red only by the heat now. Mackie waits for him to stop.

Blue is blank and unmoving, letting the water slosh over his skin and burn him.

Mackie counts the seconds then touches Blue's back.

Sluggishly, Blue raises his eyes to Mackie's in the mirror. His gaze seems far away, and he looks like he might do something dramatic. Ruin all the forest surrounding Lakeview, perhaps, or hunt down the queen that sent the devil in the first place, Sorrow.

Mackie pulls him back from the sink and turns off the water. "We're fine." He needs this to be true.

Blue leans on the marble counter and sighs. In that one motion, all the stress that's been building in him evaporates. He no longer looks murderous. Instead, he seems wrung out and exhausted. Deep bruises mark the skin beneath his eyes.

"I want to go to bed," Blue says quietly.

"Do you want to stay with me?" Mackie's never had to ask before, and the question trips clumsily out of his mouth. Despite everything, he's so aware of what happened in the car moments before the attack, and he's as afraid of that place as he is intrigued by it.

Blue tucks his bottom lip behind his teeth in consideration. "For a while," he agrees.

Mackie's heart does a flip he's unfamiliar with. He takes his soiled clothes to his room and throws them on his chair. Blue closes the door behind them. He watches Mackie dress in a pair of sweatpants and a loose-fitting T-shirt, expression still inscrutable except for the brief moments he studies the bands of bruising on Mackie's legs, left behind by the vines, then he seems murderous again.

It fades as he joins Mackie in his bed. They're face-to-face, knees pressed together. Mackie tries not to stare at him. His hair is no longer sandy blonde. As the moonlight touches it, it's marred by streaks of white-blue, the same shade it'd been the night he'd stolen Blue from the forest.

He's returning to it. It's an errant thought, unfounded. Blue is here beside him. Not trapezing through the trees. It feels like he will, though, and once he's gone, he won't come back.

Nervousness tingles into his fingertips as he locks a white strand between his thumb and forefinger. Blue's eyes flutter open and land on Mackie's. They seem blacker and more fathomless, and for an instant, Mackie feels like he's staring into the forest herself.

Blue takes Mackie by the forearm and holds him there with his palm pressed against his cheek. His lips whisper against Mackie's wrist. "Close your eyes." *Don't look at me like this.*

Mackie obeys. Blue shifts closer and wraps his arm around Mackie's middle. It takes only moments after that for sleep to come.

Near two, Blue rises to return to his bed, leaving the outline of his body on the mattress. Mackie rolls into it, falls asleep again, dry, and warm and almost happy.

The next time he opens his eyes, it's under a cloudy sky, and he's soaked and cold and confused.

A beautiful grotesque leans over him. It takes him a minute to recognize the mermaid devil. Her white hair has been pinned back from her gaunt face and she is smiling, not snarling. She looks positively beatific. "I told you I'd get you, little Caregiver."

Chapter 13

The forest is verdant green, crawling, and alive as Mackie's never seen it. The stream that cuts through it is the same blue as the sky, unnatural and beautiful. The only blemish he can spot in the landscape is the devil easing back into the water's depths.

The banks are clay and wet, and Mackie finds himself involuntarily slipping closer to her. He digs his fingernails into the soft soil, struggling to keep himself steady. The devil closes her eyes and breathes deeply from her slit nostrils.

"You know, you always have the stink of forest on you, just a little, but after bathing in her blood..." she purrs. "I don't think I've had a human quite like you before. You'll be delicious."

Crowding him are watercress and tall false dragonhead. Its flowers open and close like mouths, tasting the air around Mackie. It spooks him right to his core. He's not supposed to be here. He's supposed to stay away from the forest, and the forest is supposed to stay away from him. Those are the rules. He's not sure why they're changing now, but there is no way he can live with this as his new norm. With the way the mermaid is looking at him, maybe he won't have to.

"Nothing to say, little Caregiver? No more fingers to throw like a rude ape?" the devil presses, drawing closer with each word. "No smart remarks before I eat you?"

"Nerida won't eat you," says a much softer voice.

Even before he sees her, Mackie knows at once this is the regent the mermaid spoke of. She sounds calm and used to being in charge. She sounds like nothing scares her because she herself is the scariest thing to grace the forest.

Except, when he finally finds her sitting at the base of a huge oak tree, very similar to the one in his front yard, he isn't intimidated by her visage. She seems young, thirteen at most, though she doesn't look like your average thirteen-year-old girl.

Her skin is bumpy like oak bark, and her hair is leaves. The ends flutter in the gentle breeze. Vines grow around her arms and legs, twisting, tightening. Instead of looking afraid as Mackie was last night, she seems pleased by their strangling hold. These won't dare drag her to the ground, not like they did to Mackie. Her eyes are the purple of a brand-new sprout, and her fingernails, too.

"You're the regent?" Too much hope is packed into those three words. But maybe if this is what he's up against, he'll get out of here alive.

The child nods her head. "You may call me Briar."

Nerida twists her face, obviously displeased with the regent's decision. "If I may—"

"You may not," Briar sparks back, and Nerida sinks her sinister likeness deeper into the water. Now only her eyes and the tips of her pointed ears are exposed.

Mackie manages to draw his eyes away from the mermaid. "What do you want from me?" Does that sound respectful enough? Nerida, who is, thus far, the most fearsome devil Mackie has met, obviously fears, and respects the regent. She's powerful despite her apparent age.

"For now, I want you to be quiet and listen," Briar instructs. She straightens her shoulders as though preparing for a speech of great import and wets her craggy lips. Around her, the forest shushes and leans in, reminding Mackie of children at storytime. "Once," Briar begins when she has everyone's attention, "this whole forest was ruled by Queen Sorrow."

Mackie says, "I've heard the tales."

Her gaze gets sharp and measured. "Never like this."

"Alright, continue," Mackie mutters, hands up in supplication.

She nods. "The forest has been here for time immemorial, and it's always had a ruler to keep her devils in line. Each king or queen has been better than the last, fair, and true and beautiful. My sister Sorrow was no exception.

"She ruled this land from the east to the west, north to the south, without challenge for centuries, and me by her side. I won't say there was peace because our very nature is violence. But it was predictable, at least. Everything was always the same. Even when we were threatened by change, it never came to pass, that was the magic of the forest.

"We heard rumours of humanity and their insatiable greed, of course, and tell that they were making their way across the continent to our sanctuary, but... how do the humans say? Talk is worthless?"

"Cheap," Mackie supplies. "Talk is cheap."

Briar smiles briefly. "That's right. Still, even though nothing had ever changed, Sorrow was a shrewd ruler. She did not relish the idea of mankind coming to her home and razing it to the ground. She had our borders watched from all sides, day, and night, barring it from anyone that might mean us harm.

"The years turned into decades, and still, no man came. Despite this, Sorrow was diligent, and would not let her people rest. Even when it seemed pointless, we remained alert.

"Don't think she was cruel," Briar adds almost as an afterthought. "Or even unfair. For many of those years, especially those closing in at the end, Sorrow held the front herself, using the trees as her eyes, spying in all directions for sly men and their sharp blades.

"The morning they finally came for us, the solstice had passed, and the sap was running free. They came on foot, with their toothed metal and their chewing machines, as was told. They did not immediately set to destruction, however. The leader of the tribe was a man of stature and experience. He'd dealt with forests like ours before, some say, though that is a myth told by saplings." She waves her hand dispassionately.

"What's wrong with saplings?" Mackie queries.

"Young and fickle, prone to gossip and embellishing," Nerida lifts her mouth above the water to add.

Briar's gaze tracks to her, and she gives a solemn nod. "Regardless of that truth, the human knelt at Sorrow's oaks and spoke to them for three days and three nights in a voice like syrup. *The modern world is coming,* he said to them. *And if we do not cut a path through this land, others with less respect and more terrible equipment will. They will not love you as I do. They will clear-cut and burn and you, for all your power, and pride, will die.*

"I watched my sister walk from the trees and kneel in front of the man. *Then I will destroy first you, and then them,* she told him, but they both knew at once, neither would destroy the other. He was infatuated with Sorrow's wildness and she with his grit.

"He put down his saws, and she willingly parted her forest for him. They could live in harmony, she claimed, with the concession that no human crossed the forest border without express permission, and no devil was to exit. And most obeyed. Those that did not, did not return.

"It was the greatest love story this land knew," Briar says as though she's telling a fairy tale, voice dreamy, except this one somehow ends in devils luring boys into the trees and countless lives being lost. "Humans and devils gave gifts to Sorrow and her human consort, and their love blessed the land. The forest grew stronger and spread, and the humans flourished in her protection for a very long time."

"Maybe once, but now it's dying," Mackie tells her. And if last night's altercation is any indication, the rot is only spreading. "What happened?"

After a pause, Briar shrugs. "Humans are fragile. Even blessed by the magic of the trees, Sorrow's lover grew old, his human life whittled away, and Sorrow became despondent. She tried everything she could to heal him. She used the lives of his kin to sustain him, and the magic in their blood. She would call them into the trees and slit their throats and feed their magicked blood to her love. It helped. But it was never enough. Eventually, she had to turn to her own life, and gave him pieces of herself, until she, too, fell into a deathly sleep." She drops her voice on the last. It's a secret only the three of them can know, the skeleton in her closet, the heart thumping below the floorboards.

Mackie thinks of his great grandfather wandering into the forest. His grandfather. His father looking longingly into the trees and readying himself to do the same.

His neck and back are crawling with goosebumps.

It's connected.

He knows it's connected.

He doesn't want it to be.

"People die all the time," he says harshly. "I don't see what that has to do with me and Blue."

Briar makes her voice quieter still. "Before Sorrow closed her eyes for the final time, she planted a seed of life in her garden. When it grew, she would consume its heart, and it would replenish her life, and her lover's life the way her lover's kin never could. I was tasked with overseeing its maturation. It was to be her saviour. *Our* saviour. The forest needs her queen."

"...Couldn't you just rule in her stead?" Mackie asks. Briar seems magical enough, doesn't she?

Before he's even finished speaking, Briar is screwing up her face as though he's said something completely asinine. "The forest will reject any ruler to take it by force, and the hopeful usurper will die a horrible death."

Trees shiver with Briar's displeasure. For an instant, she does not seem like a helpless child. She is Regent, nobility, though Mackie doesn't understand what that means for this strange place.

He holds his hands up in submission. "Okay."

Briar sighs and leans back against her tree. The branches droop around her protectively. They sit in silence for a moment while she gathers her thoughts. "Without a new ruler, the forest's magic faded, and Sorrow's devils grew hungry and bold. They led innocents into the trees and ate their flesh from their bones, desperate to sustain their lives in any way they could. We *needed* Sorrow to return. The seedling would fix everything."

Briar hangs her head in shame. "But I knew as soon as it sprouted, I could not feed it to Sorrow."

"Why?"

She draws lines in the dirt by her stained knees and doesn't meet Mackie's gaze. "Devil magic is unpredictable. When Sorrow cast that spell, she could have grown a flower or made a stream. She could have planted an oak, like this one behind me, or the one dying in your yard. Instead of anything logical, what parted the ground the next morning was a boy. An innocent little boy who clawed his way from the dirt, screaming in his shrill little voice."

Other people might scoff or roll their eyes, but Mackie has seen some incredible things come from the forest and doesn't think this is beyond its capabilities. He watches Briar, horrified by what she's going to say next but physically unable to clap his hands over his ears and pretend it's not the truth.

Briar drags in a staggered breath. "I kept him in the greenhouse for a decade, hoping that his body would change, and he'd become a tree or a monster, at least, something ugly or hateful, that one wouldn't mind eating, like a fishfly, or a toad. But he was simply a beautiful boy who loved to laugh and eat beetles."

Mackie forgets about the cold water and the snapping false dragonheads. He forgets about Nerida and her shark tail and teeth. He forgets he's afraid of the forest and what lies inside.

Somehow, Briar's voice gets even smaller as she admits, "I went to Sorrow's tomb, and I spoke at her for three days and three nights, pleading my case, begging her to let me find another way. She used the trees to answer. She would not budge. She planted her seed, and it did not matter what form it took; it was a thing built of magic. It had no soul or thought, and even if it *did*, it only had one purpose, and *we all must fulfill our purpose, Briar.*"

She's getting angry. Her leafy hair twists in the breeze and the vines surrounding her curl in anticipation. The child façade peels back, and Mackie catches a glimpse of the creature Nerida respects. She is a scorpion hiding in leaf litter, waiting for a traveller to step close, barefoot.

Briar's eyes are two bright stones, amethyst under fire. "I told her very well, you know best, Your Majesty. And then I committed treason." Her expression becomes tinted with gleeful malice. "I cast a spell on the boy, his magic was sealed, and because of that, no devil could see him for as long as my spell held. And then I lured another into the trees, a human—senseless, fickle creatures, you know? Quick to fall in love and infatuated with the forest—to steal him away."

Mackie is transported back to that night, the fireflies and the widening pathway into the meadow, Blue sitting by the stream, happily eating water beetles. "The ground started shaking."

"One of my councillors knew of my treason and went to the Queen. He sat by her side for three days and three nights to make her understand, but by the time his words reached her in her sleep, the spells were done. You and the child were running. I masked your movements and parted the trees, and once I was sure you were free, I went into hiding."

"But you're still in the forest," Mackie says.

Briar draws herself up. "The Wastes are a place the queen cannot see, thanks to my magic. People like Nerida keep my secret and do my bidding."

Nerida is still wallowing in the water, watching their exchange with feigned indifference. Mackie can tell she's listening to every word, though, she's looking a little too intently at a mudminnow slipping through the shallows like liquid bronze.

"Last week, a shock went through the forest," Briar continues. "A breath of life, and for a moment, we sensed the child. The queen stirred in her hallow and the forest flourished."

Blue's magic, Mackie thinks. That day with Joe Redding, it was a geyser exploding. Since then, he's used it again to find Kevin and Austin, and then on Bobby, and the movie theatre employee. And just last night, on the devil in the park, and the police. He's near out-of-control. Briar's spell is all but useless now, and the forest has reacted to his presence.

"Her life is waning. She's more desperate than ever for a solution," Briar finishes morosely. "The boy is being hunted. My spell is holding on by a thread; it's the only reason she cannot easily find him, but it won't last. It can't."

"Kevin Evans and Austin Leek?" Mackie asks.

"Blind attempts to find the boy; her efforts were redoubled when she sensed him in her grotto."

"His name is Blue, not *the boy*."

Briar closes her violet-coloured eyes. Nerida hisses in the water. Mackie's aware he's committed some taboo. "What is it?"

"There's power in a name, especially in a place like this," Briar explains. "Anyone could be listening."

Mackie looks around as though he will spot a trespasser. There's just forest and water and flowers. "You said it was safe." Then again, so did Blue.

"Safe is a relative term, even in the Wastes," Nerida lifts her mouth out of the water to say. "For instance, the water is safe for me, but if you were to slip into the deep, you'd drown." She smiles. "And if you were to drown, stinking of magic as you do, I could deliver you to our queen, and she might believe she's found her seedling, and the true one might be free, as our regent desires."

"Enough," warns Briar.

Nerida sinks back in.

Mackie curls his fingers in the clay. More than ever, he's aware of the danger he was in last night. The whole forest now thinks that *he* is the seedling. But what's worse is that he's not certain that's such a bad thing. If the forest is after him, it's not after Blue.

That's the exact kind of reckless behaviour Blue hates in him.

"I'm assuming you didn't pull me out here just to tell me your story. What do you want from me?" Mackie asks Briar, though he's still looking at

Nerida. She seems like the kind of creature that will wait until you least expect it, then she'll attack.

"Keep the boy safe and his magic quiet for three days and three nights," says Briar. "I will ease the queen from this life into the next." The forest shudders at her words but instead of recoiling the way Mackie does, Briar sits straight with her chin raised, unafraid. "It is the duty of the regent. If she passes peacefully, the crown will come to me, as her regent, and everything will sort itself out."

"What if you can't do it?" Mackie asks. "Then what?"

"Then you must take him away from here."

The forest scares me; I can't live without it, though. "He won't go." Blue could have been convinced seven days ago, before the incident with Joe, before they ever returned to Lakeview. Not now. When Blue used his magic, he felt something, too, and he can no more be away from the forest than its trees and waters can.

Briar seems to know all this without Mackie explaining. She can read it in his face. "Then pray the queen will go peacefully."

"How will I know if you're successful?"

"When a forest queen dies, the land knows," she says cryptically. Then she stands. Even on her feet, there's not much to her. She's wisp thin and short. Mackie is tall, but even so, she only comes up to his elbow when he finally pulls himself out of the sucking mud and onto his wobbling legs.

"Be safe, Caregiver," Briar says before turning to the forest and fading in amongst the trees.

"How am I supposed to get back?" he calls after her. It's too late, she's gone. There are only the trees and flowers and...

"Alone at last. Lucky us," bubbles Nerida.

Mackie's heart leaps in his chest. He looks down upon her. He's on land and she's in the water, but he doesn't dare consider he has the advantage, not here, far from his oak. *Predators can sense fear.* He draws himself up. "You won't hurt me."

She curls her lip, and he knows it's true. That's good. Usually, gambling blows up in his face.

"This way, little maggot." She splashes noisily through the water, soaking Mackie again.

Reluctant to get in and join her on even ground, Mackie hurries along the bank to keep up with her sleek form. It's hard going, branches dangle low to scratch his face and roots rise high to trip him. He pitches near the water so many times, it's embarrassing. It might be easier to swim, but Mackie doesn't trust Nerida nearly enough to get into the water with her. Drowning accidents are frequent things even *without* the presence of devils. His chances of death seem astronomically high, knowing that she wants to take him to Sorrow in Blue's place.

"Slow down."

Nerida barely glances back. "So we can be seen together? No. The regent will skin me and steam my flesh if word gets back to Her Majesty. Keep up."

Mackie scrabbles over a huge fallen tree and kicks an oak bracket into the water. He has a clear, albeit muddy, path for a few short meters. He stretches his legs out and catches up with Nerida. "If you're afraid of the queen, why do you help the regent?"

Nerida spins in the water. She frowns at the fungus floating downstream. "Perhaps I do not share the same love for humans my queen does."

"I think the feeling is mutual," Mackie grumbles.

Nerida's eyes flash. "Is that so? You don't love your little devil?"

Any response he can muster crashes inside Mackie's throat and won't come out of his mouth. He must take a second to detangle his words and is surprised by his answer. "That's different. *He's* different."

"Is that what you think? Let me tell you something about devils, Caregiver. They belong to the forest, and the forest belongs to them. They are not bred to love humans. When they do, they suffer, they die, and they sentence those around them to suffer, too. Just because you think you know him doesn't mean you understand what he is."

For an instant, Mackie sees her crystal clear. "It hurt you when your queen began to die." He's bolstered by the way Nerida recoils. "Did you love her?"

Nerida's expression hardens. "Everyone loves the queen."

"Not the way you did." He feels mean and relishes it after her terrorizing. "That must have been hard, seeing her and her consort, knowing she was willing to give her life to save him."

Nerida's reaction is bloated. She acts like he's stabbed her with a brand. Thin white spines along the edge of her jaw protrude menacingly as the waters around her start to froth. Diving beetles climb from the churning depths and circle in front of Mackie's feet, making marks in the sand with their sharp feet while their bodies scrape together like grinding glass.

I am the water. He's erred. Mackie takes a step back. "I'm sorry. I didn't—"

His apology seems to trigger her more. Nerida's eyes slit, and the beetles and water get deathly still. "Follow the river to the edge of the forest and try not to die."

"What?" Mackie sputters.

Nerida can't hear his protests, or she doesn't care. She slips into the water as quietly as an eel. Mackie catches a flash of her poison-coloured tail, and then she's gone, and he's alone.

Eerie bird song glides between the trees. It sounds almost like talking, back and forth.

A frog leaps off the muddy bank into the water, and somewhere behind him, to his left, a twig cracks. Goosebumps run down his spine. He's sure he's being watched.

Nerida could be leading him falsely, but with no other way to go, Mackie steps over the still mass of beetles and follows the river as she suggested, making his movements measured and slow. He doesn't want to run in case there's a predator behind him, and if Nerida's still watching, he doesn't want her to know he's afraid. That would bring her great pleasure.

With as much dignity as he can muster, Mackie tracks back out of the woods. His bare feet are numb with cold, and the bottoms of his pajama pants are heavy with mud. He has stinging scrapes down his arms and across his chest. With every second that passes, more and more mosquitoes find him and try to take their dues. He slaps himself raw. He can't *stand* mosquitoes and their buzzing.

The land gradually tacks upwards. The first strands of daylight reach through the leaves and dapple Mackie's skin. He realizes then how cold he is. How long has he been in the forest? He's soaked through and exhausted, and more than a little cranky.

The river makes a sharp right, skirting the treeline. Mackie starts to follow it, too, but a gap appears in the forest, revealing the land beyond, stopping him in his tracks. Mackie groans aloud. "Fucking Nerida," he curses freely. This is where he's supposed to exit, he's sure of it. On the other side is a very busy Rebel Park, and he looks like he spent the night in the ditch.

Mackie considers the river. Can he follow it and come out of the forest somewhere else?

With that thought, the trees seem to darken and bend eagerly. It's been days since they've had a good meal and, like Nerida, would love a human that has the stink of magic on him.

"Not ever," Mackie whispers when he means *not yet*.

Mackie fixes his eyes on the road. It's at least three hundred meters away.

He steps out of the overhang with purpose and doesn't look anywhere else except for the gravel road. A hush falls over the park as, one by one, people notice his presence and stare. He can't hear their whispering, though he's sure by the second hundred meters, they're doing it in droves. A man has walked from the woods. He's beaten up and bleeding in places, but he's alive. How unusual. How *peculiar.*

How sinister.

He's crazy. He's a creep.

What they don't say is, *he's a devil*. Because to the people of Lakeview, devils mostly don't exist.

Mackie leaps over the narrow ditch and onto the road. Gravel bites into the soles of his feet. He considers running through the pain. He'll be home faster, at least.

A vehicle speeds up behind him and skids to a stop so close, the side mirror almost clips his arm. The window rolls down. He's determined to keep walking, but Mackie hears Sam's voice saying, "Get in."

Relief washes over him. Mackie opens the passenger's door and climbs into the four-by-four. Sam curls his nose and leans away. "Fuck, Mackie. What the hell?"

"I stink like magic, yeah, yeah. Tell me something I don't know." Mackie rolls his window up against the stare of the park.

"*Why*?"

"First because Blue and I killed a devil, and then you know, I got kidnapped by one." He involuntarily follows the statement with a manic little laugh.

"What?" Sam gawps.

"Can you drive, please?" He doesn't want to be near Rebel Park any longer than he needs to be.

Sam eases his foot onto the gas, and they roll forward. Mackie presses his cheek against the cool glass and shivers, even after Sam turns up the heat. His teeth chatter together loudly. Sam mutters again and fishes a plaid jacket out of the backseat. He throws it over Mackie's bare arms and Mackie works to grab it.

"Thanks."

Sam drums his hands on the steering wheel to music only he can hear. He does this when he's trying to work up the nerve to ask a question he doesn't want to ask. Like when he struggled to broach the subject of Mackie seeing Bree again after their last blowout. Or when he wondered what was going on with Mackie's dad last Christmas, when he and Blue had to stay with Sam.

"Just say it," Mackie drones.

Sam glances at him quickly, then back to the road. His hat is slightly askew, and his beard is fluffy. "Is this like the time you wandered into Michael Smith's place, screaming that the moon was going to eat you, and I had to pick you up?"

Mackie furrows his brow. "I was high then."

"Yeah," Sam says a beat later. "I know."

"I'm not fucking high."

Sam looks at him for longer this time. "You really killed a devil?"

Outside of the forest, it all feels like a distant dream. But his skin stings from mosquitoes and weeps from the branches. This isn't a dream or even a nightmare. This is real. "Blue and I were attacked last night at the pier. We didn't have a choice. It was going to kill us. So Blue..." He mimes slitting the devil's throat and relives the way the thing's eyes got wide and hears again the weak gurgle it made. It makes him feel sick. "I got the thing's blood all over me. And then I woke up this morning and I was in the forest. For real."

Sam's foot fetters on the gas and they start to slow. He's goggling at Mackie and not at the road. Mackie's only a little concerned. Sam's truck is tall enough, it can drive out of any Lakeview ditch and they're far away from pedestrians and houses now. "What happened?" Sam finally articulates.

Mackie tells him everything he can, half sure (hoping) that when he's through, Sam will tell him he has just the thing to fix everything. Or at least something that will keep them all safe for three days and three nights, but Sam is only staring at him disbelievingly again.

A long, loud horn jars him from his shock. They've drifted into the oncoming lane, and a huge truck has its wheels on the soft shoulder. Sam jerks his truck back in line and speeds up to the limit. The first thing he says is, "Nan would love to hear this story." He puts on his signal to pull into his driveway.

Mackie grabs the wheel and keeps it straight. "Forget it. I'm not doing storytime for your Nan just because it's interesting. If you don't have anything to help keep Blue out of trouble, then keep driving. I need to get home and talk to him."

"By the sounds of it, I should be more worried about you."

"No," Mackie says shortly.

Sam sucks his teeth in consideration. "The oak should ward off anything from the forest as long as you stay within its reach..." he trails off.

"I can't stay home forever."

"No." His expression turns thoughtful.

"What?"

"Try this." He reaches into his shirt and takes out a piece of clear quartz on a thong.

There are mom and pop shops around that will tell you crystals are the way to heal your soul and channel energy. Sam's never tried to sell Mackie on this before and usually snorts when he sees those booths at the fair.

"You don't believe in crystals."

"I don't believe in crystals Sara Hughes bought off some mining company making a killing on basics trying to find purpose in their lives," Sam cuts. "I believe in the crystals the forest gave Nan, and that's that."

Mackie takes the crystal. It's warm on his skin and winks in the sunlight. It looks just like a rock to him, but if Sam says it works, then he's inclined to believe him.

Sam pulls into Mackie's driveway and rolls all the way up to the front door. He eyes the frontage with its obvious patch of new paint with discontent. "I'll help you paint the whole house if you want."

Friends like Sam are hard to come by. He's loyal and always willing to offer a hand. "When it gets a bit warmer."

"Try to stay inside," Sam warns before Mackie can throw open the truck door. "Three days and three nights."

"Do you think the queen will die?"

"I think she has a better chance of it if you and Blue aren't there making a meal of yourselves."

"I guarantee that's not our intention."

"It wasn't Kevin or Austin's, either."

Mackie lets the door slam behind him. Sam waits until he's inside, then peels away.

The house is choked with cigarette smoke, and there is an incessant, maddening *drip, plop* that reminds Mackie of Nerida. Fear strums in him, resonating like a plucked guitar string.

Dad sits at the kitchen table, smoking. A pile of spent butts crowd the ashtray in front of him. He looks out the window as water drips from the ceiling onto the floor. It puddles around his feet and slowly runs toward the living room carpet.

"Why are you just sitting there when the ceiling is leaking? Why don't you have a bucket or something?" Mackie asks. He starts upstairs to look at the damage. "Is that the bathtub?" The bathroom is directly overhead. *Is that how Nerida got in?*

Dad says, "Pipe burst. Blue's gone into town to get supplies to fix it."

Mackie swings back around on his heel. "Why'd you let him go into town?"

"He's a grown man, he can go where he wants." He seems very coherent. For an instant, Mackie forgets his thoughts are tangled more often than they aren't.

"No—you—ah, never mind," Mackie grumbles. He takes the stairs three at a time and scrapes his sopping pajamas off in his room. Once he's in an old pair of jeans and a baggy sweater, he races down the stairs again.

"Sorrow's eye is on you, boy," Dad says, still in the kitchen, stalling Mackie at the garage door. "She sees you more clearly than she sees most. Protect him; she'll just eat you, too."

Mackie feels like he's been hit upside the head. Sorrow is for cultists like Sam. For people like Blue, who Mackie stole from the forest. For Mackie himself, because he's the only one in Lakeview that he knows for sure has seen the devils, aside from Sam and Blue.

Briar's story comes rushing back to him. It still feels real when he holds it in his mind.

She used the lives of his kin to sustain him and the magic in their blood.

The world turns, drops, and he blinks to focus. "How do you know, Dad?" It feels like someone else has grabbed his mouth and made him speak.

Dad turns in his seat to look at Mackie. "The Kings always know. It's in our blood."

"What does *that* mean?"

It takes Dad a long, long time to answer, and his voice is airy when he does. "The forest is an infection seeping out, putrefying everything it can reach while its queen tries to disrupt what's natural. She thinks we're made to die."

Mackie gazes over his father's shoulder to the backyard that belonged to his grandfather first before it was given to his father. In its center, the oak has split in half and is rotten through the middle. The weight of the forest is a hand pressing down on his chest, making it difficult to breathe. He's always felt its charm. Never this way, though.

"Maybe things will be different now."

Dad locks his eyes on Mackie. He's suddenly intense. "You listen to me," Dad wheezes. "Don't interfere. What's done is done."

A stone sinks in Mackie's stomach. "What's done, Dad?"

"This is our way to be free."

"What's *done*?"

Dad blinks at him.

"Answer me!" Mackie's filled with the need to know. It consumes him, and he doesn't think anything will satisfy him again if he doesn't get this answer. He resists the urge to grab his father by the shoulders and shake him. The man is frail. He might fall apart in Mackie's hands.

Dad blinks again, and a fog crosses his pallid face. His eyebrows furrow. Mackie braces himself for asinine, confused questions like *what are you doing in my house?* And *who are you?* But Dad returns to looking out the window, mouth flat and lifeless and his gaze a million miles away.

Chapter 14

The GTO roars to life. Mackie hardly waits for the garage door to roll all the way up before he speeds out and onto the road. Dark grey clouds fill the sky, casting the day in a sinister glow, dark purple, sickly green, like a bruise.

Blazing over the gravel at dangerous speeds, Mackie pulls out his phone and calls Blue. He doesn't pick up. Hundreds of terrible scenarios play through Mackie's head, each worse than the last.

He's about to press redial when his phone lights up with Blue's picture, taken last year at the beach, a huge beach ball clutched to his chest, and his mouth pulled into a wide grin. His hair looks whiter than the clouds in the sky, and his eyes are almost the black of night. He's not like anyone else Mackie's ever known. The truth is so apparent, it's hard to believe anyone was ever fooled.

Mackie answers the call with an abrupt, "Where are you?"

"At the hardware store." Blue slaps some gum in his mouth. "The pipes burst in the bathroom; can you believe it? It wasn't even cold last night." Before Mackie can answer, he says, "Hey, where were you this morning? I tried calling you a hundred times." He sounds totally normal. Just a little concerned. "Is everything alright?"

Mackie ignores the question. "Stay where you are. I'll be there in a minute."

A brief hesitation. "Sure. I have to go, though. I'm almost at the cash register. I'll see you in a few."

"No, Blue—" Mackie stammers. The line is dead. Blue is gone.

Shadows reach from the trees and cross the road. Though it's barely ten in the morning, it gets twilight-dark. The clouds overhead are thick, black, and ominous. The GTO's auto headlights come on. Trees sway ahead, skating errant leaves across the road and breaking a few thin branches in the sudden, violent wind. Something is happening in the forest. It wails like a mother giving birth. The sound is heard over the roaring motor and through the tempered windows.

Mackie jams his foot down on the gas pedal, pushing the needle dangerously high in determination. Whatever is coming, he doesn't want to be near it when it emerges.

He's too late.

Ahead, the forest shudders and spits out a grotesque. In Mackie's periphery, it looks like a big buck, but as it turns its bulbous body toward Mackie and rears back on two legs, he can see it is anything but.

Its middle bulges weirdly with its innards, forcing the fur on its belly to be sparse and patchy. Its mouth is full of jagged teeth. Rather than hooves at the ends of its legs, huge, furred hands with protruding nails, black with rot, grip the ground.

It bows its antlered head and charges the car. Mackie yells and jerks the wheel. Tires squeal, and the frontend noses dangerously close to the ditch. Mackie thinks he's going to lose it, months, *years,* worth of work gone, and then? Will the devil tear open the door with its deformed hands and rip him limb from limb? Feed him to Sorrow?

At the last minute, his tires catch traction on the pavement, and he swerves around the devil and makes it to the end of the road. The devil's piercing screams follow. Mackie looks in his rear view and sees it spinning on him and giving chase. It reminds him of a furious cow moose. It's rampant. It's rabid. It only has eyes for him, and it's catching up with frightening ease.

Will they run through the streets? He wonders. How far will the forest go to stop him? And, by running, is he leading it straight to Blue?

He slows down just enough that he won't roll his car at the stop sign, then guns it out onto the highway, narrowly avoiding getting squashed by a honking transport truck. The devil isn't as lucky; it hits the front grill, splatters, parts of its body flying in every direction. The truck wavers. The trailer swings into oncoming traffic before settling out again, and the driver pulls off to the side of the road.

The forest shudders, shocked. There's a car and a lot of ground between them now, but Mackie can feel it recoiling and rethinking its tactics. It's lived beside the modernized world for as long as it's existed, but it hasn't had much interaction with it. He uses the precious seconds he has to make up some distance and only has to slam hard on his brakes once when a cop car mounts the hill ahead. If he were to be pulled over for a ticket now, the forest would snatch him out of the cab of the GTO and make him a distant memory.

Mackie is still ten kilometres above the speed limit when he and the officer pass. The officer is checking their computer more intently than they're checking the road and doesn't notice Mackie's wide eyes, pale and sweaty face, and overhot engine.

As soon as they've passed each other, Mackie pushes the GTO again. Eight cylinders growl beneath the hood, and the rear wobbles, threatening to spin out on him. He holds the steering wheel tight and muscles the car back between the lines. Despite himself, he feels a thrill. He's outwitted the forest, for now, anyway. Above, the sky is still dark, and to his left and right, the forest still seethes like an infected wound, watching him, biding its time.

Milford's Hardware is a bit off the beaten path. It's rural-urban in that there are three other stores around it, and then a whole lot of nothing, flattened fields, and way, way down the road is a house that belongs to the Gericks, but the Gericks haven't lived there since Jean-Paul Gerick senior, the wife and child beater, up and died last year. None of his surviving family wants to live in the house and hold onto it while they wait for when the market turns in their favour.

Mom's cherry red sedan sits idly in the hardware's parking lot. Blue's white-blonde head is leaning into the trunk as he puts his purchases away.

Relief hits Mackie first: Blue is safe from the forest.

Relief quickly turns to fear, as ahead, a dually swerves off the road and into the parking lot and three men pile out of the truck, Jayden and Jace Slater, two-thirds of Lakeview's identical triplets (Mackie only knows them apart because Jace has a small, furry mustache and Jayden has a sleeve of tattoos, whereas John, the final triplet, has neither). Shawn is at the back of the group, looking unusually out of place.

They holler something aggressive at Blue; Mackie can't hear them, of course, but he can see it in their body language. Blue straightens and takes a step back. Mackie's whole body pricks with nervousness. He's still a few hundred meters away and arriving too slow. He jerks his GTO around a small blue four-door creeping through town below the speed limit, earning himself a honk and a middle finger from a lady well into her late-seventies, and squeals into the parking lot, pulling up alongside the bunch. Dirt and gravel kick into the air and obscure the scene for just a breath before the rising winds grab and scatter it. Jace, Jayden and Shawn are much too close to Blue, and they're closer by the second.

Screaming bleeds through the closed window, though the words are incomprehensible until Mackie throws open his door and steps into the pregnant air. Maliciousness fills every breath, and his skin crawls with adrenaline.

"You tell me what you did to him!" shrieks Jace. His whole neck is red, stark on his pale skin, and his hands are balled into tight white fists. His hair is on end, as though he's shoved his hands through it time and again.

"I told you, I didn't do *anything*," Blue responds. He's not his usual collected self either, words laced with tension. He takes an uncertain step back to keep some distance between him and the three advancing men but every time he does, he puts himself closer to the trunk and blocks an easy escape.

Jace's hands are in his hair again. He turns once, walks two steps as though trying to convince himself to leave this ill pursuit. Something in his mind tells him *no,* and he wheels back around and stalks aggressively at Blue. Jayden stops him by planting his hand in his brother's chest and pushing him back.

"Wait." Usually calm, even Jayden looks frazzled. He breathes to steady himself and makes eye contact with Blue. "Just—just tell me. Just tell me where he is, and I won't even be mad. No one even has to know. Only us. We just want him back."

Blue fumbles helplessly for something to say. He *wants* to tell them something useful but he's at a loss for words.

"What's going on?" Mackie speaks loudly to make his presence known. Jayden and Jace hardly glance at him, only Shawn's gaze lingers.

"John's missing." Shawn almost seems reasonable; his voice is flat and without accusation; dead. These are the facts. This is where they've led us. If he's glad of it, Mackie can't tell. He must be, though. He still bears the marks of their last run-in; his eye is black, his cheek is swollen, and his right hand in a cast. Shawn isn't the type that easily forgives or forgets.

Jace loses his barely kept cool and erupts, "And he won't tell me where the fuck he is!" He sidesteps his brother and pushes Blue into the back of the Civic with all his might. The metal buckles and there's a Blue-shaped dent in the trunk.

"Hey!" Mackie lurches toward them. Jace shoves him into the grill of his car, too. By the time Mackie is on his feet again, Jace is at Blue. He has him by the collar of his white dinosaur print shirt and is trying to bully him into the dually.

"You're going to show us whether you like it or not!"

"I don't kn—*oof*–" Jace hits Blue in the ribs and cuts off his words. He reels back to hit Blue again. Blue curls and ducks at the same time and narrowly avoids getting punched in the face.

"Get off me!" Blue pushes Jace back and manages to put a few inches of space between them.

Jayden's been watching from the sidelines and finally jars out of his shocked stupor. He's never been this person; fear makes us ugly. He blinks at Blue, shame colouring his expression. Blue doesn't seem to notice. He's angry. His shoulders are rigid, and his muscles are knotted together. He shoves Jace back again with more force and puts even more distance between them.

Jace snarls and lunges. Jayden stops him with a solid hand against his chest that knocks his air out in a surprised gust. "Wait. Just wait a second."

Amazingly, Jace listens.

Everyone gets still. Jayden gulps in haggard breaths as though he's run a marathon. He keeps his hand against Jace's chest and puts most of his attention on Blue.

"Blue, please," Jayden pleads. "I'm sorry. We just want our brother back. Just tell us what you did with him."

"Nothing," Blue says weakly. "I didn't do anything."

Jace's hands squeeze tight; his knuckles blanch. Jayden redoubles his hold. "Tell us *now*, or I can't be responsible for what happens after."

Blue's expression turns cold and remote. Mackie's never seen him this way before. This is someone new.

"Fine. If you want to know where your brother is, let me show you." Then, inexplicably, Blue rips open the door to Jayden's truck and gets in, sliding into the middle seat. The door bounces back and closes softly behind him.

Mackie is the first of them to move. He grabs the door handle and yanks it back, opening the cab on Blue. "Get out."

Blue acts like Mackie doesn't exist. His eyes are fixed on the forest.

"Now, Blue."

Jace shoulders Mackie out of the way. Mackie trips and goes down in the gravel. Stones cut into his palms. "Jace!" Mackie roars. Jace doesn't spare him a glance as he leaps into the passenger's side and closes the door in Mackie's face. Mackie scrabbles to his feet and tries the handle. Jace has slammed the lock down. He can't get in.

Jayden climbs into the driver's seat on the other side. Before Mackie can dare to race around the back of the truck (he's sure he'll be run down if he tries to go around the hood), the dually is growling and moving forward, tires squealing.

As it goes by, Shawn grabs the back rack with his good hand and hauls himself into the bed of the truck, grimacing as his arm is nearly pulled from the socket. The Slater brothers haven't ever thought much about Shawn Macintyre, not in grade school or high school, and not now, when their minds are on their missing brother.

The truck kicks up gravel and dust and fishtails out into the road, where it cuts off a black sedan and sends an SUV halfway into the ditch. It bounces out again with its horn blaring.

Mackie is even less cautious as he leaps into the GTO and gives chase, tearing into oncoming traffic at sixty above the posted limit to pass the same slow-moving vehicles Jayden has passed in his rush to follow Blue's instruction.

Where are they going? Mackie wonders. *Not to the scrying pool.* It's on the opposite side of town. There's nothing except road and forest in this direction, and Yarrow Lake, glittering like a wide, vacant blue eye between gaps in the trees.

Scattered houses blur by, and then it's just forest pushing in on all sides. Mackie drives one-handed while he tries calling Blue. The phone goes to voicemail again and again. He's close enough to Jayden's bumper that he can clearly see their three heads in the cab and Shawn in the truck bed, but any time Mackie tries to speed up to get in front of them and cut them off, the truck pulls away until they're careening down the curling road at unsafe speeds. When Mackie backs off, they maintain their speed and pull further away. He gnashes his teeth. What can he do?

Unexpectedly, the truck makes an erratic movement to try to get around something on the road. It doesn't quite make it. Whatever the thing was, it squashes under the passenger's front and rear tire. In the back, Shawn is thrown against the side of the box and is dangerously close to falling out. He casts his hands out to get his balance.

"Goddamn," Mackie curses when half a second later, it's his turn to dodge the mess on the road. It's the size of a small child, could have even *been* a child, were it not for the definite claws and coarse-looking fur tufted up all over its body.

It's a devil. It has to be.

The forest is leaching out. Ignoring whatever agreement Sorrow and her lover made long ago, the devils are stepping out from under their protective canopy and into the human world. Will everyone still willfully ignore the peculiarities, or will they finally accept that things in Lakeview Township aren't always gardens and playgrounds and historical societies? That sometimes, they're masses of rotten skin, scales, and claws?

Mackie swallows an alarming laugh before it can break free.

They reach a part of the road Mackie hasn't ventured down before. Asphalt narrows into one lane and turns to packed dirt. The trees are thick overhead, blocking out what little daylight has leaked through the clouds thus far. It gets dark, and in the dark, hundreds of red eyes glow from the treeline.

The truck is slowing; Jayden's foot flutters on the break as though he's not quite sure if he wants to keep going but is too afraid to stop. Even those that deliberately ignore the forest can't deny its pull when they're surrounded by it.

Mackie can almost taste their fear. Or is that his own? Thundering heartbeats are the only thing he can hear, and it's hard to draw breath in the thick of all this magic. The forest is wild here. Hardly recognizable. Whatever part of Lakeview was here before, it's been reclaimed by the wild, inch by slow inch, year after year, until all that remains is this broken road and what might, possibly, be the remnants of a failing driveway to the right, leading into what might be a rotted cottage set in a way.

They've slowed to a crawl. Mackie is on the truck's bumper. In the box, Shawn grips the racking with white-knuckled hands while he looks out into the wilderness.

Turn around, turn around, turn around, Mackie pleads silently. He calls Blue again. There is nothing but dead air, though. He has no signal, as though this place is completely separate from the rest of the world and things like cell phones don't belong here.

Green and brown swamp water laps at the road, and vines curl lovingly around tree trunks. Mackie watches maples bloom in real-time, lily pads, swamp marigolds nestled in the ditch burst with colour. It's beautiful but undeniably ominous. He grips the wheel and lays on his horn. He's right up on the dually's bumper, looking at a decal of a cowboy hat-wearing skeleton wielding two comically huge pistols, a *Honk if You're Handy* sticker, and a dust-covered trailer-hitch that looks like it's never been used before.

There's a sharp bend in the road. The truck slows further to make it around.

A tree ahead starts to rise and move, its roots are feet, branches are arms. It bends. Bark pops so loudly, Mackie can finally hear something other than his throbbing heart. Jayden's taillights blaze as he jams on his breaks.

"Why are you stopping?" Mackie yells ineffectively at the back of the truck. He lays on his horn again, long, and hard.

In the cab, Jace reaches across Blue to the steering wheel. The truck swerves around something else Mackie can't see. Both the front and the back tires sink into the wet ditch. Shawn grips the back rack.

He can't hold on and is catapulted out of the truck.

Horrified, Mackie watches as something scaled and wicked erupts from the water like a bass reaching for a fly and snatches him up in wide jaws.

They disappear; only the turbulent sediment marks that anything was amiss at all.

Shawn's never been a nice person. Once, in grade nine, Mackie saw him trying to pelt seagulls with stones. Later that year, Shawn made it his goal to sleep with shy Lina Poremski, who was pretty in a quiet way but never had much attention from boys. He spread rumours afterward and ruined her. By the beginning of grade ten, it was easier to be the thing that everyone said Lina was than to pretend she was who she used to be. He beat people up for being smart. He beat them up for being dumb. Ridicule and bullying are the only ways he knows how to interact with others.

People like Shawn deserve to suffer, Mackie tells himself when the horror feels too much, when he imagines a beastly forest creature tearing the eyelids from his eyes and sucking out the gelatinous bulbs, when he imagines a nasty beast using Shawn's stomach as a pouch and his bones as back scratchers.

They deserve it.

He knows he's only trying to convince himself.

The truck lurches once again in Mackie's periphery. He tears his gaze from the sediment where Shawn disappeared, watching in dismay as the tree creature reaches across the road and picks up the truck as though it's as small and light as a Hot Wheels toy. Metal squeals and grinds. The passenger's door flings open, and Jace leaps out with abandon. The truck is too high now. When he hits the road, his one leg buckles. Whatever he's holding in his hand flies away from him and lands a few feet away.

Jace doesn't seem to immediately feel pain. He stands. There's blood soaking his jeans. He chooses a direction opposite of the tree and starts to hobble but doesn't get far. Tree roots slide over the road, grab him by the ankle, yank him to the ground and then into the woods. He doesn't even have time to scream. His head leaves a smear of blood on the packed dirt.

The tree flips the truck on its side and the open door bangs closed. Then it turns toward the forest and tracks a path. It moves as easily as a child through wheatgrass, and before Mackie can blink, it has disappeared somehow, its top melding in with the rest of the forest.

"Fuck!"

He sits in his GTO for a moment, brain grinding over a plan, but there is no plan for going into the woods; you just don't do it, especially when she is this way, angry and vicious, unless you have a death wish.

"*Fuckfuckfuckfuckfuck.*"

He has to do something, though.

Mackie opens his door and then just stands there, one foot in his car, the other on the road, peering around at the still forest and the quiet swamp. Aside from the smear of blood on the road and the settling sediment in the ditch water, this doesn't look like a place of devastation. There are no lurking monsters any longer, at least none that he can see, and the immediate threat of the forest is curling back, settling down. She finally has what she's been looking for and is satisfied. There is only the clean, crisp air, fragrant with newly bloomed flowers, and the stink of the swamp.

Four men could disappear here today, and people might look for a week or so, but eventually, Lakeview will go back to its usual drowsy state. They won't make international news for strange disappearances, and none of its residents will whisper about it. The forest will linger, a crocodile just below the water's surface, waiting for the next time its belly feels empty.

A chill starts at the base of Mackie's neck and works down to his lower back. He moves his feet to banish the feeling but doesn't get far, his attention snagged by the thing Jace dropped as he fell.

A long, deadly-looking shotgun shines dully in the overcast light. Mackie's never been hunting, but nearly everyone in Lakeview knows how to shoot a shotgun. It's almost a right of passage into your teen years. He's shot pop cans and targets, and though he hasn't held a gun in years, when he picks it up, he still remembers exactly how to hold it and how to aim.

Mackie checks the ammo. It's a Remington magazine-fed pump-action, and aside from a few scuffs here and there on the butt, it looks nearly brand new. There are seven slug rounds in total, five in the magazine and two in the chamber.

It goes against everything he's been taught growing up, but he takes the safety off before stepping off the road and into the forest, making it ready to shoot when he needs it.

Mackie tucks it under his arm and sets off.

While not deviating from the path the tree took, Mackie chooses a route as well out of the water as he can possibly be. Remembering, too well, how Shawn got taken away. Despite everything, the enormous thing's track is subtle, as if the forest is trying to mask the devil's movements, but if he is patient and looks hard, Mackie can see lines in the mud from the tree's trailing roots and the occasional branch snapped off high above.

Silence permeates the forest. Even when he stops to listen, he can't hear the devil that stole the truck, any screams that might be coming from its inhabitants, or even a cricket for that matter. Just harrowing nothingness. It's like the whole forest has gone to sleep.

Or every devil inside its borders is distracted following Blue.

Without being told, Mackie knows it's the queen's minions and not Briar that has him. *The queen is hungry.* All she must do now is wake from her sleep and eat him, then she and her lover will be restored. The unreality of it all makes Mackie's head spin. He tries to focus on facts, but none of them are hard and fast anymore. His world is changing at a rapid speed, and he doesn't know if he can run fast enough to keep up.

Something pale shines ahead through the lattice of tree branches.

Mackie risks leaping over the trickling river he's sure is twice as deep as it looks, and three times as populated by monsters. He lands in squishy mud and must hold the shotgun out for balance. He draws it back into his shoulder as he approaches.

It's Jayden's bumper, folded like a piece of cooked spaghetti. The bumper stickers are all scuffed up and almost unrecognizable. Broken glass from the truck's rear window shines all around, giving Mackie the dizzying notion he could be looking at the starry sky.

Someone moans, breath staccato. Mackie tightens his hold on the shotgun and looks for them frantically until he finds the source of the noise: Jayden is cast over a fallen log. His fingers dig into the wood, grounding him. His shirt is torn and there is a lot of blood, but Mackie can't tell where it's coming from.

"Jayden?"

Jayden's bloodshot eyes roll wildly in his skull, grazing over Mackie.

"Jayden? Can you hear me?" Mackie inches closer, trying to make sense of what he's seeing. When he succeeds, he wishes he hadn't.

Jayden's left leg is torn off at the knee and his blood is spurting over the ground, wetting the leaves and the dirt in rhythm with his pounding heart. The forest floor sucks the mess up greedily. Bleeding hearts pop up all around him. They have no eyes or mouths yet, but it's only a matter of time before they develop.

Mackie's blood pressure spikes. Black spots appear in front of his eyes. He blinks them away. Draws in an iron-soaked breath. "Jayden?"

Jayden finally acknowledges his presence. His bloodshot eyes square up on Mackie. "Help me," he gasps.

"I-I-I-I'll—I'll try." Mackie stutters. He hasn't stuttered since he was thirteen.

Fuck.

Breathe.

Think.

He has his first aid training and renews it every three years. He's been over scenarios like this a hundred times in class.

Remember?

Yes. But also not really. It's different when a person, especially one you grew up alongside, is bleeding out in front of you.

Don't panic. Just work.

With a sharp movement, Mackie tears a long strip off the hem of his shirt and ties it around the ragged end of Jayden's leg as tight as it can possibly go. Visibly, the blood slows. He expects Jayden to scream or hiss or move, even. He doesn't. Mackie's afraid to look up to see if his eyes are closed and his chest is still.

He pulls out his phone and looks at the screen without much hope, remembering the dead air when he tried to call Blue just moments ago. Miraculously, there is one bar of service, just barely enough to call for help.

A woman picks up and makes a stuttering Mackie repeat himself five times before she agrees that help is on the way. Even still, Mackie's not confident they'll dare venture into the forest, even for one of Lakeview's golden boys.

He leaves his phone on beside Jayden's head in hopes that they can track the GPS to his location, then he resumes his hunt.

Chapter 15

It's hard to know how long he's been running. Mackie's leg muscles are burning, and his lungs feel tight. Sweat wets his forehead and his upper lip. The forest stings him for every step he takes that brings him closer to Blue. A scratch of a branch, a prick of a thorn, uneven footing twisting his ankles, on and on and on, hindering his movements but never managing to stop him completely. Not because it doesn't want to and not because Mackie has a magic of his own, though he feels this might be at least a little true, all things considered. The forest is distracted by its prize. It's been a long time since it has felt this kind of hope.

The sky gets dark. Night comes fast under the thick canopy, making Mackie's travels even more arduous. He must move with his arms up, batting away branches that try to gouge his eyes, and step more carefully than he would usually be bothered as he looks for rocks, roots, and fallen tree limbs that would be more than happy to drag him to the forest floor.

The river has snaked around again, and now it's in front of Mackie. To get to Blue, he must get to the other side. There is no easy way around. He's decided to risk leaping over it when it burbles, and a creature rises from its folds. Last second, Mackie bails. He throws himself to the side and lands in the soft mud. When he looks up again, he's staring into Nerida's yellow eyes. She seems more enraged than usual.

"You had one task, Caregiver. *One.* It has yet to be a day, but already, you've failed." She looks upon him as though he's as useless as a tick on a dog's back.

"I tried," Mackie pants. He's too panicked for shame or contrition. "They got him anyway. They took him into the forest—"

"Yes, the entire forest knows of your blunder," she seethes. "Now the regent is forced to act ahead of schedule. You may have doomed us all."

"Just help me get to Blue," Mackie pleads. "I can help."

Annoyance colours her usually pale features. She flicks her tail in the water and makes a scoffing noise. "Humans."

Mackie is preparing another line of argument to sway her to his side of things when a huge gush of water surges around him and drags his exhausted body from land and into the mire. There is no air in his lungs and Nerida doesn't give him time to breathe before he's pulled away with his head forced below the surface. It's quite possible she is trying to drown him so she can carry out her original plan and give him to the queen in Blue's stead. Instead of being outraged, Mackie wonders, will the ruse still work? Do I still stink of devil blood and magic? He will go willingly if it means Blue won't have to.

The revelation is cold and startling, and he resists poking at it for fear of discovering what it might mean.

Mackie fights, kicking and pushing at a lot of nothing. Nerida is nowhere near him. It's just currents pushing him along at breakneck speed, It's just currents pushing him along at breakneck speed and greedy tree roots skipping over his exposed skin.

He needs air. It's the all-consuming kind of need, that he cannot rail against no matter his best intentions.

It goes on for too long, and then longer still. Unending. *This is how I die.* No one will know where to look for his body. They will suspect, though, right up until the moment the forest spits out his bones, and no one will be surprised. Taking from Lakeview, it's just what the forest does, as though it's long been slighted, and it's just taking its dues.

He thinks of his mother alone, watching her husband die, and he thinks of his father, caught in the maze of his own mind, suffering until he walks into the forest and disappears like the rest of the King patriarchs, and he thinks of Blue, who is lost in the trees, soft Blue, who will throw himself at the devils' mercy if he thinks it will make everything better. How unfair life is. Her moments of fleeting joy weighed against a deluge of suffering. And for what? Death at the end of the tunnel? The thought makes Mackie mad enough to split heads.

Black spots dance in front of his eyes, and his lungs are just about to expand, gulping in water. A selfish thought pervades his panic: *Please don't hurt.*

As if the forest intends to spite him, Mackie's shoulder hits a solid boulder. The water turns turbulent, and then suddenly, the currents sweep him up into the open. He grasps with weak hands and closes them around the flimsy trunk of a sapling.

He swallows down air as fast as he can, sputtering and choking and reaching for the edge of the swamp. His shoulder throbs from the boulder, and the quartz Sam gave him is burning his chest. He fishes for the necklace and yanks it out of his shirt. It blazes against tree trunks, a candle in the darkness. Mackie takes it off and puts it in his pocket where it's less likely to burn his skin.

As soon as the offending jewelry is out of sight, a cattail reaches out and slaps him across the face with its cardboard leaves.

"Fucker," Mackie hisses.

The cattail bends forward like a small and unusual person and pushes him in the opposite direction, toward the other bank. Mackie spares it a dark glare before getting out on the suggested side.

"A please and thank you would be nice," he finds the grit (and breath) to mutter, earning himself another slap upside the ear, this time from a different cattail. This one splits the skin. There's no sense arguing with a plant. Mackie drags himself through the now stagnant water and up onto the soft mud. Nerida is nowhere to be found.

Deep lines are scratched into the ground, and Jayden's truck door lies sheared off just a few metres ahead. Beyond that is the truck itself, mashed and mangled, scratched, torn open. The roof is missing, the hood, half of the bed. One of the front tires sticks out on its axel like a crooked front tooth.

Rejuvenated by the sight, Mackie scrabbles to the truck. He's terrified to look inside the mangled cab, half sure he's going to find Blue's broken body, but there's also a flame of hope he keeps his hands clasped around. Blue is extraordinary, and if there's anyone Mackie knows that can survive being abducted by a murderous tree and flung about like a rag doll, it's him. The cab is dusted with broken glass and shorn off tree bark. The remainder of Jayden's leg lays against the driver's door, blood still bright and wet. It looks lonely, detached from the body, and pale.

Otherwise, the truck is empty. No Blue.

The bushes rustle. Mackie hopes for a moment Blue is hiding in them. Instead, a small sharp-toothed gremlin with olive-coloured skin leaps out like a tick jumping from one grass blade to the next. It scuttles into the cab and teeters on the doorframe, eyes wide, drool dripping from its jowls onto its bare and sparsely-haired body.

Mackie's stomach flips when the gremlin decides there is no immediate threat and launches itself into the cab. Jayden's leg is much bigger than it is, but it unhinges its jaw and swallows the appendage, blue Air Jordans and all. Something in its gut crushes the bone as easily as a seed crushed in a pestle and mortar. Mackie can not only hear, but watches as it gets broken down into something that just makes the gremlin's stomach bulge.

Mackie gags.

The gremlin turns toward the noise and lifts its pug nose to the sky, whiffing noisily. Mackie's blood drives hard through his veins; he feels lightheaded, and everything becomes surreal. He stands deathly still, paralyzed by fear. Any hopes he has of being overlooked wilt when the gremlin turns its chin down again and flings itself toward Mackie on its powerful legs.

With the shotgun forgotten in his hand, he swings on his heel and starts to run in an undetermined direction. His only thought is to get away as fast as he can.

The forest works against him, the trees and the ferns and the sopping mud and before he knows it, sharp claws are digging into his back through his shirt, and he's cascading to the ground.

Muck breaks his fall. It's cold, and he's soaked. His fingers slick through the soft soil as he pushes himself up and over, crushing the weight on his back. The gremlin kicks out from under him, snarling and snorting, before opening its mouth wide and biting at Mackie's thigh.

The gremlin's teeth break the skin, but don't sink in hard. Mackie's leg burns like he's rolled in coals, and the gremlin jerks back and starts writhing on the ground. Twists of smoke erupt out of the creature's mouth. Gross pustules form and burst on its tongue and lips; its teeth have rotted black.

In its pain, the gremlin rolls close to a hawthorn tree. Roots tear free of their earthly confines, alive, and wrap around the gremlin with crushing force, reminding Mackie of a Venus flytrap. In seconds, as the roots curl like fists, the gremlin's eyes bulge, its bones break.

Before the creature is fully dead, the hawthorn tucks its roots back under itself, gremlin, and all.

Fuckfuckfuck.

Mackie's breath clouds in front of his face, each coming faster than the last. He's afraid to go anywhere, and yet, he *needs* to. His leg is burning, and the mud is slowly sucking him in.

Mackie moves carefully, turning from his back to his side. When the hawthorn shudders but doesn't lash out at him, too, he sits up and examines his burning leg.

It's the quartz Sam gave him; it's seared straight through his pants and left welts on his skin. The stone itself is latticed with hairline fractures, and when he touches it with the tips of his finger, it breaks apart into tiny pieces, magic spent.

He wishes he had gotten ten more from Sam. It's well worth the third-degree burns.

It starts to rain in small, fast drops.

He thinks he should be too afraid to stand but hears a small cry that both gives him hope and frightens him. Carefully, Mackie clambers to his feet. The hawthorn shudders once again while considering if it's satiated, then settles. Mackie takes a wide berth around where he thinks its roots should extend before letting out the breath he's been holding and following the cries to his left, where a narrow path, likely made by the frequent traffic of the gremlin hunting and drinking, cuts through the trees. It spills out into a grassy lea, its borders draped by snapping vines and thorny black locusts.

In the centre of the lea, rumpled, bloody and wild-eyed is Blue. He is escorted by the pale bear-like creature they spotted in grade twelve—or another creature that looks just like it.

Its robust snout is full of jagged teeth when it snarls, and its claws are at least five inches long. They press into Blue's back, push him forward, and shred his shirt, leaving behind shallow gouges in his skin that could very easily turn to life-threatening wounds with just a bit of pressure.

Mackie hefts the shotgun to his shoulder and dashes into the clearing.

Several things strike him at once.

One: there is a massive (anatomical) heart-shaped tree on the north side of the lea. Its trunk is wider than his GTO is long. Part of it is bursting with life, flowers and vines and birds leaping from one knobby hunk of bark to the next. The other side is infected with mushrooms and blight.

Two: the tree's centre has been hollowed out and seems to be covered by filamentous spiderwebs.

And finally: a woman rests beneath the spiderwebs.

Her hair is long, black and puddles at her feet. She is beautiful in the same way summertime skies are, just before the moon comes up, and everything is indigo and glittery and soft.

Her eyes are halfway open.

This is Queen Sorrow, Mackie thinks.

Once her eyes are open, he knows that'll be the end of Blue. Already, the spiderwebs around her tomb are starting to sag and break apart.

"*You've returned to us,*" whispers the queen. She cannot yet move and uses the wind's voice to speak. Goosebumps rise on Mackie's arm.

Blue stares at the queen, hands open at his side. Rain soaks his clothes and his hair. He doesn't seem entirely surprised to see her. "Please, don't do this."

The bear stands straight and opens its mouth. An almost human voice rumbles out. "You're the seedling. Your only purpose in life is to feed the queen so she may return to herself. Come."

Blue continues for a few paces almost automatically, then he seems to come back to himself and digs his feet into the ground, risking splitting his skin anew. "No."

A hush runs through the clearing. *No?* It's clear the devils have never been denied before.

The bear says, "It's your fate"

More firmly, Blue says, "There's no such thing."

Branches whip with the queen's anger. She again uses the wind to speak. "*You're a seedling born of my body. Your only purpose is to sustain me.*"

"That can't be all," Blue says, but his words lack the conviction they had even a second ago. "I have a life. A family. Friends."

"They'll hate you without your glamour," the queen says. *"The only time they won't is when they've forgotten you've existed at all."*

Blue's eyes flutter closed. His cheeks glisten wet with rain and tears.

"*You know it's true, Seedling. But it's alright. You never belonged with them anyway. Your place is here.*"

His hands shake as he wipes his cheeks, looking young and scared.

"Come," the queen beckons.

"Will they be safe?" Blue almost whispers.

"Always after."

Sorrow's tree extends its branches like a mother reaching for a child. Her eyes track open another millimetre.

Blue's shoulders quake. He takes a halting step forward.

He's thinking about it, Mackie starts. *He's honestly considering it.* And if he doesn't act now, he'll lose Blue forever. He bursts out of the shadows of the trees. "Don't touch him!"

Blue spins. His face goes slack. "Mackie, what...?"

"She's lying, Blue. You don't belong here." His voice echoes across the lea, stronger than expected.

"He is of the forest."

Mackie speaks to the queen directly. "He came from here, but he doesn't *belong* here. He's not your property." Mackie holds out his free hand to Blue. It shakes slightly with adrenaline, mostly. The fear will come later.

At the sound of his words, the grass greens at Blue's feet and stretches out across the clearing, so verdant, so vital. But when it reaches the queen's tree, it withers and dries, as though she's sucking the life out of it. She grows stronger as the seconds tick by, and her eyes open fully. They're the rusty brown of sunburnt leaves.

Something snorts, pulling Mackie's gaze from the queen. Briar eases out of the trees. Her eyes are fixated on Mackie, and she's not the only one.

He finally realizes the lea is seething with devils. Some burn like forest fires, their shapes obscured by a dancing flame that never catches the saturated grass and underbrush. Others peek at him from behind trees or in between blades of grass. Some hang from branches, grotesquely beautiful, long limbs, lidless eyes, sharp teeth, and stares, all fixed unerringly on him.

A whisper goes through the lea. *There's a human in the forest.* And then another. *A King. An assassin.*

They mean me. And why shouldn't they? He has come to steal Blue back and doom their queen. Somehow, he's the villain.

Killed his ilk before, they whisper. *Kill him, too. Will only make our queen stronger.*

Mackie waits for Briar to speak in his favour. She never does. As, one by one, the devils emerge, he tightens his hold on the Remington. "Don't come any closer!"

They still do. Slipping from their perches and slithering through the grass. He feels like a lamb in a slaughterhouse, faced down with their sharp teeth and claws, on land that they know, and no obvious way out. Even the bear releases Blue to turn on Mackie.

There are only seven rounds in the shotgun, and now that it's wet, Mackie doesn't know if it'll fire at all. He swipes the barrel across the crowd, trying to decide who is the biggest threat.

Everything here seems unfairly deadly.

"*Kill the human, then open the seed and bring him to me,*" hums the queen with the forest's voice. The webs of her tomb break. Her eyes stick on Blue.

A ripple goes through the bunch, and then the devils launch as one. Razor teeth, razor claws, hateful eyes. The forest loathes humanity. And why shouldn't it? They build their houses out of her bones, murder her charges just because they can, wear them as trophies and then throw them away afterward. They whittle her away to nothing—push her to extinction—before realizing that they need her again, but tamed. Harmless. Docile.

A familiar-looking bird demon makes it to Mackie first. It's snarling, and its red eyes are dancing with bloodlust. Using its wings, it pulls itself backward and kicks its feet out. Large spurs decorate its devilish feet, and they're aimed right for Mackie's heart.

That familiar electric hum that precedes Blue's magic fills the air, hot and white, and then an unnatural wind starts up. It throws the bird devil away and bends the trees to the ground. Some snap and splinter and fill the air with a pulpy wood smell. Devils scream. Those that are too close to the breaking trees die.

Mackie expects the gust to let up. It only gets stronger. Leaves and twigs cut at devils, pushing them back, and soon, the air is filled with detritus and rain and the stink of blood. Mackie almost can't stand or see or breathe. He gets low to the ground and braces against the wind.

Mackie wipes rain from his eyes and squints, trying to pull Blue from the blurry shapes. It's his ghostly hair that makes him stand out. He hasn't moved from his spot. He looks wrathful, hands out and wind whipping by him at breakneck speeds but never pushing him down.

A tree tears from the ground and crashes into the lea, pinning a fox-eared devil that had been crawling toward Mackie. It squeals and scrabbles, trying to get free. A tree limb twists at an odd angle and crushes its head. Its kin trample over its still body, suddenly in a rush to get away.

The bear devil scrapes forward against the torrent, swiping for Blue. Mackie yanks up his gun and fires in the bear's direction. He hits it in the shoulder. It roars and flinches even as it continues forward. Mackie pumps the action and tries again. The bear staggers and goes down with a huge wound weeping in its chest. Blood and bits of gore glitter on the grass. Regret flashes across Blue's face but Mackie doesn't feel it. He'll lay the lot of them down if it means Blue can come home with him. Maybe that's the difference between humans and Sorrow's devils.

They need to get out of here.

Mackie risks being taken away by the gale. He surges to his feet and gropes for Blue's hand. His fingers are limp and clammy but when Mackie pulls him away from Queen Sorrow, Blue trails after him. He trips and almost goes down, gathers himself up again. The wind slows; the rain never does. Mud sucks at Mackie's feet, and little roots lash at his toes. He won't stop. He won't let Blue, either.

They're at the edge of the lea when a deafening roar fills the air.

"Stop them!" the queen demands.

Grass deadens below Mackie's feet. He's sure if he were to look back, he'd see the same blight that chased him from the forest the last time he dared to enter, killing everything behind him. He doesn't look, though, and doesn't slow.

The forest looms ahead, trees with their limbs clasped together like children playing red rover. Mackie chooses ones that look thin and malleable, drops his shoulder, and barges forth, remembering his high school rugby days.

Trees buckle inward when he collides, and he thinks for an instant that they're going to make it, but then the trees regroup and push back, and Mackie smacks into Blue. They lose their footing and collapse tangled together on the ground. Grass razors their legs and arms and cheeks and draws blood that the thirsty forest quickly absorbs.

Feet pound on the ground behind them. Something large is approaching.

Blue breathes loudly in Mackie's ear. He rocks forward on his haunches and presses his long-fingered hands to the tree roots. More electricity. Reluctantly, the tree roots and limbs peel back just wide enough that Mackie's shoulders might fit through.

Whatever chases them sees the newly made opening, too, and snarls.

Panicked, Mackie takes Blue's hand again and scrabbles forward. Moss buckles under his palms, water and mud soak his skin, and bugs race desperately out of his way. Tree limbs scratch, and cut, and almost hold him back, *almost,* but then he's through, and Blue comes through behind him.

Beyond the lea, the forest opens wide into a tunnel like the one they used to elude the forest the night Mackie stole Blue. The curtain of death escapes the lea and chases them anew. Trees fall all around them, newly, and suddenly, husked out and decayed.

From somewhere, Mackie finds the energy to run.

Twice, Blue's hand slips from his grip as he falls, and Mackie must stop to return for him. Each time the death gets a little closer, until it's just at their heels, and he's more than sure they're not going to make it.

An earthquake shakes the ground and splits it in two. Trees collapse all around them. Mackie throws his free hand over his head for protection as boughs rain down and tree trunks threaten to crush him.

It's over in a second, and when it passes, a lot of trees are down, and starlight reaches the floor of Sorrow's Forest. The death following them slows without trees side-by-side to spread its cancer.

Seeing their opportunity, Mackie redoubles his efforts, and moments later, the pathway spits them out onto his road. The driveway is only metres ahead, bracketed by the solar lights Mom uses to press against the darkness.

Mackie would plow ahead, but Blue is gasping and lagging. Mackie is forced to stop with him. One foot is in the driveway, the other on the road. The forest is too close. Still too volatile. Still looking for them, and the tree Sam gave him is too ill to do any good at this distance.

"Come on, Blue."

Blue doesn't move. He looks pale and sick. "You shouldn't have done that, Mackie."

Mackie is bigger than Blue and stronger, and he pulls him into the driveway without responding. Blue still drags his feet and looks toward the trees as though Sorrow herself might burst from them at any second.

Mackie wishes he were brave enough to dare her.

The house is quiet and still. No lights are on, though it's only seven-thirty, and all the bedroom doors are open. He doesn't know where his parents went but is admittedly relieved they aren't here to see him and Blue walk in like this. They're both filthy and bleeding. Worse than that, both cars are missing, the Civic still in the hardware parking lot, and the GTO...

It's probably part of the forest now.

Mackie's too relieved at being free to be angry. There are other vintage cars that need refurbishing.

Blue allows Mackie to pull him into his bedroom and close the door. The window drapes are still closed against the forest, and the room sinks into darkness. Normally, Mackie would leave it as it is, but he's suddenly cautious of the dark. He turns on the bedside lamp.

Blue stands in the centre of the room with his arms wrapped around his chest. He's quivering, soaked through, hair matted to his forehead, and eyeliner smeared beneath his dark eyes.

"Are you okay?" Mackie asks.

Blue nods even as he pinches his bottom lip between his teeth until it turns white. He looks in the direction of the forest as though expecting it to reach up and through the open window.

Considering how Nerida got to him, Mackie isn't sure that's not possible.

When he thinks of the forest retaliating, his chest feels tight and small, and there isn't enough breath in his lungs.

He can't wonder if it'll come for them. It'll drive him mad.

"I'm going to shower," Mackie says to feel normal. He needs to get the grime off him.

Wordlessly, Blue follows Mackie into the bathroom. Someone has picked up the rolled-up towels that were catching the leak and the floor is dry, though Mackie has to turn on the water valve before he can turn on the shower. Immediately, cold water drips from the showerhead. Everything broken is still that way.

He vows to fix it in the morning.

Blue sits on the closed toilet seat while Mackie throws off his clothing and climbs into the shower. He doesn't question Blue's presence. He wants him close by as well. He doesn't like the hollow look in Blue's eyes, nor does he want to be alone.

His skin is so cold that the water scalds him, but Mackie keeps it hot to chase out the chills. Soon, the mirror is fogged, and he's almost sweating under the spray.

Blue is still shivering. Something pulls tight in Mackie's chest.

"Come here."

Blue stands and strips his clothes. They stain the floor with blood and dirt. One more thing to fix, but Mackie doesn't mind. He's happiest when he's repairing something.

Blue climbs into the shower and stands inches apart from Mackie. He quivers each time a drop of water lands on his skin. Exasperated, Mackie pulls him further beneath the spray.

Long minutes tick by before Blue's teeth stop chattering enough for him to speak. "I didn't take John."

"I know that, of course. You wouldn't."

Blue shakes his head and drops his eyes to their feet. "I'm not innocent, either."

In Mackie's memory, he sees Bobby pulled into the ditch again. "What do you mean?"

"I saw it happen. I saw the devil lure him into the forest, and I didn't stop it. I thought..." Again, he shakes his head.

Mackie says, "If you tried, it would have taken you, too."

"It *should* have. It *wants* me. *Me.* You should have left me." Two furious spots of red appear on Blue's cheeks. His knuckles are white; his fists are clenched. He looks small, paper-thin. His shoulders wrack, and Mackie has the absurd notion that if he continues, he'll shake himself apart.

Cautiously, he reaches for Blue and pulls him into his chest beneath the pounding spray. Blue complies, chin digging into Mackie's shoulder. Mackie is once more reminded of how much larger than Blue he is. His arms easily wrap around Blue's shoulders. He holds him tight enough to almost stop the tremors that wrack his body.

They stay as they are until the water runs cold, then, without communicating, dry, dress, and return to Mackie's room, where they're pulled together in much the same way on Mackie's bed.

Chapter 16

Curtains scraping on their metal rod rouse Mackie from a dreamless, exhausted sleep.

Squinting, he spots Blue at the windowsill looking upon the forest. Morning light plays through his blonde hair, making it glimmer, and kisses upon his milk-pale skin. He wears only sweatpants, plain black. His wiry muscles flex as he grips the curtains; his lips are a tight line.

"What's out there?" Mackie hears himself ask.

Blue starts and turns. For an instant, his eyes are pure black. Then he blinks, and they return to the brown facade he's maintained for the last eleven years. "The forest is dying."

Mackie's horror is much duller and quieter than he suspects it should be. All he can think is, if it dies, it can't take Blue. It can't take anyone.

Mackie can't know his expression, but whatever it is that Blue sees on his face, it makes him release the curtains and come back to the bed. Beneath the sheets once more, he faces Mackie, one arm tucked beneath his pillow and the other curled against his chest. He studies Mackie intently, and Mackie studies him back. Blue's birthmark is darker than it's been previously, staining half his face, and his eyes are wide. He looks like he's seen a ghost, or ten, and isn't processing the situation very well.

"Everything will be okay," Mackie says uselessly. It's the kind of reassurance Mom gave him when Grandpa died, made for children who believe their loved ones with unfailing certainty. The kind of reassurance that's nine parts bluster and one part truth. Things will go on. Nothing will be the same. But it will, in some semblance, be fine.

Blue finds a loose thread on the pillowcase and plucks it. "Why did you come for me?"

The question takes Mackie aback, and after a fumbling moment of silence, where he tries to find the words to say how he feels, he settles on an insufficient, "You know why," and hopes that it's true.

Blue matches his gaze and understanding passes between them. He closes the spare distance between them and kisses Mackie like he kissed him the night on the pier. Except, there is no car between them, awkward gear shifts, or radio to distract. His lips are cool, and his hand, as he rests it against Mackie's cheek, is hot.

Holding onto each other this way feels like they're both full of hopeless desperation. Mackie's drowning in it, but he goes willingly, wrapping his hand around Blue's bicep and pulling him closer as he rolls onto his back.

Blue follows until he's on his knees between Mackie's legs. His skin is still as cold as it was last night, while they shivered beneath the shower spray, but now he smells of soap and not blood and mud. He grips both hands in Mackie's hair and kisses Mackie expertly, teeth nipping, tongue sliding, body bucking against Mackie's.

He inches down the line of Mackie's chest, paving a pathway with his fingers and smoothing it with his tongue. Each swipe fills Mackie with anticipation until he's shaking and gasping.

Blue takes his time. Everything is a tease; everything is a game. His tongue dips in toward the head of Mackie's cock, flits away, his lips purse around the tip, and then he blows cool air across Mackie's body. It goes on for what feels like forever but is only minutes, and then Blue hooks his arms around Mackie's legs and gives him what he wants.

The morning is well gone by the time Mackie gets out of bed. Blue is already in the kitchen, sitting on the counter, coffee between his hands, swinging his heels gently into the cupboards. When Mackie joins him, he meets Mackie's quiet shyness with his usual rakish and confident grin. Something is bothering him, though, and Blue is trying hard to pretend it's not.

Mackie's gaze is drawn, naturally, over Blue's shoulder to the window. His breath catches.

The forest is slumping, rotting, *dying,* just as Blue said, and not in the quiet, temporary way old-growth forests do when it's time to renew the cycle, but dramatically, in a way that seems uncontrolled, without purpose and very permanent.

Huge trees sag together with their roots pulling at the ground like bones in emaciated creatures fighting against skin. With one good wind gust, they'll tear through the thin layers holding them in place and crash, where they'll sink back to the earth, taproots broken. Leaves curl yellow, brown, and black and fall. The grass that hugs its borders is crispy and burnt-looking.

The worst of it, though, is the grey lump at the border. It takes Mackie's study to identify it as the dog-like devil he saw on his first night home as it hung in the shadows of the bird feeder. Now it's lifeless and bloated like a balloon ready to pop.

Blue follows his gaze. "Do you think that will happen to all the devils when it dies?"

The question is unexpected and difficult to answer. Mackie only blinks in response.

From upstairs, Blue's phone shrills. Mackie jumps at the sudden noise.

It goes off again.

It's the same ringtone Blue always has—the old school Spiderman theme song, minus the lyrics, but, inexplicably, hearing it makes Mackie's insides curl. Without knowing why, he doesn't want Blue to answer the phone.

Voicing his suspicions seems too superstitious, though, and he says nothing as Blue slides off the counter and mounts the stairs three at a time.

To distract himself, Mackie goes through the motions, getting himself a cup out of the cupboard, filling it to the brim with black coffee, sipping it. It scalds his tongue.

Blue reappears. He's even more white-faced than before. "Mackie?"

Mackie swallows another scalding mouthful of coffee. *Don't say anything,* he thinks. *Don't, and maybe...*

Blue forges on ahead, immune to the pleading in Mackie's expression. "Your dad is in the hospital."

Looking at the quiet house, part of him knew, he realizes. Or suspected, at least. George King is dying. Dying for Sorrow.

His breaths are short and fast.

"Your mom wants you to go to the hospital. She needs you there."

Mackie bites his lips together. Shakes his head minutely.

I can't, he thinks.

I have to, he knows.

"Mackie? Did you hear me?"

He's immobile. Scared. Horrified. And beneath that all, quietly, secretly, glad. The nightmare is close to over.

God.

He closes his eyes.

"Just... try to breathe. Sit down or something. I'll call a cab," Blue says.

Mackie doesn't hear or understand, until ten minutes later, a cab is sitting in the driveway, waiting for them to pile in.

A nurse directs Mackie up a flight of stairs and to the left into the Palliative Care Unit. Leaden, he ascends, with Blue at his side. Mom meets him outside of the room. Though she's angry, she doesn't ask where he's been, why he's scratched to hell, or why he nor Blue have answered their phones since last night.

Blue sits on the loveseat in the lobby, and Mom joins him, taking the spot Mackie normally would. "You should go see your father," she says, indicating a room on the far wall that looks like all the rest.

Do I have to? The words Mackie will never say stream through his mind on repeat alongside *I don't want to. I'm scared. I can't.*

But he does.

Machines beep and wheeze quietly. His father is strapped to the bed and immobile.

Mackie sits beside the bed. He studies the lines of his father's face and can remember a time when he looked powerful, young, and strong. A time when he was terrifying, vital, a force worth fearing.

Now he is broken, though not very old.

Beneath the Velcro straps, Dad's hand rests against the bed rail. It's frail, skin thin, bones exposed. Mackie forces himself to touch it, pushed on by morbid curiosity and a strange sense of duty.

When Dad's fingers twitch, Mackie almost lets go. He swallows the yell that tries to climb from his throat and instead focuses on his father's face. His eyes are open just a millimetre, reminding Mackie, strangely, of Sorrow in her tree coffin, peering out at the world, mostly dead, but a little not.

"Mackie?" he rasps.

It takes two tries for Mackie to make his voice work. "Yeah."

"You've been in the forest, haven't you, boy?"

He can see no sense in lying. "Yeah."

Dad's fingers squeeze. He doesn't feel so old or frail for an instant, but the strength quickly bleeds out of him. "Fool."

"It was going to take Blue."

Dad wets his lips with a tongue gone grey. He struggles to find the breath to speak. "She'll take me, understand? She'll take me, and then she'll take you. Unless you do the right thing."

Hopeless and confused, Mackie says, "I don't know what that means."

"Yes, you do," says Dad.

"No—"

Dad turns his gnarled hands on Mackie and grips him hard. "Give her the seedling, boy. Do what's right. She'll let you go."

Mackie bites his cheek. Hard. "And if I don't want that?"

"You'll do what's right." Simple, inarguable.

"It doesn't *have* to be the only way," Mackie tries anyway, but Dad closes his eyes and doesn't open them again.

Mackie feels dug out. He doesn't cry, shiver, or clench his fists in denial or fury. He lays in his bed, Blue's arms wrapped around his middle, and stares at the ceiling, at the poster of the 1949 Oldsmobile Rocket 88, cherry red. He feels none of the wanderlust he normally does when he looks over her sleek lines. It simply reminds him of his father, and he doesn't know how to feel when he thinks of him.

"Do you remember when we used to go swimming at the quarry?" Blue asks in a whisper.

"Yeah."

"And we would skip stones, and the loser had to double the winner home on their bike?"

"Yeah."

"I always lost," Blue says.

"You weren't very good at skipping stones."

He shrugs a little. "I didn't mind doubling you on the bike. You always laughed, and I liked it."

Mackie furrows his brow. "You did it on purpose?"

"Occasionally. Remember the sword battles we'd have with the tree limbs that would fall into the yard?"

Sometimes, those felt so real, Mackie could almost hear the scrape of steel on steel. "Don't tell me you lost those on purpose, too."

"No. You were stronger than me. I still liked to do it, though, because you liked to do it. Remember when—"

Mackie turns on him. He can see the flecks of black in Blue's brown eyes, like the deep spots on a bruise. "Why are you telling me this?"

Blue takes a breath and holds it. "Mackie..."

Whatever he's going to say next, Mackie's sure it'll break his heart. "Don't."

"I have to go back," Blue says anyway. "I have to go back to her. Everything is suffering."

Mackie squeezes the bedsheets and bites his tongue furiously to push back the burning in his eyes. "Don't talk like that."

Blue gets closer, cheek on Mackie's shoulder, and says no more.

Chapter 17

Mackie doesn't remember falling asleep, but when he opens his eyes, he's in his bed alone, and it's morning. The sun is streaming through his window in pale bars, and birds are chirping. His nose is stuffy, and his cheeks feel sticky. He doesn't remember the specifics of his dreams.

It takes a few minutes, sitting there fuzzy, staring at the fallen oak in the backyard, its bark spongy, for yesterday's events to rush back to him, Dad, the queen, the forest, and

Blue.

He throws off his blankets.

Blue's bedroom door is open, and his room is empty. Mackie fumbles down the stairs into the kitchen. Mom is making coffee; Dad's spot at the table is alarmingly empty. The TV plays in the background, reporting the disappearance of the Slater triplets and Shawn Macintyre.

"These boys get drunk and wander into the woods and can't find their way out," Mom mutters with a disappointed shake of her head.

"They're dead," Mackie says. His words don't have the effect he's hoping for, she doesn't flinch or ask how he knows that because *everyone* knows that, just mostly, they're too polite to say it.

Mom looks over her shoulder. "Where's my car, Mackie? I have to go to work."

"You're going to work today?"

"What else am I supposed to do?" Mom clings to her coffee cup white-knuckled.

"Shouldn't you take a day or something?" Dad *died* yesterday, he thinks of adding, but is too afraid to say so.

"No point."

He sighs. "I'll pay for a cab. I have to get it from the hardware store."

"My car?" She's getting close to screeching.

"Sorry," he murmurs.

She turns her back on him. "You better call right now. I'm going to be late."

He uses the corded phone on the wall. "Five minutes," he tells her a moment later.

She simmers quietly. Mackie speaks even when he knows he should leave her be. "Have you seen Blue?"

"What?" She's distracted, rummaging through her purse for God knows what.

"Blue," Mackie repeats. "Where is he?"

She finds a package of cigarettes "What is that?" Then understanding crosses her face and Mackie's almost relieved until she asks, "Did you bring home another cat? Please say no, I—"

Mackie must walk away or risk screaming.

He checks the garage.

Inexplicably, his GTO is sitting in its usual spot. The tires are muddy, and its paint is dusty, but aside from the front seat being pulled up to a position closer than Mackie would put it himself, there are no other signs of life.

The same sick feeling he had when the hospital called about Dad settles in behind his ribs. He does his best to ignore it and moves his search into the backyard, where the stench of the decomposing oak is almost overpowering.

Three woodpeckers scatter from its head where they're excavating grubs and find other sagging trees to perch on. They look down on Mackie with intelligent eyes. It's hard to say if they're devils or not. Birds are halfway there, to begin with.

At the risk of sounding crazy, Mackie asks the birds, "Where is he?"

They cock their heads and chatter their beaks together as if speaking to one another. They never try to include him in the conversation.

From the front yard, he hears a car door slam. He races out front. It's just Mom getting into her taxi. When the car rolls out of the puckered driveway, a deep sense of aloneness settles over Mackie. Suffocating.

Without anything else to do, Mackie returns to his GTO, gets into the driver's seat, and starts cruising through town, looking for Blue without expecting to find him.

Gradually, he notices the small changes. The forest looks less sad than it did yesterday, and spring has come to Lakeview for real. Flowers are blooming, trees are returning to leaf, and the patch of forest that's been dead for ten years has a small spot of yellow where marsh marigold is coming up.

But no Blue.

He returns to the grotto, parking on the side of the road with his wheels nearly in the ditch. Here, too, the forest has begun to heal itself. The line of dead trees has fallen, making room for saplings, forest flowers, and moss. Mackie tries not to tramp on it as much as possible as he claws his way into the grotto.

The forest opens, and the pool appears. Gone is the red water; now it's sparkling blue. Mackie wades in up to his thighs, and then he just stands there. He doesn't know how to make this work—he's not magical. He pictures Blue in his mind, soft blonde hair, dark eyes, *loud*. Aside from making him ache, nothing happens. Even when he plunges his hands into the water and searches blindly, as though he can pull Blue out of the deep like Blue pulled Kevin, it's gloriously anticlimactic.

A frustrated yell climbs out of his throat, scaring the birds above his head. He looks up to see the same woodpeckers staring down at him. It must mean *something*, but when he stays there in the pond for hours, soaking and shivering, and nothing happens, Mackie is forced to admit maybe it's not what he thinks.

Sam is in his backyard securing his goats when Mackie pulls into his driveway. The sun sits low on the horizon, a squashed grapefruit bleeding all over the sky. Its pink light guides him over the hillocks to the goat pen.

"Hey." Sam snags his sweating beer bottle off the fencepost and turns on Mackie. His favourite baseball cap is pulled low over his head, dark hair curling out the sides. He leans on the gate and dutifully ignores a new billy goat chewing the edge of his flannel overshirt. "I heard about your dad, Mackie. I'm really sorry, man. That's shitty."

It is, but unchangeable. "Blue's gone," Mackie blurts. That's something he might be able to fix.

Sam lifts his eyebrows. Mackie prepares himself for *Who's Blue?* He might scream, or he might laugh. The feeling pressing at the base of his throat is very similar.

Sam has never been like everyone else. "What happened to him?"

Mackie works the lump out of his throat, slightly horrified he's so emotional, and tells Sam everything. It feels like something that happened to someone else, all of it. The night in the GTO, Jayden and Jace, the queen, how they narrowly escaped the seething forest. Blue's words. That he must go back.

"And now he's gone," Mackie finishes.

Sam is quiet for some time. The billy goat gives up annoying him and clops over to his food to chew that instead. The sun gets lower still.

"Did you ever consider maybe it's for the best?" Sam says at last.

His words threaten to crush Mackie. "It's not." A world without Blue doesn't seem like much of a world at all.

"Mackie..." Sam says. There's not much conviction behind his name, nothing to stop Mackie from spinning on his heel and returning to his car.

It's past midnight, and Mackie's fingers and toes are cold. He sits on the patio, staring into the forest. Mom watched him for a while from the living room window but has since given up and fallen asleep on the couch.

The cold helps keep him awake, along with the cigarettes. Mackie smokes one after the other until his tongue is numb, and his heart is pounding with the nicotine rush.

He hears a splashing at the treeline, and his heart pounds instead with excitement. He gets out of his seat so fast that it tangles around his numb feet, and he falls. His cigarette extinguishes in the soggy grass.

Mackie pushes himself up again and crosses the backyard in a few short steps on his stinging legs.

Nerida waits in the deep pool of the stream.

"Where's Blue?" Mackie demands.

Her eyes glow menacingly. *Shameful you didn't drown in the grotto today, Mackenzie.* "Hello, Caregiver."

Mackie narrows his eyes. "Where is he?"

"Of course, I'll bring you to him." She twists one finger over the water's surface, beckoning. Small fish dart up to the surface, turning it silvery with their bellies. "Step closer, come into the trees."

Mackie willfully ignores the warning in her words and steps beneath the branches. The forest breathes around him. It is not a kind place, even if it's not as hungry as it once was.

Nerida's lips peel back into a smile. "And into the water?"

Mackie's nervous, stepping over the bank and into the water, one foot after the other. It's cold as hell, and deep. He slips on slick clay and goes under. He claws his way back to the surface, fingers brushing the bodies of scattering minnows, gasping, and shivering.

Nerida is *right there*, breathing her putrid breath in his face. She clasps his arms with her clawed hands and opens her mouth wide, revealing her serrated teeth one at a time. She lunges in, fast as a shark. Mackie closes his eyes against the bite, cursing himself for being so desperate.

The bite never comes.

Splashing.

Mackie peeks between his lashes. Nerida jerks back, hissing. A thick tree root pries her mouth open. It threatens to tear her face in half.

He hears her jaw crack and her skin, like tissue paper, begins to rip at the corners of her lips. Blood trickles down her chin. Mackie can't look away from the gruesomeness. But it never reaches its peak. Nerida somehow manages to slither away from the root and once she's free, a sudden wave rears up and takes Mackie's feet out from under him. He's rushing through the trees, half underwater and half panicked for air.

He hits a bank and gets pinned for three unnerving seconds. He must use most of his strength to push himself off. The water spins him around, dunks him under completely.

Mackie opens his eyes against the stinging cold. Out of the murk appears a ghostly shape that strikes fear into his heart. He pushes off the bank again to avoid it and just narrowly passes by Shawn's body. He's been mostly torn apart, hunks of flesh ripped off right down to the bone, and his one remaining eye is sagging out of his head.

Before he can see what other horrors lay in the water's depths, Mackie is pulled forcefully from the current and deposited onto the bank. He turns on his side, sputtering and coughing his lungs raw.

Someone kneels beside him. Mackie jerks away, sure it's another grotesque. It's just Blue.

He looks different now, washed in the silver light of the moon. His hair has lightened to its natural blue-blonde state. Gold-wrought leaves are threaded throughout it. His eyelids have been brushed with wintergreen shadow and his lips with black. He's traded his clothes in for soft silks the likes of which Mackie's never seen, and though they look comfortable, Blue does not.

"Are you okay?" Blue asks. Even his voice sounds different, tinged with etherealness that sets Mackie spinning. Blue has always been from the forest. He's always been unique. He's also always been Mackie's, in one way or another, and now Mackie doesn't know if that's true any longer. He doesn't know this Blue.

"Mackie?"

Mackie swallows the lump rising in his throat. "I'm alright." He's trembling almost as bad as the time he got hypothermia falling into Yarrow Lake in the spring.

"You're scared."

"I'm *mad.* Where the hell have you been? Why did you leave in the middle of the night? You think you can just drop off the GTO, and disappear?" Even Mackie is surprised by his eruption. He's never been angry like this with Blue. Mad enough that he shoves his shoulder.

Blue stumbles back but, otherwise, does nothing.

"Don't you have anything to say?" Mackie wants to push him again. He refrains.

"You should go home."

Mackie laughs abruptly. "Yeah. We should." He reaches for Blue, and his hand gets slapped aside by a tree root thin and whiplike. It stings enough to draw Mackie's attention outward. They have an audience, a collection of various devils—mountain lion and snake creatures, something like a scaled wolf that watches with curiosity, and Briar, who stands a few feet away, boiling with rage, roots twisting around her.

They're in a part of the forest Mackie doesn't recognize, though it reminds him very much of the Wastes. The ground rolls with gentle hills. Tall willows slowly sway in a warm breeze. Behind the largest is a green structure made of twisted vines. It looks like a palace, elaborate, tall, speckled with flowers and ramparts, spires, and baroque accents. There are no windows, just holes to the inside where vines don't grow.

The whole thing is very fairy tale-esque, right down to the horrors peering out from the windows of the façade.

Briar says, "You will not touch the seedling."

Mackie gawps at her. "Pardon?"

She stands firm and doesn't bother repeating herself.

"Blue?"

"You should go back, Mackie," he says. "You don't belong here."

"Neither do you."

In opposition, Blue holds out his hand and leaves curl up from the ground, grown from seeds unseen, and bloom into bright pink flowers. "I belong here."

Mackie dashes the flowers aside. They droop. "Sorrow wants to *eat* you, have you forgotten?"

He shakes his head. "When she does, everything will be okay again."

His words make Mackie feel cold all over. "Do you hear yourself?"

"It's the only way."

A very tall and very thin, green-skinned woman with a back full of lush black wings walks from the vine castle and stops just behind Blue. It's so odd, Mackie can only stare. "Should I kill the human, Seedling?"

"No. Return him home, please."

"Blue." Mackie can't stop the hurt that seeps into Blue's name.

Blue rolls his lips between his teeth, looking down. He turns remote, repeating, "Take him home, please."

"No," Mackie protests again. "I won't go until you at least *talk* to me."

"There's nothing to say."

"You can't announce you're letting a forest witch *eat you* and then say there's nothing to say!" Mackie's throat aches. He's screaming. He can't bring his volume down. "Dad *died,* Mom is acting like nothing's happened, and now you're—you're trying to suicide. Just *stop.*"

Blue looks at him sadly. "Please, go home, Mackie. The forest isn't any place for a human."

He tries to shove Blue again, instead.

Something invisible closes around Mackie. Whatever it is, it feels like sunshine in summer. It stops Mackie in his tracks and makes him feel drowsy. He doesn't panic when Sorrow's familiar shadowy death moves into the grove.

Briar's eyes go wide. "She's here."

"Send him home," Blue pleads.

Briar shakes her head. "There is no time."

The magic holding Mackie in its grip changes. He feels his perception altering. He shrinks rapidly, getting small and light. His legs dig into the ground, and his arms are pinned to his sides, hands tilting outward.

"A flower?" Blue hisses. "She'll step on him."

"Stop looking at him," Briar orders.

Blue goes still and faces forward as the trees part and Sorrow enters the grove.

She's even more sickly than before, stringy hair pointing to the ground because she cannot hold her head up. She's carried by two moving trees, suspended between them almost in crucifixion. Tattered spider silk clothing hangs off her shoulders, and her bones shine through her thin skin.

The trees stop in front of Briar and Blue and lay the queen on the ground. She sits with her legs folded out beside her and her hands limp in her lap. With great effort, she raises her eyes to look at Blue through her thread-like hair.

"Seedling." Her voice is still the voice of the wind.

"I'm ready now." Blue steps toward her. Mackie tries to scream, but he has no mouth with which to make a sound. His efforts earn him a warning glare from Briar, though, and he suspects he's at least making some sort of fuss. Whatever it is, it's not enough. Sorrow only has eyes for Blue.

It takes all her effort to lift her hands toward him. Blue takes in a fortifying breath that stiffens his spine, and then he gets on his knees in front of her and lifts her arms over his shoulders.

He seems much larger than she does. So vital. So full of life. How? How can this be happening? It's not right.

Mackie can't bear to watch, yet it's impossible to look away. Whatever Briar did to him, he's paralyzed, and now he's forced to watch as Sorrow gasps in haggard breaths and grips Blue's shoulders with her frail hands. He's forced to watch Blue pull his shirt from his shoulders. He's forced to watch Sorrow's mouth open wide.

Her teeth, black, jagged, sharp, sink into Blue's shoulder and ruin his smooth flesh. Blood runs down his back and front, and Blue gasps. Sorrow, like a vampire, latches her lips around the wound and sucks his blood down her throat in greedy swallows.

Her hair starts to turn luscious, her nails pink, while Blue gets wan and thin.

No. No! Mackie thinks. He struggles to move and feels one of his legs rise. He realizes then, they've turned to roots, and he's pulled them from the soil.

Sorrow's eyes—black like Blue's—dart up and latch onto Mackie. Recognition shoots across her smoothing face, then anger. No human is supposed to enter the forest. No devil is supposed to harbour them.

She's just releasing Blue to turn on her sister when a thin root shoots from the ground around Briar and burrows itself in Sorrow's chest.

The grove gets still and quiets with shock. Sorrow's lifeblood pumps rhythmically out around the roots. It's bright red and stains Blue's knees and the ground between them. The forest eagerly soaks it up.

"Traitor," Sorrow gasps the accusation at Briar, who takes it with quivering stoicism. What's done is done, but she can't believe she's done it.

"Your reign is over, sister," Briar's voice shakes a little too much. "You've led us to near-destruction for your love. As all things must, it's your turn to return to the ground."

"Traitor!" Sorrow repeats, this time screaming. "Traitor!" Blood dribbles between her lips and down her throat.

Briar accepts her accosting with a bent head.

"The forest will never be yours!" Sorrow says, now quiet. "It'll never obey you."

"It was never meant to," Briar agrees. "It's not mine to take."

Sorrow's limbs start to solidify. Before Mackie's eyes, they become bark-like. She's turning into a tree.

The transformation takes only seconds to complete, and once it's finished, he stares into Sorrow's dark face. Her eyes are solid bark, but he can see the betrayal etched in her features.

Blue wavers on his knees. Briar rushes forward. Mackie waits for her to capture him, but she merely removes the leafy crown from her sister's head and places it on Blue's. It sinks into his hair and fuses to his skull with thin vines.

"All hail the king of the forest," she whispers softly.

Her words are repeated by the devils all around. "All hail the king."

Mackie, consumed suddenly by a dangerous feeling of weightlessness, then sees nothing but black.

When Mackie can open his eyes again, he's back in his house, crunched up on the armchair in his room. The sky is still dark.

He's wet, and his head feels cottony. Digging through his memory, horrors surface. Nerida, the stream, Shawn rotting under the water. And then...

His memory is segmented. Sorrow's blood. Blue...

Sitting up, his head pounds as though he's been drinking for three days straight.

A feeling of unsettledness drapes over him, too gauzy and thick to find the starting point. Mackie's attention is drawn to the window, where light trickles from the trees, as dull as a candle flickering in the wind.

A man steps out from beneath the leaves, and all Mackie's memories crash back into line. Blue and the forest, Queen Sorrow. Now he's here.

Mackie's heart is a war drum thudding in his veins. It slows when he hears the sliding glass door open and close, then footsteps on the stairs.

Blue appears in the doorway, looking taller and wispier than before. It could be the shadows, but his eyes look beetle black, and Mackie's hit with the memory of Blue sitting streamside, crushing the insects between his teeth.

"Hi," he says. There is a whisper of the same etherealness that tainted his words before, distant, and weak now. This Blue is *his* Blue.

"Where have you been?" Mackie doesn't mean for it to sound so accusing. "I looked for you. And then when I found you—" He trails off, unsure of exactly what happened.

"I know," Blue says, and nothing more. The acknowledgement is more infuriating than a half-assed lie would be.

"What happened?"

"A lot." Blue steps in and closes the door. He's still in his new silvery clothes. They suit him, but not the world beyond the forest. He shakes his head, the gesture pure, helpless frustration. "So much, and I just..."

Mackie's not so desperate for an explanation that he wants to see Blue tormented. He offers him an out. "We don't have to yet."

Relief relaxes Blue's face. His shoulders sag some. "Okay."

A hush follows. It's prolonged and almost awkward, like the space between one dying breath and the next.

Mackie strives to shatter it. "Come here." He reaches for him, and Blue steps closer, letting Mackie envelop him in a hug. He presses his cheek to Mackie's shoulder and clutches him tight. His breath breaks warm on Mackie's neck, making Mackie shiver.

They stand unmoving, Mackie feeling Blue's chest rise and fall and Blue squeezing Mackie hard and restricting his breaths. Blue says, "You're still wet."

"I didn't have time to change." And he isn't even sure if he would have bothered if he did. He probably would have just run into the forest again, looking for Blue.

"The forest is dangerous," Blue says as though he's read Mackie's mind. He works while he talks, taking the hem of Mackie's shirt and pulling it over his head. It drops to the floor with a sodden splat.

"I know."

If he's frustrated, he doesn't show it, helping Mackie step out of his sopping pants, too. Mackie keeps his movements minimal. Now that he can feel his bare skin, he's aware of how many times he's been bruised and cut in the last twenty-four hours.

Once he's nude, Blue ushers him toward the bed. Mackie lies against the wall. Blue joins him nose-to-nose and pulls the blankets over them both.

They lay that way long enough for the moon to pass its apex. At some point, Mackie's chills subside, and his stomach unknots with the residual fear he didn't even realize he was feeling—fear he'd die, fear *Blue* would, fear they'd never see each other again.

Mackie mostly keeps his eyes closed, stealing peeks at Blue only on occasion. Every time he does, Blue's eyes are open. The whites around his irises are stark, making his eyes electric. Sometimes, they're focused on the ceiling, but sometimes, they're on Mackie.

Blue skates his fingers down Mackie's exposed spine, a gentle touch to soften the coming blow. When he speaks, it's in the voice he reserves for terrible news. "Things can't go back to the way they were."

Mackie works the lump out of his throat. "I know." Perhaps even way back when Kevin first disappeared, he knew. Things were changing. "Are you scared?"

"I hate it, so maybe," Blue admits. "But I can't stop it, so what's the point?"

The part of Mackie that always wants a favourable solution shuffles through courses of action as fast as a Blackjack dealer. The only worthwhile thing he comes up with is running away, but Blue won't. *Can't.* Especially now. He needs the forest, and the forest needs him.

"These last few days have been nice, though."

"Monsters and death?" Mackie says sarcastically, thinking not just of Nerida and her ilk, but Shawn and his, and Dad, whose cremated body will likely be ready for pickup by morning.

"I meant this," Blue answers, voice pitched low to match the way he kisses Mackie, heady and hopeless. His lips are wet and warm, and his hand splays across Mackie's bare back, pulling him closer still.

"What are you afraid of?" Mackie finds himself asking when he can. Blue can pretend and glib his answers, but his fear taints his kiss.

Blue closes his eyes and leans his forehead against Mackie's. "That I won't be able to do this again."

"Of course, you will. I'll always be here."

Blue squeezes Mackie's side hard, trying to hold him as though Mackie is sand, slipping through his fingers. "I know," he says at last, and it could be he means it, but there are other things he doesn't say, too.

Verbal assurances won't work, so Mackie tries to take the sadness from him with an equally slow kiss, barely thinking about Blue's darker eyes and thinner limbs. While he's different on the surface, deep down, he's still Blue.

Blue leans into the kiss and lets out a small moan. Encouraged by his response, though it's stuttering, Mackie deepens the kiss, brushing Blue's bottom lip with his tongue. Blue grants him entrance.

As the seconds go on, Mackie's mind empties until there is only Blue's hand sliding down his side and the growing ache between his legs.

Blue pushes him onto his back and follows, putting one leg between Mackie's and planting his hand above Mackie's head. The other he uses to trace a path down Mackie's leg. He pulls it up and holds it, spreading Mackie and pressing into him. It's a vulnerable position, but it's also enthralling. Mackie does his best to shove aside his insecurities as Blue's mouth ventures away from his, down his neck to his chest. Each spot he's touched tingles with electricity that should probably hurt but only makes Mackie dizzy and giddy.

Blue uses his tongue on Mackie's middle and leaves a slick wet trail from the centre of his chest to his belly button. His kiss turns open-mouthed again. Mackie arches his hips, unable to help himself, and his erection brushes against Blue's cheek, close enough that he can feel the humidity from his mouth.

"Take off your clothes," Mackie orders.

Blue looks up at him through a fringe of dark lashes. He smiles, showing off teeth that are a little sharper than before, and Mackie is reminded once again that they're not quite the same. He likes it, though.

Blue strips, never taking his eyes off Mackie. Mackie remains as he is, legs spread, naked, feeling like he's in someone else's body. Blue's tattoos move when he does, almost like they're alive, right down his middle to where he's at attention.

He returns to Mackie, kissing him once on the mouth, and then turns his ministrations between Mackie's legs where he works tirelessly until bursts of light dance behind Mackie's eyes. Chills wrack his body in reverse, starting at his toes and ending at his temples. Blue squeezes his thighs before moving.

"Come here," Mackie rasps, just in case he's going to slip away.

Blue hesitates, then follows Mackie's instructions, climbing up Mackie's body, legs across Mackie's hips, and then his ribs until he's straddling his chest. Mackie looks up at him from his prone position. His heart is a racehorse at the gate, waiting for the signal to gallop right out of his chest. He breathes shallowly, reminding himself that there isn't any reason to be nervous.

Blue looks down upon him. His hair is chaos, and his lungs expand and contract wicked fast. He looks exactly like what he is: a devil, beautiful and strange.

Mackie puts his hands on Blue's chest first, wanting to learn the feel of his skin. He's warm and sweat-slicked. Blue's own heart strains against his ribs, and his lungs fill insufficiently with air. When he gets to Blue's hips and pulls him closer, Blue's eyes flutter shut. Mackie's skin prickles with insecurities. What if he's not good at this? Or Blue decides he doesn't like it? What if he can't learn to be better? Then Blue threads his fingers in Mackie's hair, and Mackie forgets to be scared.

Blue lays next to Mackie, still face-to-face, arm around Mackie's middle. It's such a familiar pose, they've done this a million times, and yet because their intent has changed, it's foreign, too.

Mackie shutters his eyes, pretending it is pure bliss, and that this aching, sorrowful feeling sloughing off Blue doesn't mean anything at all. But it does, and he can't ignore it, no matter how he tries.

"What's wrong?"

Blue surprises him with an answer. "If I'd known how this last week was going to be, I would have stayed away."

"From the forest, or me?" Mackie asks with his eyes still closed. It's easier.

"Both."

"Somethings, you can't run away from," Mackie thinks aloud. The sky won't always be blue, garbage won't always be on Fridays, Shawn won't always be there to beat you senseless, but the forest will always be hunting for its lost devil.

"I can't stay," Blue segments, drawing Mackie's eyes open again. The moon is touching his knife-like cheekbones and slashing across to his dark mouth. His eyes are once again as black as the backs of glossy beetles. "I have to go back to the forest."

"But you'll come back."

Blue shakes his head.

Mackie doesn't feel the stab of shock he's expecting and can only conclude that he knew, somewhere deep down, that he couldn't actually keep the boy from the forest.

"Then I'll come see you."

"Humans don't belong in the forest," Blue says, and the words are harsh, but he says them so gently, Mackie almost doesn't feel the knife twisting.

He knows that. *Everyone* knows that. He just thought... "I don't want you to go."

Blue pulls him close. "I know. I don't want to, either."

"Then don't." It doesn't *have* to be complicated.

"The forest is dangerous."

That's not all of it, though. "Say what you really mean."

"I won't be like Sorrow," Blue blurts. "I won't keep you around past your time, and I won't fall into the same trap, hurting people and using my own life until I can't, and then using the lives of people I've stolen. Getting bitter and mean, causing everyone pain. You had a life here before I was thrown into it, and you'll have one after I leave, too."

"I'll be miserable; I'll just think about you."

"No, you won't." Blue says the words with such significance, it's hard to misunderstand what he means.

"You plan on wiping my thoughts out, how you did to Kevin?"

"It'll feel like a missing limb for a while, like something's not right. It'll eventually fade, and you'll move on, Mackie, and you'll open your garage, and fix your old cars, and you'll live your life, and you'll meet someone, maybe a girl or another boy, and you'll have each other, and it won't hurt so bad."

"It's never worked before."

"I didn't have the magic of the forest behind me before."

Could that be true? Will it really make a difference? Mackie tries to be mad—these are his memories, after all, but is horrified to only feel his throat closing. "I don't want someone else."

Blue has nothing to say to this. His silence makes it clear there is no argument here, he's decided, and there's nothing Mackie can say. He tries anyway.

"I think I love you."

Blue's eyes flit to his briefly before closing again. He pulls Mackie closer, his only response.

Mackie lies awake for a long time, until he's sure his eyes are dry, and his thoughts stop stumbling over each other. He thinks Blue's asleep, his arm still tight around Mackie's back and their legs tangled together.

He's exhausted. He lets his eyes close. Just for a moment.

On the brink of sleep, he feels Blue shift, his breath break over his lips. "Me, too," he says.

Electricity fills the air and pricks on Mackie's skin, and he thinks he knows what it means, but every time he tries to chase the thought, it slips away from him, like water leaking through sand.

Credits

Cover Art—Brittany Lane; Instagram @brittanylaneart
Cover Design—Jessica Moon
Cover Design—Chad Moon
Editing—Susan Floyd
Editing—Mandy Russell
Formatting—Mandy Russell

Acknowledgments

Sometimes, you have a book that just *comes together.* I don't mean to say it was perfect, and I mean to say it was easy, but when I sat down to write Sorrow's Forest (without much of a plan because I'm a horrid Pantser, and I was just looking to get some words down) it just *grew.* Like the reaching roots of a tree, planted in the right soil, in the right location, at the right time of year. I wasn't wondering *what happens next* or *how do I write this.* This was a story that demanded my attention and told me exactly what to do. I'm proud of how this one turned out.

There's a litany of people I need to thank. I'll start with the one that suffered the most.

Raymond, thank you for the fishing trips and your patience listening to this story. Though I know it's not your preferred genre, you were there for the monsters, both human and mystical, and gave me the insight I needed to make this story the best it possibly could be.

Next is Shane. My first beta reader, and Blue's first fan. Thank you so much for reading this weird little tale and getting hyped, and suggesting the changes on the first, and roughest draft.

Tara. This isn't one of the projects you helped me edit extensively, but the changes you did help with really shine. You're a goddess.

Lastly, thanks to my found family at Shadow Spark. Being surrounded by like-minded creatives is something special. You've all been amazing and I'm so happy that Sorrow's Forest has found a home with you.

About the Author

Kaitlin Corvus is from Ontario, Canada. The north holds the best part of her. She writes about nobodies, monsters, and gutter glitter, loves the stars, the deep dark sea, and a good horror mystery.

She can be found on twitter @KaitlinCorvus

Made in the USA
Middletown, DE
08 October 2022